STARK RAVING ELVIS

TCB. There has been something uncanny, a special tone in the way Elvis had said it. A glint of recognition had gone back and forth between them. It struck Byron that this was more than just a casual exchange. Something enormous had happened here. Elvis had given him a secret message and it clearly said: I am surrounded by assholes — but Brother, I know you and you know me. We know each other in a secret way. We are fated. Like father, like son, like brothers, like lovers. In that moment, Byron understood. There was the final answer: Byron would be King, it was only a matter of time. Amen.

STARK RAVING ELVIS

William McCranor Henderson

A STAR BOOK

Published by

the Paperback Division of

W.H. ALLEN & Co. PLC.

A Star Book
Published in 1985
by the Paperback Division of
W.H. Allen & Co. PLC
44 Hill Street, London W1X 8LB

First published in the United States by
E.P. Dutton, Inc. New York, 1984

Printed and bound in Great Britain by
Anchor Brendon Ltd, Tiptree, Essex

ISBN 0 352 31720 5

'Once you get into
this great stream of history,
you can't get out.'

— Richard Nixon

1958: The Gift

Byron 'Blue-Suede' Bluford — soon to be Prince Byron, heir to the Throne of Rock 'n' Roll — was reborn in the Elks Club Talent Assembly, Portland High School, Spring 1958. It was the kind of renaissance that turns a boy's life over like a spadeful of dark, rich dirt — which is fine and good, Byron's pop used to reflect (in the days when the old coot could still think straight), so long as too many worms don't crawl out.

It started like any dumb high school amateur show: Teresa Binkly, a candidate for Miss Maine Potato, opened with a giggly fire baton routine (minus fire, due to regulations). Billy 'Zits' Parker honked out 'Lady of Spain' on a musical bicycle pump, his own invention. Then Butch Marcel and the Heartstoppers trooped on and roasted the place with a smoking hot version of 'Red River Rock'. Butch was a chubby kid in a zoot suit. He had greasy pomaded hair that tumbled over his forehead, braces on his teeth, and baby-fat cheeks that jiggled as he blew his big tenor sax. Behind him the Heartstoppers made more noise than a 747, twanging and thundering, amps up full, cymbals hung with stopper chains for extra sizzle. The effect of rock 'n' roll in a high school auditorium in 1958 was stunning. Until the Heartstoppers appeared the kids had been orderly. Now they were howling for raw meat.

Butch Marcel approached the mike. After waiting for quiet he motioned to the wings.

'Blue-Suede Bluford!' he announced.

Byron stepped out on stage (with a push from his buddy

1

Fat Larry McCann) and scowled into the darkness. Even with stage fright, something in his image — a manfulness, a dark, full-lipped sensuality — hushed the crowd, made them wait for him. In front of the lights, he seemed to loosen up. Almost casually he ambled to the centre of the stage and raked a comb through his hair. His muscular coolness drew whistles and catcalls of admiration. Then the music started. He grabbed the mike and belted out 'Hound Dog' with all the trademarks — Elvis's withering grin, blistering eyes, rubbery legs and swiveling, humping pelvis — in a voice that seemed to be stolen right off the record. This was no joke. With a band behind him, Byron was a man dancing on a thousand volts. In the dreams he would have for years, they tore the seats up with switchblades — like something out of *Blackboard Jungle*. In reality they stomped and cheered so hard the teachers had to cut the whole thing short and send everyone back to homeroom.

Only later, much later, did Byron realise that if he had just been born in the right place, at exactly the right instant, there was no doubt — he would have *been* Elvis Presley. Long after Talent Assembly was nothing but fodder for old yearbook memories, after America had reeled through assassinations, discovered dope, counterculture and Asian war — after Byron had toughened into a thirty-ish factory worker with long hair, a softball cap that said 'BYRON' and a wardrobe of T-shirts with Elvis's face on the front — he still clung to the memory of how the King's power had flowed through him that day in 1958. He couldn't get over it — that one searing instant of glory, because he stood on a stage for three minutes and did what Elvis Presley did.

Byron had grown up a dusky-eyed, dreamy kind of kid — shy, two left feet, fog in his head, a clothespin on his tongue. The older girls, the ones in lipstick and puffy sweaters, had been watching him from the time he was twelve, but he never had an inkling. It was mumblety-peg, toads, BB guns, then solitary dates with his right hand. Even Elvis, when he came along, was Byron's personal secret. The looks, the attitude, the moves — Byron put them all together in the privacy of home, like a Charles Atlas body-building course. Elvis emerged, a set of fresh muscles.

But where could he strut his new stuff — show off the bumps and grinds, the hip sling, the shaky leg, the Tupelo drawl? How many Talent Assemblies came along in one lifetime? Even in the aftermath, when Butch Marcel had begged him to join the Heartstoppers, it was as *himself*, Byron Bluford — to sing Chuck Berry songs, Buddy Holly songs, Roy Orbison songs. Where was that at? Being Elvis was what mattered, after all. Why stand up in front of people and try to be anything else?

Yet how the hell could you make a life out of being Elvis? What could you do with it that wasn't just a gag? After high school, as real life crept over him like a mist, each major encounter — with the wife he married young and divorced quick, with the mother he couldn't satisfy, with the future he seemed to drown in — each dim milestone brought it up all over again. As long as he continued to exist without a life that made any sense, the question wouldn't give way, wouldn't crack. Without the answer to it, Byron Bluford was nothing. And because he lived without the answer, he hardly considered it a life. It was something else. Time spent killing time. Watching himself go nowhere. Waiting . . . for what?

Eighteen years later, the answer came — from the King himself.

1976: The Gun

Byron met Elvis Aaron Presley face-to-face in the summer of 1976, at a Boston Garden concert. A distant cousin of Larry McCann's (the same Fat Larry) was working for Elvis, one of the black belts on his security crew. He ushered Byron through the cavernous back corridors of the Garden and slipped him into Elvis's dressing room. It was full of pre-show hangers-on. The air was heavy with the smell of sweat. Byron felt suddenly sick — a jangling in his head, a taste of metal in his mouth. The thought of backing out flickered through his mind, but the door had been locked behind him.

The area where Elvis sat glowed as if they had lit it with a spotlight. Elvis looked puffy and tired, in a bulging white jumpsuit with gold and blue trim. He was reading aloud from a book called the *The Golden Voice of Ra*. His face was dripping with sweat and his eyes had a dull polyurethane glaze. There was a gun strapped around his paunch.

'And the mountains shall split asunder to make way for the coming of the Final Spirit, the Fire-Lighter of History, the igniter of the Universe . . .'

His eyes wandered toward the door. He noticed Byron immediately.

'C'mon over here, son,' he said.

Byron steered himself into the light and shook hands with the King. Then he looked, close up, and what he saw almost made him choke.

Elvis seemed stuck to the jumpsuit, as if it had melted and hardened, a poisonous second skin, tightening its grip on his tired flesh, draining the life out of it, killing him slowly. Sickness seeped through the hooded eyes. Byron tried to shake the image of death out of his head.

The boys from Memphis were fluttering around Elvis, cracking a stream of dumb jokes and snickering nervously at each other. They seemed to want to pull the boss's attention away from Byron.

'Elvis! Hey, Elvis —!' they were calling. Elvis this, Elvis that. Byron had no sense of time. The moment seemed to spin in an endless circle, as he and Elvis exchanged a few words.

'Y'know. Somebody's been trying to kill me,' Elvis said in a soft monotone. 'I thought for half a second it was gonna be you.'

Byron laughed uncomfortably and shoved his hands in his pockets. He couldn't look Elvis in the eye.

'Nah . . . not me. Not me, man.'

'You carry a gun?'

'Nah.'

'Y'ought to. This ain't a world for gentle people. I got a damn Browning Automatic Rifle.'

Then somebody took Byron by the arm and moved him gently toward the door.

'Stop right there —' said Elvis suddenly. He stared oddly at Byron from across the room and then removed the .22 Savage revolver from his bulging waist, belt, holster and all. He folded it and held it out to Byron.

'TCB, my friend,' he said, with a nod. *Take Care of Business*, read the belt. 'TCB' was tooled all over it, with lightning bolts in ornate clusters.

And then Byron found himself out in the hall, cradling the cold weight of Elvis's own gun in his hands.

TCB. There had been something uncanny, a special tone in the way Elvis had said it. A glint of recognition had gone back and forth between them. It struck Byron that this was more than just a casual exchange. Something enormous had happened here. Elvis had given him a secret message and it clearly said: I am surrounded by assholes — but Brother, I know you and you know me. We *know* each other in a secret way. We are fated. Like father, like son, like brothers, like lovers.

He had said: You've got to finish it for me, man. I'm too far gone to be what I was. Go out and do it! Byron had seen it in that look as clearly as if it had been written across Elvis's face in magic marker. In that moment, Byron understood. It was like a picture in his mind: Elvis, weakened; Prince Byron, strong and ready, standing over the suffering king, receiving his potency, the full force of his earthly mission. And then, if there were any doubts, in front of those gobbling turkeys, Elvis had silenced them by passing on his gun. There was the final answer: Byron would be King, it was only a matter of time. Amen.

Except that now, over a fucking year later, Elvis was still out on the road, struggling and thrashing like a weary old dray horse, embarrassing himself in front of the whole damn world, while Byron simply hung in the wind, his vision deadened by forty desolate hours a week at Cavanaugh Pump Works. Month by month, the promise was running dry. But he kept the gun shining, the leather rich and soft. He practised quick draws in front of the mirror, over and over, dropping to one knee and fanning the Savage like a gunfighter.

'How 'bout it, man?' Byron would plead with the face on his T-shirt. 'How long are we gonna play this game?'

A Walkin'
Dead Man

You could lose a piece of your nose if you nodded off at the Cavanaugh assembly line. Byron usually managed to hang on somehow till lunch, when he could grab a nap out by the vending machines. But this time he had a regular blackout. One second he was watching the stream of ring bearings, one after another — next, his whole body was slumping over and falling right into the line.

Larry McCann and some of the other guys saw what was happening. From a distance it looked like the BYRON softball cap was melting right into the KING OF ROCK 'N' ROLL T-shirt.

Down the line came a shout: 'Byron!'

His head jerked up and he glanced sharply around. Rings were piled up on the line in front of him. Turner, the foreman, rang the alarm bell and stopped the line. The other guys looked up and took a breather while they waited for the old goat to start bitching. Turner was a walking bummer: a bloated, gross-featured humiliator of men.

'You fuck-up,' he muttered.

Byron blinked at him. 'Why'd you stop the goddamn line, man?'

The two men eyed each other for a moment. Byron was thin, but powerfully built. Even Turner wouldn't cross him lightly.

'For you, your highness,' said Turner. 'Your stupid face fell into it.'

Byron's mouth flared into a grin. 'You're shittin' me,' he purred.

'Would I shit you?'

'Could be, could be, a guy as ugly as you.'

Turner grinned horribly and spat to one side. He dropped his gaze to Byron's chest and poked Elvis's nose with one stubby finger. 'Who's that asshole on your T-shirt?'

Byron's comsposure slipped a notch. 'What do you want from me, scumbag?'

'I want *work*,' snapped the foreman. He turned his back and walked off to restart the line. Byron raised his middle finger high in the air and turned in a slow circle.

'Psst! Byron —' From down the line Larry McCann tossed him a Dexadrine the size of a football. Byron reached up with one hand, grabbed it, and gobbled it.

'I swear to God — I'm losing my balls in there. I'm a walkin' dead man.' His eyes rolled as he paced back and forth among the vending machines, raging at the lazy lunch-shift crowd. 'For two cents I'd fuck this job! Two goddamn cents —'

'There ya go, Blue-Suede.' Two pennies flashed through the air — Ronnie Spaulding's idea of a joke. Mouths stopped chewing as Byron picked up the pennies and glared back at the goofball.

'Boy, I don't deal with small change,' Byron drawled, firing the coins back at Ronnie. 'Bank it up your ass!'

The laughs broke over him in cleansing waves. The speed was exploding inside him like a warm ball of light. Now he felt better. He threw his head back and cackled with pleasure, running in place like a sprinter.

'Damn, that's good!'

He drew a half-pint of bourbon out of his pocket and squatted in the corner like a hobo.

'Gentlemen, I tell you what — it's all bullshit, total, all-out bullshit, there ain't no way around it. So, goddammit to hell! Let's get drunk. I'm having my first drink of the day.'

He drained the half-pint in two gulps.

8

No More Bing Crosbys

People said that Byron drank in the style of his pop: quick and dangerous, prone to the bender. In the state of Maine, known for eccentrics, 'Plum' Bluford had fit right in, even though he was from 'away,' a transplant, a tobacco-chewing Georgia cracker. Cashiered out of the wartime navy, he had drifted North to work in the Boston shipyards where he fell in love with a vivacious half-Indian girl from Maine. Betty Crow was her name. She had a jolly face and dark eyes, sharp as a hawk's. Plum bowled her over with his redneck charm, playing to her weak side — a desperate optimism, a tendency to stretch promising visions past all sensible limits, right off the map. She looked at Plum and saw not the flashy backwoods drifter, but a man with a limitless future — a corporation president, chairman of the board, a sleeping giant.

Betty worked hard stitching shirts for the Navy, but after hours she let herself go, carousing with Plum in the old Scollay Square honky-tonks and 'combat-zone' joints like the Hillbilly Ranch. Quickly enough they blew her savings and ran up a small jungle of debts. On Betty's urging, they headed 'down East' to Portland, her hometown, where Plum made an honest woman out of her (she was pregnant) and set out to make himself an honest man.

Around Portland, Plum picked up a double-edged reputation: on the one hand, a serious, flint-tough poker player; on the other, a raucous, overdressed, hard-drinking maniac, with his flashy pin-stripes and lunatic laughing fits. At his gambling peak he was good enough for local money-men to back him in blue chip poker games around the state — a high ride for a young hayseed from nowhere.

But by the time Byron was born, things were already unravelling. In her sixth or seventh month, Betty abruptly ran out of whatever had fuelled her infatuation for Plum. In public she treated the man with icy coldness. No one knew exactly why, but people had their notions: she had found a few long blond hairs in her bed most likely, or spotted Plum feeling up a factory girl. Some clear act of betrayal had turned Betty Crow around so sharply that Plum was written out of the future. All those visions of greatness she simply transferred to the life that, three weeks overdue, sprang from her belly.

Again, she was off the map: this boy would be the most brilliant of professionals, a man of consequence; a Congressman, a Senator, and maybe someday (why the hell not?) President of the United States. Little Byron was a miracle. She had nothing but joy for the future. Plum be damned — let him come and go, he no longer mattered.

So, Plum came and went, still quite the swashbuckler, until his youth began to fade. Then the cracks yawned open in his personality and a paralysing darkness could be seen behind the slick face he showed the world. Middle age robbed him of his nerve. He lost his touch at poker, blew big money in a series of high-stakes disasters, and was reduced to scrounging work in the Lewiston mills. Before he died, Plum Bluford had turned into a raw stumblebum, sleeping in the street, crazed on rot-gut brandy.

And growing up somewhere in the midst of all this was Byron — mortified by poverty, stunned by his pop's spectacular flameout, fearful of his mom's growing moodiness and anger. He would be no lawyer, no Congressman, that was obvious to him at least — and finally, grudgingly, to his mom. Everything around him said he was nowhere, nobody, nothing. He learned to strut like a scrawny little rooster, but he was white trash and the world made sure he knew it.

After they found Plum's body one morning, frozen in a

culvert, Betty aged fast, greying, losing her fun, her girlish shape, the brightness in her eyes. She went into and out of depression for months, then years, unforgiving of her son, like his dad a denial of her dreams, a flash that burned out quickly. Byron knew that was her view and now, he figured, she'd take it to the grave.

This is where Elvis blew into his life like a storm. Here was a man who made pure style out of being white trash. He was dazzling. He didn't apologise for anything. He turned it into gold. With Elvis as your guide, there was no need to hide your bush-hog status in front of rich kids — you strutted it right in their faces. No more Bing Crosbys. Being Elvis was a way of life that Elvis had made clear as A-B-C. As Elvis, he was sexier, smoother, better-looking, more relaxed than when he was just Byron. Being Elvis was being *somebody*. It was an achievement, a distinction. Everything the young Elvis did had the mark of the highwire artist about it. Byron admired Elvis for that, and he respected himself for walking the same highwire.

As Elvis, he was an authentic American hero. That was why he had such contempt for jerks like Turner: here was a true bush-hog with no roots, no culture, no respect for a hero, no reverence for the undisputed King of Rock 'n' Roll. And in the so-called real world of Cavanaugh Pump, this slob outranked him!

Three nights after Byron's meeting with Elvis, Betty Crow Bluford clutched at her chest and keeled over dead. At the wake, Byron got drunk with his Indian relatives. His eyes rolled. He wailed and clawed at his mother in the coffin. Before they closed the lid he tossed the .22 savage in with her, but someone pulled in out for him. He drank steadily for two weeks, and was seen around town night and day with burning, bloodshot eyes, stumbling, sitting in the gutter.

'Like Plum all over again,' said the folks who knew him, watching what was surely a rerun of the old man's flameout.

Then one day — a miraculous change of weather: It was

over. He pulled himself together, took the job at Cavanaugh, and held it — a week, a month, two months. 'Byron is steadying up,' was the revised forecast.

Until, that is, they saw him going public with this Elvis craziness — actually standing up and trying to pass himself off as Elvis Presley, or Prince Byron, or whatever the hell he was calling it. In the Spring of '77, with Presley himself still performing all over the place, it just seemed witless, pointless, another piece of flaming futility out of Byron Bluford. How the hell could one boy come up with so many ways of going to the devil? You had to wonder at it.

Divine Stuff

But Byron had a plan, and a message for Elvis. The message was this: No more waiting.

He began simply by working anywhere a house band would let him step on a stage; that meant the milltown bars and roadhouses around Portland or Biddeford or Old Orchard Beach — tough joints where they'd just as soon throw a ten-pound bluefish at you as look at you. He brought with him a tight medley of 'early Elvis' hits and a rough, dopey charisma that worked on these crowds, the beer-sotted fishermen and tough-talking factory girls. His crafted image of Elvis came across without a crack: solid, youthful, attractive, and dangerous. They liked this guy. He spoke Maine: Rod and Gun Club picnics and rock 'n' roll barn dances, plastic pools and dories in the backyard, stinking mud flats at low tide and pine forests bigger than the moon. Maine, where God had his duck camp — the pride and dirt-poor shame of it. Ayeh. He could rap to them, all night. He kept them guessing. What the hell was he going to do next? They couldn't tell — but they wanted to know.

TR's was in South Portland, less than a mile from Cavanaugh Pump — which gave Byron the home-court advantage. It was a place to unwind after your shift — dark, stinking of beer and motor oil, a place to get loaded fast and swing a pool cue at somebody's head, a place to mess around in the back of a van before stumbling home to the wife and kids.

The club had been around for years under one name or

13

another. In recent times, T.R. 'Bob' Hogan, a Buick dealer, had bought the place and tried to elevate the clientele by offering live rock on weekends. The music attracted gangs of rowdy kids who clashed with the Cavanaugh regulars, but Hogan stuck to his guns — rock 'n' roll was putting his place on the map in Portland and Hogan liked that. He began to fancy himself a regional impresario. He launched a talent search, turning Mondays into what he called 'Hoot Night', and made it known he was looking for a regular act for mid-week when business was slow. After a few failures, the word got out that he was desperate for a solid success. Byron was quick to smell the ultimate possibility: real money — a chance to make a living as the Prince of Rock 'n' Roll!

Tonight, for the fourth straight Monday, he and Larry McCann pulled into the parking lot and drained a ritual half-pint of bourbon. The sounds of Hoot Night filtered out into the warm summer twilight. In the darkness of Byron's old Ford pickup it seemed as if time had gone nowhere since high school. There they were, Byron and Fat Larry, waiting in the wings, just like 1958. Byron grinned.

'C'mon, old guy,' he said softly, 'Let's check it out.'

Fat Larry was essentially the same wide-eyed high school fan who had goaded Byron onto the stage back in '58. Bald and pot-bellied now, he had looked hard into 'the mystery of history' and devised a theory, which went like this: Early rock 'n' roll had produced the last generation of American creative geniuses. The early rockers were heroes who had chiselled themselves into history the hard way, 'originals' who had created themselves from dust. Nothing like them had appeared since. Now, however, an astounding thing was happening: Elvis, the first, last and greatest of all, was running out of steam. With the gift of the .22 Savage, he had passed the torch to Byron. Thus, went Larry's logic, working alongside Byron on the assembly line was like a ticket into history: He was working with the undiscovered Elvis himself — the reanointed, reappointed rockabilly genius, future unbounded, potential unlimited! That's the way Larry saw it. And he spoon-fed the vision to Byron.

'Me, now, I couldn't possibly become anything, man, I'm a squat failure. But you —' His rheumy eyes would glisten. 'You're sheer action, you're put together out of divine stuff, original stuff. Just like Elvis . . .'

Byron stepped gingerly across the parking lot gravel so as not to dirty his blue suede shoes. He was wearing pink slacks and a shiny purple 50's-style early-Elvis sport jacket. At the door he stopped for a moment and took several deliberate breaths. When he turned around and glanced at Larry the transformation was like a makeup job: the cheekbones were higher, bonier, the smile more crooked and dazzling, the eyes glowing in their sockets. Even though his hair still hung almost to his shoulders, Byron Bluford seemed to be gone. Elvis was there.

'Everybody drunk yet?' Byron called as he sauntered in, peacock-like, followed humbly by Larry.

'Yo! Blue-Suede!' shouted a few bloated regulars clinging to the bar. 'Goddamn. C'mere, Elvis!'

Byron and Larry joined the drinkers for a pit stop, then wandered on down to the stage, where a nervous-looking girl who couldn't have been more than nineteen was picking away at her guitar and trying to cut through the din. There was a thin film of sweat across her face and her cheeks were flushed. Dimples appeared and disappeared in her cheeks. Every so often she tossed her head to clear the thick chestnut mop out of her eyes. Byron stopped dead. Something about her seemed to freeze him in his tracks. He watched her intently until she couldn't avoid his eyes any longer. With a flush she let her gaze lock onto his, then looked straight through him and kept on singing.

'Sweet little fox, huh!' Byron said to Larry. He threw some nuts into his mouth and washed them down with a glass of Old Milwaukee. 'Can't sing, but what a beauty!'

Aside from the girl, who at least looked terrific, the talent was pretty raw tonight. You could tell from the bored faces on the house band. There was a groaner who did 'My Way', the losers' national anthem. The band pitched it too high for him so it came out sounding more like a howling dog. But no matter how you mutilate it, 'My Way' goes over in any tavern, so he got a hand. Then came a couple of college boys with a banjo and fiddle. They drew a few yahoos, but TR's was not a shitkicker's scene so the crowd fell mostly into raucous chit-chat. Then a beefy trucker who called himself Billy Utah tried to struggle through 'Truck Drivin' Man', but blanked on the lyrics and had to sit down.

The girl meanwhile had squeezed in beside a couple of pouty-looking girlfriends at a table near the front. Her large dark eyes occasionally glanced back at Byron, cooly, as if she were just scanning the room. There was something proud about her. Byron liked that. She was young and a little awkward, like she hadn't quite grown into her body. Except that she had. Byron kept noticing her shoulders, the way she held her neck. He watched her flick the beer off her lips. He followed her with his gaze when she went to the bar. He couldn't keep his eyes off her. She was unusual and she was doing something unusual to him.

'Damn . . .' he whispered. Now a pudgy little Canadian with sprayed hair was squeezing out a polka on the accordian. Hogan drifted around to Byron's table.

'You're up next, Byron,' he said with a nod. Once the polka-boy had bowed off, Hogan stepped up to the mike.

'Okay, last but not least, we got the Prince Byron Rock 'n' Roll Revue — Byron Bluford!'

Now the house band was wide awake because this was fun. The Cavanaugh Pump crowd came alive with a howl and on rushed Byron, lugging a guitar with no strings, his hair slicked back and held with a rubber band. While the band vamped he stood at the mike and rolled his hips around, Elvis-style, pulling some squeals out of the factory girls. He waved the band into silence and grinned his lopsided Elvis grin at the crowd, letting the movement stretch and stretch until it fell apart into hoots and whistles. Then, with a sudden swing of his hips, he blew straight into 'Hound Dog' and the place went wild.

This was head-and-shoulders above the other acts. Byron knew he had it, the definitive version of Elvis — the hips, the shaky legs, the throaty baritone, the grins and winks — Elvis, the young King, the insolent punk teen idol. He had what the others lacked — the power to command attention. He could turn it on or off at will. He played with it like a young dog tossing a hambone.

At the finish he had the crowd up and sloshing their beer as they cheered. He raised both arms like a fighter and grinned out into the rowdiness, loving it.

'Thank you, folks!' he mugged. 'C'mon, I know you love me better than that! Lemme hear it!'

Byron caught the girl's eye. He grinned straight at her.

She fingered her blouse and looked away, blushing again. Suddenly she leaned over to one of her girlfriends and whispered something in her ear. They all got up and left. By the time Byron had finished taking his bows and worked his way through the crowd to the front door, she was gone.

'Well, goddamn!' Byron said, pulling the rubber band off his hair and throwing it into the dirt.

Karen LeBec was hanging around the front door with her halter top almost down to her stomach, working on Hogan's bouncer. But all of a sudden she wasn't into the bouncer anymore, she was chattering in Byron's ear. Her husband was on the road somewhere in his eighteen-wheeler that Santa Claus gave him for Christmas and she was mad at the sucker anyway — Byron got the whole story on the way out to the truck as a vague depression crept over him.

'She walked out on ya, didn't she,' said Karen shrewdly as she slid across the seat. Byron pretended he didn't know what she meant. 'Don't play dumb, Byron. The little honey walked out on ya so Karen gets a free trip, right? I know you, baby . . .'

She smirked at him a little sadly and started rubbing her lipstick off.

Damn it, she was right. Byron suddenly realised he'd give anything right now, anything to have Karen LeBec off his neck.

'Tell you what, Karen. How 'bout right here in the truck? That way you can still go back in and circulate, huh?'

She looked at him and blinked once. Then she pulled her lipstick out, smearing up her mouth all over again.

'S'long Byron.' Her heels hit the pavement.

'Sorry, baby. Guess I'm just not into it.'

She slammed the door and walked back to the bar, giving him a rearful of what he was missing.

At 4 A.M. Byron brought his truck to a bucking, lurching stop in front of his house. *Elvis Is Back* was blasting off the cassette stereo, full volume. Byron staggered out of the truck, tripped and crawled the rest of the way to the front door. Lights popped on up and down the dusty blacktop street.

'Turn if *off!*' a voice shouted.

But Byron was already inside the house dragging himself through the dream-jungle of Elvis posters, back to the bedroom, where a dartboard hung with four darts piercing Elvis's face.

Steadying himself in front of the full-length bedroom mirror, he shot a hard look into his own eyes. For a minute someone else was there, on the other side of the mirror. His lip curled slightly. He set his legs apart and did a few slow gyrations. Elvis was there.

Outside, there were more shouts from up and down the street as the music blared on. Byron pulled away from the mirror and sloshed some water over his begonia plants, gifts from a lady he couldn't remember, now his only companions.

'Have a little drinky, boys,' he mumbled.

A wave of dizziness forced him back against the bed and, just as it occurred to him to do someting about that goddamn racket out front, he toppled over on his back and passed out cold.

The Mystery of History

June 15, 1977

Dear Col. Parker:
I understand Elvis will be appearing in Portland
again for two shows August 16. Welcome to Maine!
I wonder is it possible to talk to you and him about
my views concerning the style of show he has taken
on lately, which I think is a serious mistake (as you
know). As ever, my offer stands to take over for
Elvis in any situation where he might become
unable to perform.

Yours truly,
Byron 'Prince Byron' Bluford'

Byron finished soaping up the truck and tossed the sponge
back into the bucket. He unscrewed the cap from a new pint
of Old Buffalo Gums or whatever it was and took a gulp. He
aimed the hose at the chrome-and-plastic Elvis hood
ornament and watched the water carom off it into a fine
mist, making rainbows in the late sunlight. Wearily his eyes
followed the soap as it ran of into layers of scum across the
gravel. He went back to the front porch and tipped some
more whiskey into his mouth, sloshing it around before he
let it go. A quaalude went down for dessert. Sunday.
Fucked up again.

He sat on the porch steps and watched the sky filling with
cotton. Bud Kimball started up his chainsaw — what would

Sunday be without a little chainsawing?

'Timber!' Byron shouted.

'Fuck you, Blue-Suede.'

Byron took a deep breath. The air had an ugly trace of paper mill sourness in it, the usual stench. He squinted lazily at the neighbourhood he had grown up in: peeling paint, busted asphalt, rickety leaning overgrown shacks, wood chips everywhere, uncut weeds, kids scuttling around the sawdusty yards on their Big Wheels. There was a tightness in his gut, a Sunday hopelessness that defied every attempt to booze it and dope it away.

'Fuck you, Blue-Suede!' The Kimball's oldest kid buzzed past on his moped, imitating his dad. Byron shot him the bird — cocky little bozo. The kid shot it right back. Byron laughed. The booze ran around his head. He stood up — and the world stood up along with him, trying to wrestle him to the ground. He staggered once and regained his feet.

Okay: at least the letter to the Colonel had gone out on time. The Presley organisation would damn well know where to find Byron if they had to — whether they answered his goddamn letter or not. TCB. He staggered again. The earth seemed to turn a slow flip. A little girl in a brownie uniform came skipping up to the porch.

'Here's your Girl Scout cookies, Mr Bluford.' She handed him a box of mixed creme sandwiches and rubbed her nose, hopping from foot to foot.

'Well, thank you, honey — d'I order these or something?' Byron tossed the hair out of his face and fixed her with a bleary stare.

'Yeah, dontcha remember? Last month, I come up and you was asleep in your car?'

'That sounds about right.' Byron reached into his pocket and pulled out whatever was there — a ten. He gave it to the Brownie. She blinked back at him.

'That's too much, Mr Bluford!'

'You just keep it all, honey.' Byron folded his arms and nodded firmly. He thought he could feel the quaalude coming on already. 'Keep the whole damn thing.' His legs wobbled.

'Wow! Thanks a lot —'

'Thank you, sweetheart. You have a good day, you hear?'

The Brownie jumped up and down and scampered away, clutching the ten. 'Yippeeee!' she squealed.

Byron chuckled. Another few years and she'd be climbing into some dude's pants. But now — a croaky little elf was all she was. Made him think about . . . what? Larry's ten-dollar phrase, the mystery of history. By which he meant how you start off a little pip, get ripe, go stale, rot, die. Ah, hell, how depressing, contemplating shit like that.

Watching the little tyke scamper off he began thinking of the girl from TR's, the slender little chestnut fox, impish, like a child in the way she moved — but womanly all the way up and down. Oh God, here it came, depression, like a chain around his neck, freezing him to the spot while Sunday rolled over him like a heavy incoming tide.

'Fuckin' ran out on me,' he muttered.

The last glint of red had gone from the sky when he forced himself back into the darkened house. The place was falling to pieces. His dead parent's rickety old lobster shack, gone all to hell, and here he was, still rattling around in it, letting it flake into peels and chips and rubble right around him. Some plaster dropped into his hair. He pulled a string and the kitchen light blared on. He wasn't hungry.

On the walls, Elvis was everywhere. Elvis the kid, the youthful punk. Why? Why not? Beat wallpaper anyway. Images of things could work wonders on his mind. Back in the bedroom were his private snapshots. Sometimes if he got the right picture moving, he could melt into it, loosen up a little. Sometimes if he sat watching long enough, the posters would spring to life with electric force, bucking and moving and grinning at him. Other times he could even conjure the same effect out of the mirror, commanding the Elvis behind the glass to come alive and dance, free of any trace of Byron.

He reached for a snapshot of himself Larry had taken: Prince Byron live onstage at TR's, hips cocked, guitar slung

21

low and off to the side. He waited for it to move, ripple, wink at him. Nothing. No sign of recognition. The picture's deadly stillness reached out and grabbed his stomach. Nothing stirred. No feelings. No desire to take even a single breath. Only a slow realisation that he would go no place tonight, be nobody. It was Sunday. Tomorrow was nothing but another Monday — a Cavanaugh Pump day.

And Elvis? Elvis was still out on the road, a goddamned semi-invalid by this time, still out making a fat fool of himself.

C'mon, man,' he whispered. 'Throw me a little something.'

He walked back into the twilight and sat in the grass. A breeze was blowing at the Kimball's wash. Byron had watched chunky old LaVerne Kimball hang it out, one more baby swelling in her gut. Bud Kimball had done a job on her, for sure. Byron closed his eyes and let his mind drift back to high school: she had been LaVerne Ray then, a trim, soft, soulful girl who one time let him go under her sweater in the back of the bus . . .'

History. It made him almost want to cry. Choked him all up. The booze, the lude, the memory of LaVerne, melted him into a lump of sadness and desire. He rolled over, soaked with sweat. His mind reeled as he spread-eagled in the dusty grass. The tension broke finally as, with nightfall hiding him, he made love in the spinning darkness to Mother Earth.

The Girl

'This is it, boys!' This is what we have been waitin' to see, right?'

Byron zigzagged back and forth among the vending machines, gesturing with a ham sandwich as he raved. Larry and Ronnie Spaulding and a scattering of other guys were lounging around on lunch break.

'What is it we been waitin' to see?' Ronnie had to ask Larry.

Larry opened his mouth to answer the question, then decided to ignore the dumb fool. Let him hang. He shot a wink at Byron.

'Well, hell,' Ronnie persisted, 'I got a right to ask a simple question, don't I?'

Now Byron was jogging from machine to machine, fired with energy.

'Goddamn, don't get in my way, boys! I've gotta run. I've gotta run this off. One side, please —!'

"What? What is it?" demanded Ronnie.

Crumbs sprayed from Larry's mouth. "An exclusive audition, you numbskull!'

'Personally offered,' Byron puffed. 'T.R. Hogan called me up at home!'

Ronnie's mouth cracked open as he thought about that.

'It's a full set, flea-brain!' Larry shouted at him. 'If it works out there'll be money, a regular gig. Two full nights a week.'

'I'll tell you something else, too, man,' Byron ran on. 'This is the begining of a damn legend. I'm gonna rise out of

23

this shit heap. You won't see me on this line much longer.'

Ronnie was still struggling with the concept. His big hands grasped the air as he talked.

'Okay . . . s'posing you do get your two steady nights a week as Prince Byron — where d'ya go from there? I mean, don't it seem like Elvis's got the Elvis Presley field pretty well sewed up?'

Byron stopped chewing. Larry jumped in like a terrier.

'No way, man. Let him have the stadiums and the field houses. That's not the real Elvis anymore.'

Byron raised a fist in agreement: *Yeah. Stick to the clubs. Give them something they could see up close — the young, tough, pure Elvis with hard edges. Early Elvis.*

'You pay twenty-five or thirty bucks and he's ten blocks away. And even up close what do you see — a tired old dude dressed up like Liberace!'

Give 'em the thin, hungry, sexy Elvis, from before he'd been chipped and worn away into the harmless movie bozo, then the aging fatso in the creamcheese jumpsuit.

'Why not give the folks the Elvis you can't see anymore?'

Give 'em the real thing. Give 'em Prince Byron! The future was ripping open like a vision of birth.

The next day Byron drew an advance from Mrs Bertie, the cashier, and made an appointment at Cosmic Cut to have his hair styled. He had a photo of Elvis from a 1962 fan magazine that showed exactly how he wanted it done — in a shaggy, sweeping duck's-ass. At quitting time he punched out and left Cavanaugh on the run, dropping by the K-Mart, where he pulled some loud printed shirts off the rack and grabbed a pair of purple polyester slacks that looked right.

At Cosmic Cut Brenda Harper was in the middle of combing out a pudgy-faced college kid.

"You're late, Byron,' she said without looking up.

"Well, I can't sit around —'

Brenda had had a hot interest in Byron, but she considered herself a notch above him now that she had been to beautician's college in Boston.

'Just sit down and wait —'

'Aw, hell,' Byron shouted. The college kid paled and shrunk in the chair. 'I can't wait — I've got a crucial appointment, y'understand? Finish him off!'

Brenda refused to look at him. 'Either wait or let Wendy take you.'

'Who's Wendy?'

Brenda called to the back: 'Wendy!'

From the back room Wendy emerged, and Byron rocked back on his heels. Wendy! He smiled suddenly and made her a gallant little nod. It was the girl singer, the slippery little fox from TR's.

'Cut the man's hair, honey.'

She seemed dazed for a second, knowing Byron and yet not knowing him — and trying to make sense of the fact that he was beaming at her in such a chummy way. Then it hit her.

'Oh. Elvis, right?'

'You got it.'

'Well . . .' She motioned toward the cubicle, which was off behind some planted plants. She seemed shy. Byron realised how young she must be — just out of high school. He got a whiff of her when she leaned him back to wash his hair — a sweet, fresh smell. This was rare. A wave of magnetism surged through the room, lining up the future like iron filings. He could hear the wheels turning in heaven.

'I might as well tell you, I've been looking for you.' Lay it on like butter.

She smiled at that. 'Really? First I heard.'

'You ran out on me, didn't you?'

She screwed up her nose. 'Huh?'

'At TR's.'

'I didn't.' She was blushing. 'Put your head back.'

'Admit it. You knew I'd be heading straight at you soon as I got down from the stage. I could see you knew it. Right or wrong?'

She sighed. 'I saw you staring at me if that's what you mean. But my roommates had to leave —'

Byron lay his head back into the wash basin, laughing.

'Ah, bullshit, you knew I'd be coming after you and you took off like a rabbit, right?'

'Well? What did you expect? One thing I'm not is a groupie, okay? And if you want to know the truth, man, I thought you were a little crazy. I think you still might be. Now shut your eyes.'

Byron grinned like a fool as she ran the warm water through his hair, soaped him up and worked his scalp with her fingers.

'Someday I'll do this for you,' he said. He heard her give a little snort.

'Someday they'll sell ice cream in hell.'

But she was still smiling, he could tell from the way she said it. When he peeked, he caught her watching him with her heavy brown eyes.

She gave him the Elvis-style cut, just like the magazine photo, but Byron hardly even noticed. He couldn't take his eyes off her. She was slim and her neck curved just right and her breasts nudged softly against her blouse. All he could think of was taking her someplace far away from here.

She chatted as she cut — not really as shy as she seemed. Right off, he was getting her life history. She was from way the hell up in the woods somewhere near Canada. Gordon Lightfoot fan at age eleven. Wrote her own songs in a 'country' Joni Mitchell style, whatever that was. Just doing this gig temporarily, till she got a break, and so on. Then she got into her witchy roommates, who made life nasty for her because she came home drunk sometimes and worked on songs in her room. She had attitudes, all right. Cutting hair was a bore. Elvis was a 'cornball.' Maine was the pits — and on like that. But Byron was so mesmerised by the sight and smell of her he had stopped trying to follow what she was saying.

'What time do you close here?'

'About an hour from now.'

'I wanna take you home. Don't say no, 'cause I just don't hear the word no.'

She blinked. 'I didn't say no. Of course, I probably should . . .'

'Don't even try, honey.' There were insolent bright lights twinkling in his eyes.

Wendy stepped back and took a good look at him. She shook her head. 'This is unique, for sure,' she said with a laugh. 'Or uniquely crazy maybe, I don't know . . .'

She was hooked. Byron could see it in the way she glanced toward the front and made a quick decision.

'Okay, wait for me in the parking lot,' she said softly.

Animals

'Hey, Krasdale!' Brenda whined from the front.

Wendy didn't answer. She never answered to 'Krasdale' anymore — not since taking the new name. You had to reinforce a major action like that. She was now Wendy Wayne, Singer/Songwriter. Period. Brenda knew that.

'Byron got you wet yet?'

Working for Brenda was a breeze, except sometimes the bitch could be so blunt it was really irritating. Wendy shrugged coolly and pushed some hair out of her face. Then she couldn't avoid a glance at Brenda and they both cracked up. What the hell?

'I dunno, he's a cheap thrill all right, if that's what you mean.'

The guy wasn't her type. She normally went for the quiet, passive ones. The poets. This Byron was a complete wild man. But there was no denying he had an interesting look: the big jaw, the crooked smile, the high cheek bones, the headlights for eyes. Plus he was openly outrageous. That really appealed to her.

'What do you know about him?' she probed.

'Everything you're gonna find out,' said Brenda. Very cute indeed.

'Like . . . ?'

Brenda grinned. 'He'll try to nail you in the truck. Make him wait. It'll be worth it.'

Wendy slapped her forehead, laughing at herself. 'I can't believe this —'

'Hey, pure lust is all. Be an animal!' Brenda tapped her

28

head with one finger. 'Just don't forget — he's got a few loose screws, okay?'

'Thanks.'

'Yeah, I know, you can take care of yourself. But don't say I didn't warn you Krasdale.'

'Just don't call me Krasdale, asshole,' Wendy shouted after her, grinning.

Pure lust. Why not? He was a pretty animal. Put him through his paces, make him kick and prance. Wendy was a pretty animal, too, and she knew it — full of the same animal grace that steamed off Byron like a cloud. So, maybe the point was just to come together with another beast, feel like a creature for a while, running, licking, nuzzling.

It had been a long time since a man had made her feel like that. She cut plenty of hair, she met her share of men in the bars — she had opportunities — but it was never quite right. Every now and then, on a whim, she would bring somebody home, some 'poet' with a gentle manner, but in the light of day it was always just, see ya sometime, Jack. She was losing the habit.

This guy, however, was something else. Brenda was right — she was moist with anticipation. Her cheeks were hot to the touch. Images were flashing through her mind. She saw herself on a golden bed, stretched out, her wrists tied together with pink ribbons. Jesus, what a song she might get out of this! Bring on the brute — bring on Prince Byron. What the hell, it was all grist for the mill. Let the animals run!

For almost an hour, Byron fidgeted in the truck. He couldn't cool down. He was totally unhinged over this girl. She blotted out everything else in his head. Dangerous! And this day, of all days. He had to keep his head together.

'Keep it together, bozo.'

Every few minutes he made himself remember he would have to go home, eat, change, and be at TR's by eight-thirty.

'Go home, eat, change . . .'

29

Yeah, but not so fast: Anyway you cut it he had to clear time for this woman. She was more than just an accident. She was: a key to the whole gathering event — a charm, an omen, a confirmation of his place in the future. Just as out of nowhere, Elvis had been given Priscilla, now here was what's-her-name. It had to happen like this!

Then the back door opened and she stepped into the air, timid, like Beauty coming to the Beast. His heart stuttered. He honked the horn and waved her over. Hurry, baby. As she stepped into the pickup, he bowed sweetly and made an instant move, slipping his arm around her. She turned her head, avoiding his lips.

'Not so fast . . .' she whispered.

The whisper was as good as a promise. Byron cranked up the truck and pulled away. The sky was copper-coloured and fading into thick grey darkness. They rode off into what was left of the sun, toward the Western Prom where she lived. The silence was delicious, full of every possibility.

'Sing me something,' he said.

She shook her head, smiling, inviting him to coax her.

'Come on. Something of yours. You're gonna be a star, huh? Sing to me.'

She had a thin, shy little voice that made him want to touch her lips. At the first red light he reached for her hand and kissed it. That brought her sliding over to his side of the truck, leaning lightly against him. Maybe the voice was off-key. Maybe the song was awful, he couldn't tell, the touch of the girl made him unable to hear.

It was dark when they pulled up in front of a row of sagging town houses. Byron turned off the engine. Now the girl grinned honestly at him and there was no nonsense. Byron leaned her back against the seat and her mouth opened to him. His hand fumbled at the buttons of her blouse. Momentarily she stopped him.

'No, I'm taking you inside,' Byron insisted.

Wendy pushed him away and sat up brightly. 'Good — you'll meet Katy and Marcia!'

'Who's that — cats?'

'Roommates.' She tossed it off with a throaty little laugh.

Byron halted. Teasing him. He shook his head. No, he was too close to let it fall apart now. Instantly he re-started the truck, revved it, and took off, tyres squealing.

'What the hell are you doing?'

'Taking you home. My home.' He swerved onto 1-95 and anchored his foot to the floor.

Wendy watched him out of the corner of her eye and let herself relax. A smile played around the edges of her lips. No need to think this over — her body was already doing the thinking. The guy had pulled her in like a fish. Watching him now, she was full of the same gritty physical desire she had felt at TR's. He was right — she had run away from it then. Now she drifted toward it, down the interstate, wide open.

This is how she wanted it to be: slow and tender the first time, then faster, breathless, a little kinky. At Byron's she stepped down from the truck and hung back shyly, hands in her pockets. He came to her. Good. Gently, he took her arm and led her into the house. Now she let him touch her wherever he wanted to and they kissed long and wandering kisses, still standing on their feet. Somewhere outside she heard a chainsaw sputtering and whining into action. He unbuttoned her and unzipped her and slid everything off her, kneeling between her legs. She leaned back against the sofa, pulling his face against her. Good, good, good. Next door, two kids were snivelling over a toy. A dog howled. Her head fell back and she was gasping and coming, astounded at the quickness of it.

Byron carried her to the bed, spread her out, and settled himself between her legs. A tree fell outside.

'The Little Prince,' he announced, flourishing his own tree.

'Not so little —'

'Nope.'

Her voice was tiny. 'Careful, baby.'

He entered slowly, running his hands under her hips,

arching her against him as he thrust, until she came again.

'Twice, huh!' he said admiringly.

'Come,' she whispered.

He came in several great groans, waited a minute and was ready again. Tenderness gave way to a bucking, panting horse race, almost too much for her — but finally not too much at all. She was exhausted, captured, addicted. But not quite finished. She reached for him again, wondering how much she could take.

Suddenly the man was on his feet, wilted, distracted, scurrying off to the kitchen, opening cans of cold spaghetti and peas. She watched him with amazement. The lover was gone; his total absorption with her had simply vanished. Now the guy was all business, all nerves, all action. He spooned the food onto two plates, grabbed a couple of plastic forks and a bottle of bourbon and hustled back to the bedroom.

'Cold plate special,' he grunted, setting the plates on the bed beside Wendy. 'Eat up, baby. I've gotta be at TR's in forty-five minutes.'

Wendy lay back, half-covered with the sheet, following him with her eyes. She shook her head.

'Just pass me the whiskey,' she said. 'I'm not hungry anyhow.'

Who Is This Guy?

Byron hardly noticed the girl now that she had gotten so quiet. As he dressed, an ugly foreboding spread through his skull. Then in the truck, on the way to TR's — a full-force attack of the horrors. His head was vibrating. Someone had planted a box in his brain and they could fuck him up with a simple twist of a knob. Somewhere, every few seconds, a secret hand was turning out new waves of static and pain. With each wave he squinted, waiting for his brain to explode and leave a purple blast mark on the new fleece upholstery. It was this way: the harder he strived, the farther he reached — the more implants in his brain. The horrors. Jibberish running backward through him mind. Always when he was reaching for strength. Going beyond himself. A test. History . . . algebra. Elvis.

He was still vaguely aware that the girl was in the truck, but she wasn't important now. His mouth was set in a thin line. A layer of cold sweat covered his face. He glanced at himself in the rearview mirror: the eyes had lost their shine — they were dull, unfocused pools of fear.

As he walked through the parking lot, he heard footsteps, the girl tagging along behind him. He turned and cast a quick glance at her. She smiled, but with a look of confusion.

'Do you want to get rid of me?' she asked.

'No.'

'If you do just say so.'

'I said no, girl!'

She looked strange. Her eyes seemed to flash like a catwoman's. She had strong claws, strong teeth. Ah hell, was it hallucinations now? He stopped and put his hands to his temples. Too much noise in there. He was helpless.

'Well? What's wrong?'

He shook his head. He couldn't talk to her, not now.

'Nothing . . . nothing's wrong.'

Then Fat Larry was there. Byron almost collapsed on his shoulders.

'Larry, Larry —' he kept repeating in a hoarse whisper. 'I'm gonna blow it, I'm blowing it already.'

'No way,' Larry snapped. He pulled a silver pillbox from his watch pocket. Byron's hands were trembling in fits. Larry whispered something and the two of them headed off toward the parking lot, leaving the girl to fend for herself.

Wendy found a booth and had a quick bourbon. Get drunk, kid, she told herself, wondering if this guy was going to drop her a bare forty-five minutes after setting off all the fireworks. Fucking *men*.

She had no idea how much time went by, or how many bourbons, before someone finally jerked the jukebox plug out of the wall and Hogan stepped up to the stage mike.

'Awright, here we go. Introducing —!' he growled theartrically, 'the Prince Byron Rock 'n' Roll Revue!'

Wendy gaped. She couldn't believe what she was seeing as Byron bounced on, miraculously transformed. Where did it come from — the freshness that radiated from his eyes? Cocaine? Was it coke inside that silver box? Whatever did it, Byron's fear was simply gone, replaced by a smooth cockiness that put him instantly in control of the room.

He opened with 'Jailhouse Rock,' roaming the stage like a cat. His mouth hung slack and the upper lip curled. His eyes searched the room for contact. Then he got sassy and lowdown and the eyes glazed over. He talked Southern. He stood with his legs apart and ground his hips around. He grinned out of the side of his mouth, like Elvis, and kept his head low so his eyes seemed to smoulder out of the dark sockets. He was beautiful, all right!

But there was something else: In the middle of the set

there came an eerie moment when Wendy realised Byron was literally gone, replaced by another personality, a kick-ass, scary hillbilly — Prince Byron, the bootleg Elvis. *Who is this guy?* she thought.

'Smile, baby, and I'll buy you a drink,' said a raspy voice.

A lean urban-cowboy type had slid in beside her. He attempted a sexy grin but it came off as a leer.

'I'm buying my own drinks,' Wendy said. keeping her eyes on the stage. The cowboy wiped his sweaty palms and followed her gaze.

'He's a fag, you know,' he said after a moment.

Wendy let that sail past.

'He is, you know. You're wasting your time.'

She looked him square in the face. This was how you destroyed a lounge lizard.

'Funny, I was just at his house and he fucked my brains out.'

She watched him blanch while he tried to stay cool. After a minute he stood up and slithered off to the bar.

Fools like that kept Wendy Wayne, Singer/Songwriter, on the far edge of boredom in Portland. She had come to this town from noplace and she was damn well going someplace. New York, L.A., someplace real, where there was real action, where the clubs were plush and full of possibilities. What fascinated her, watching Byron, was that his obsession seemed so close to hers: an absolute star trip — but in his case so spectacularly twisted!

Prince Byron finished up in a blur of raw insolence. It had worked, everybody knew it. The big cheers died away but he lingered in front of the stage, radiant, letting the crowd come up to him, press around him. Just like Elvis.

Hogan ran a quick check on his cash register tape and realised the Prince Byron Rock 'n' Roll Revue had moved more beer in forty minutes than his club had sold over the entire weekend.

'I'm into it, Byron,' he said, flourishing a thick roll of bills. 'I like what you do to this crowd. You're definitely onto something. I'm sold.'

Hogan peeled off five bills. 'This is for tonight. You've got Tuesday and Wednesday nights if you want 'em. Two shows a night, starting tomorrow. Give 'em hell!'

In the parking lot Byron exploded into ecstacy, leaping and shouting in the darkness.

'I'm a star! Baby — I'm a star!'

'I believe it,' Wendy said with a touch of genuine awe.

Suddenly he was beside her, the lover again, his arm around her, sweet, attentive. He drove her out to the Howard Johnson's on 1-95 and led her around like a princess. Wendy realised she was reeling drunk for the first time in ages. Her body was flashing on and off like a Christmas tree and every second she wanted him to touch her again.

Hojo's filled up with the crowd from TR's but she didn't even notice. She was dizzy with Byron — silly with desire. She didn't care who saw the wet hungry kisses. She fed him french fries from her plate. She licked and nibbled at his fingers. She let her hand play between his legs. In the truck, quivering with excitement, she went looking for the Little Prince with her lips — the fate worse than death, Brenda called it, but of course that depended on your point of view.

Later, at Byron's house, in Byron's bed, she watched him sleep, defused, curled up beside her like a three year old. Byron . . . Prince Byron . . . whoever the hell he was.

Princess Wendy

He woke up in a room full of smoke.

'What in the *hell* are you doing —?'

The girl looked back defiantly from behind his most secret stack of Polaroids (Karen LeBec from all angles), curling them into black wisps as she torched each one with a Bic and dealt it into the kitchen sink.

'They were lying around. I don't like them.' She kept her eyes on him, her lips pressed firmly together. A spark of humour softened her face and one dimple appeared. 'I'll replace 'em for you.'

'With what?' Byron realised he was smiling. Nothing this girl did could make him mad! Good things she didn't know it — God knows what she'd get away with. Burn the whole goddamn house down while old Byron stood around giggling like a silly fool!'

She unbuttoned her blouse and parted it like curtains.

'Get your camera,' she said.

Byron moved close to her and shook his head. Gently he slid his hands down her back and pulled her against him.

'Forget the goddamn pictures,' he said.

She rested her head heavily on his chest. A disoriented look drifted into her eyes.

'I'm crazy, you know. I don't even know what I'm doing. I'm temporarily insane.'

'Crazy, huh,' said Byron, hoisting her into the air. 'Well, you're in the right place here, honey.'

Crazy. He could look at her and tell she didn't know what the word meant. She was too fresh. What could she possibly

37

know about craziness? He felt her clean flesh pressing against him, swelling, receding. He smelled her healthy milk-smell and knew she could never be crazy. He wished he could put on her healthiness like a magic cloak.

Byron had been without a steady woman since before his mom had died — drugging himself to sleep, living out of cans, wearing week-old dirty underwear, taking home wenches like Karen LeBec. Now he knew he wanted this one. He couldn't even keep her last name straight but he wanted as much of this girl as he could get. That's what serious love was — the whole seven-course lunch! Why be cagey about it — why hold back? For the moment his whole mental focus had swung totally in her direction. She obsessed him. He wanted her with him every second. She would be the vision, the inspiration, the fire that lit up his ballooning vision of himself.

For a week he stalked her, haunted her, mesmerised her. This love was going to be a force to reckon with. He knew it when she started hanging onto him like a little girl hangs onto her daddy. Lying in bed she would watch him, big-eyed and silent. This was his lady. She went to TR's with him. She met him after work and cooked his dinner. It was serious love. The kind of love that could make you fearless, surround you with strength. With love like this you could sail forward into the future like a spear.

As the weekend approached, the heat became unbearable. Byron got the idea into his head to take the girl out some-place fresh and cool. On Friday they threw sleeping bags into the back of the truck and drove north along Route 1. Everything smelled like health — the blowy July breeze, the spruces that lined the highway, the blasts of sea air, the sunshine. Byron couldn't imagine a moment in his life when he had been happy in this particular way — namely, that if God had made an offer to stop time, he would have chosen this moment, frozen it — the sun, the calm, the girl beside him, Prince Byron standing at the door to the future.

'So tell me about your wife.' She had to know everything.

'*Ex*-wife. I've got the lawyer's bills to prove it.'

38

They had drunk half a bottle of wine. Byron's mood was so warm he was ready to talk about anything, even the former Mrs Bluford.

'I'll tell you about her: I was nineteen and she was pushing thirty. She had a voice that sounded like it was coming from the moon. I fell in love with that voice. She asked me to come home and meet her father. So we went into the living room and she says to this brass jar on the mantle, "Dad, I want you to meet Byron. We're getting married." That's the way it was.'

'Yeah, enough about her.'

That night they slept in a pasture that didn't seem to be near anything. A haze hung over the hills and weird animals seemed to be peeking through the hedgerows. The night loomed over them. Byron dreamed of a howling beast that ripped flesh and was unstoppable. He slept through the morning.

In the afternoon, they woke up to the sound of a crowd of people, partying somewhere in the distance, a tiny yammering in the vastness of the outdoors, like a pocket radio in a deserted house.

'Let's go find it,' said Byron.

It was a wedding reception, well underway. Several half-sloshed guests clapped Byron on the shoulder as he and Wendy approached a low brick building that turned out to be a Disabled Veterans Hall. A guy in a powder blue tux was holding a baby and puking into a bush. Inside, the crowd was shit-faced, including the bride, who was having a loud shouting match with the groom. Some older folks were sitting against the wall like potted plants. A country & western band stood around looking sullen as their leader negotiated from the stage for some food.

'I never played a damn wedding where we didn't get fed!' he blatted over the PA.

A minute later the best man tossed them a mound of roast beef scraps wrapped in tin foil.

Byron and Wendy drifted through the eats and ended up parked at the open bar. After a few bourbons, Byron was warming to the band. Especially when the leader started doing rubber-faced impressions — Cary Grant, Jerry Lewis, Jimmy Cagney: *Aw right, yooo guyyys*. Then suddenly the guy disappeared and, as the band played the theme from *2001*, came charging back in a spangled white jumpsuit and a black wig, as Elvis.

Byron darkened. The jerk was playing this for laughs. He even had a pillow or something to give him a gut. The crowd charged the stage to gawk at the bozo — they stared at him with their jaws flapping, as if he was some kind of comical Jesus Christ in his stupid-fool jumpsuit.

Suddenly Byron roared with all his might: 'Asshole! Get off that stage!'

The wedding guests swung around to face him. On stage the leader tried to kid his way through. 'Well, hey, if it ain't mah retarted cousin, Enos the Penis. Y'all go outside with the dogs, Enos — ' He cut himself short as Byron sailed an empty beer bottle several inches over his head. 'Jesus, man!' he gasped.

The crowd froze as Byron glared past them at the shaken Elvis. Then a couple of beefy enforcers were walking toward him, and the moment would have turned bloody if Byron himself hadn't pulled away in disgust.

'I don't wanta look at this shit,' he said, motioning to the girl to follow him. The wedding guests gave him plenty of room.

In the truck she had more questions — more goddamn questions! How come the impersonator made him mad? How come he did Elvis anyway, why didn't he be himself?

'Everybody plays off to somebody. You play off of Joni Mitchell —'

'It's different.'

'It's not different.'

'It's different because I don't wanta *be* Joni. I write my own songs. I'd like to be *like* her, I'd like to write as good as her — but I don't wanta *be* Joni. I want to be Wendy Wayne.'

'I thought your name was Crabtree or something —'

'Not any more,' she fired back, hitting each word.

'Well, it ain't as different as you think. I wanta be Prince Byron because that's true Elvis. I mean, Elvis doesn't even do his early act anymore. He's lost it. Well, I found it. I'm the one that does it now. I own it. If Elvis wants it back, he'll have to take it from me. D'you understand what I'm saying?'

She shook her head.

'Look,' he went on, 'Guys like that clown today, they don't take it seriously. They put on the jumpsuit and do what Elvis is doing nowadays — that's a total drag. What I'm doing is preserving something that no longer exists. These other yahoos can kiss my ass, that's the only way to see it.'

The girl just nodded and looked away. Byron guessed he had made his point. She turned back and now she was smiling. She came close to him and whispered in his ear.

'You know what? I don't give a damn one way or the other.'

However she meant it, Byron took it as a compliment.

At Camden they turned into Mt. Battie and parked at the top. They found a spot with some shelter that looked out over Penobscot Bay and Byron rolled two fat joints. The bay got bigger and bigger and seemed to wrap around them as they smoked. The sky was puffy blue and the white clapboard mansions of Camden shone in the clear sunlight. There seemed to be nobody on the earth but themselves. They lay in the grass and the girl came closer to him and clung to his neck, nestling in the hollow between his ear and his shoulder.

'Byron, listen,' she whispered. 'I'm out of control. Just don't hurt me, that's all.'

The words sunk in slowly through the pot haze that had his mind beginning to echo and snag on itself the way it did when he had to think behind the stuff. Whew. If he were a pothead he'd have to live in the desert.

'Hurt you. How'm I gonna hurt you?'

'You know. Just . . . y'know, the way a man can hurt a girl. They're all classics.'

Byron's head flew back and suddenly he was laughing in great whoops. Wendy's eyes widened as if he had reached out and pinched her.

'Hey — I don't want to hear that bullshit — I'm not about to hurt somebody I *love*.' He fired the word love like a pistol shot.

She was speechless. Her mouth hung open.

'I love you, honey. I do!' he rushed on, full of eagerness, a little boy's wide-eyed excitement. 'I think about it every second. I'm so much in love with you I'm blind!'

She held him. 'Oh, Byron —'

If some other guy had said it, Wendy would have laughed. But she was rivetted to him now as his voice took on a vibrant harshness, like a gospel revivalist.

'Listen, things are coming together all over. If you look around the world, you can see big plans shaping up. I need you, honey, because what I'm trying to do is hard, it's almost the hardest thing a man could do, it's almost impossible.'

A thought flew across Wendy's mind: Who was this talking now? She felt a shift in his identity that sent a little chill down her spine.

'What is it?' she said. 'What are you trying to do?'

Love and ambition seemed to flow together in Byron's face. He stood over her and his eyes sparked with flecks of inner light.

'What *he* can't do anymore. What he told me to do when he gave me his gun. One day there's gonna be a hole in the sky where Elvis Presley used to be and I've got to be prepared.'

Wendy didn't know how to take what he was saying. Something about it was upsetting her. His eyes weren't focused on anything. His voice was a monotonous drone. It was like listening to someone hypnotised.

Suddenly he looked her in the eye. 'You know, I'm a miracle. I had every goddamn strike against me. I'm a

42

nobody, a nothing. But I'm riding a wave now, this is a wave we're on. Hang on, baby, because I'm going somewhere!'

Something was frightening her, the fierceness, the ranting. 'I'm going somewhere too,' she added.

'Well, hell, let's go together!' he crowed. A hint of fun softened his face. 'Do you love me?'

The fear coursed lightly through her stomach. She brushed it aside.

'Yes . . .'

'Say it.'

'I . . . love you, Byron.'

The End
of the Road

August 10, 1977

Dear Col. Parker:
    This is to inform you that I have been signed to appear regularly with my band at 'TR's' one of Portland's premier supperclubs. As you will recall from my earlier letters, I am (to my knowledge) the only exclusive example of early Elvis style, including Elvis himself, in the USA.
    Re: your visit to this area next week, I invite you to view the 'Prince Byron Rock 'n' Roll Revue' at TR's on Tuesday, Wednesday or Thursday (as I am now featured Thursday nights as well). It might possibly give Elvis a few ideas as to the strong points of his youthful show of the mid to late fifties. Mr T.R. Hogan joins me in welcoming you to Portland.

                Yours truly,
                Byron, 'Prince Byron' Bluford

The air in TR's was so thick you could slice it with a broken beer bottle. Years back, someone had installed a pair of smoke eaters, but nobody could remember when they stopped working. It was no place for the squeamish or refined, even though 'Portland's finest live entertainment' had theoretically upgraded the status of the joint. Before Byron, Hogan had experimented with various attempts to give the room a touch of sophistication. But all experiments had ended with one dropped-out New York acid-casualty who called himself 'Sir Lancelot'.

Lancelot never quite grasped the personality of the club. He would burst forth grandly from the back of the house, strumming his way forward like an angry troubador. Hitting the stage in full trot, he would unleash a sneering version of 'Masters of War' or 'Maggie's Farm'. The subtext was indignation with society, which he figured would be picked up and shared by the working-class crowd. But something about his presence, or lack of it, had the curious effect of scattering attention. He was worse than a zero — he created chaos.

On what turned out to be his last night at TR's, he tried to gain control by demanding requests. When that fell flat, he tightened up his jaw and ploughed into 'Dead Skunk', a sing-along (what could the fool be thinking of — get TR's to *sing along?*). He reached the chorus and shouted, 'Everybody . . .!' as if he expected the Mormon Tabernacle choir. Nothing happened.

'Sit down,' somebody said, loud and clear.

Sir Lancelot's face reddened. He belted the chorus again, alone, as if determined to force the place into submission through sheer petulance. Then he made his big mistake. On a sudden impulse he leaped off the stage and began to circulate, snarling the chorus directly into people's faces. Once off-mike he couldn't be heard. The general roar of the room swallowed him up and he was lost — no longer the featured performer now, just a roaming nuisance.

A big Cavanaugh worker rose up and started to sing along, trailing after Lancelot until he crashed heavily through several tables. At this point, Hogan intervened.

'The set's over, Lance,' he said gently.

Sir Lancelot appealed madly to the crowd: The Man says I can't play music.' His face crinkled into a look of gleeful defiance. He was breaking out in a sweat. 'He says I can't play my *music!*'

'Come on, pal. Pack up.' said Hogan.

Lancelot turned on him savagely: 'I'm not going anywhere, you loathsome old toad —!'

At that point, Lance's lady moved in, a wan hippy girl with fear in her moon-shaped face. She had his guitar case and his railroader's cap. 'C'mon, Chuck,' she whispered. Hogan, who had grabbed the troubadour by the T-shirt, loosened his grip. The boy slumped a little and let his girlfriend put the guitar away.

'Am I fired?' he said after a moment.

'You're fired.'

He fixed Hogan with a cool stare. 'Why?'

'Because nobody wants to listen to you or look at you — you're a black hole. Try another job, son, this ain't for you. You're just not good enough to get away with being crazy.'

Lance half-smiled, as if Hogan had just tried to sell him the Brooklyn Bridge. His contempt was unbounded. They had rejected Bobby Dylan, they had crucified Christ. The gap that yawned between his grand vision and his mundane, irritating stage presence simply didn't exist.

'You'll hear from the people!'

Hogan exploded: 'I already heard from 'em! Whaddya think just happened here?' Hogan pushed him toward the door. 'Get out — I don't have time for this!'

Sir Lancelot walked off into the night with his neck at a sad, defensive angle.

Good-by visions, hello life.

No such problems existed for Prince Byron. When he was on, his presence restructed the space of the room. The house band suddenly came to life behind him. Attention flowed only one way — toward Byron. Hogan knew he had a gem. As July wore on, the Prince Byron Rock 'n' Roll Revue pulled in growing numbers of fans, until Tuesday and Wednesday nights were beating out weekends. Hogan added Thursday and gave Byron a small raise.

'When he gives me weekends,' Byron told Larry, 'I'm gonna quit Cavanaugh. But *damn*, if I just didn't have to be workin in a fuckin' pump factory when Colonel Parker hits town!'

'If you want weekends,' said Larry, who liked to pretend he was Byron's manager, 'we're gonna have to bargain for 'em.'

'Ah, hell —'

'Listen, weekend business takes care of itself. Hogan's got you right where he needs you — in the middle of his week. And as for Colonel Parker, what he doesn't know won't hurt him.'

Byron shook his head solemnly. 'Colonel Parker knows everything, man. Everything.'

July turned into August — going on late summertime in Maine, but hot and stinking inside TR's. One Thursday night, with Elvis and the Colonel's visit just days away, Wendy pulled Byron out behind the club where there was an empty lot and some fresh air. She was in a foul mood. The lot was alive with the sound of puking drunks.

'You could do better than this, Byron,' she nagged gently. 'Not just more nights here — I mean someplace else altogether. This is the pits, man, this whole place, this whole town —'

From the dark side of the club came a loud tinkle — some turkey watering a hubcap. 'Listen to me, Byron —'

What she didn't know was that old Byron was way ahead of her.

'I've already been working on it, baby.' His eyes sparkled. It was Prince Byron talking. 'I'm already halfway there . . .'

In fact, he had a plan. He needed representation, namely a booking agent. Colonel Parker and Elvis were coming to town! When they arrived, Byron wanted to be in the position of an equal, a fellow professional. It would kill two birds with one stone: enhance his status with the Colonel and turn up better work while he waited for Elvis to call it quits. He was already thinking *Boston*.

Boston was where the New England agents were. If he hooked up with an agency out of Boston, doing what he did now, he could work steady, whatever happened, for real

47

bucks. For the first time in his life, he wouldn't be scrambling uphill, and when the Colonel came to town Byron could just drop the news casually — a big-city agent connection.

He had already gotten Larry to take pictures — slick publicity-type shots — and make a couple of tapes ('Live at TR's). Monday morning he dressed up in his supreme best gear and grabbed the early Boston bus. The plan was to drop into several booking agencies — Larry had told him to forget phone calls, you just show up and make a strong impression, then you're in. He'd simply look them over, sign with the sharpest outfit, and the rest'd be history.

There were half-a-dozen agencies within walking distance of the Boston Greyhound Terminal. Byron had eaten into his stash of uppers on the bus and was ready to strut as he walked through the station. It was a bright hot day in the old Bean Town. There was energy in the air, and he picked up plenty of looks as he walked down Boylston Street beside what had to be the Bostom Common, past the mouldy old statues, past the winos and panhandlers. Through the trees he could see a building with a shiny gold dome. State House, most likely. The idea occurred to him to drop in on the Governor. Why not, the way he felt? Greetings from the State of Maine.

But right away he was running into snags. The agency offers were full of musicians. There were blacks, folkies, hard rockers — just hanging around. It was hard to get anybody's attention. The phones were ringing off the hook. The secretaries said he couldn't see the agents without an appointment, just leave his picture and his tape. But, hell, he only had two tapes — and less than a dozen pictures. These didn't look like first-class agencies anyway. Too much confusion. Byron just smiled and kept moving — back the other way, through a trendy part of town where everybody dressed just so and sat around in sidewalk cafes sipping little glasses of wine and soda water. From looking at the storefronts you couldn't even tell what the hell was on sale inside. Unless swank bullshit. Then up above what they called Copley Square, Boylston turned into a youth street, full of college kids buying records. Byron had a feeling this was a more promising part of town.

Superstars was a very zippy young rock agency — so hip it looked like they got their hair styled there every ten minutes. Byron had to sit and watch while one of the agents, whose name was Tad, helped the secretary hang up a big purple neon sign that said:

SUPERSTARS
CONCERT PROMOTION, BOOKING,
ARTIST MANAGEMENT

Tad wore spiffy little English high-heeled shoes and kept touching his shaggy hair.

'How's that, Byron? Is it straight, man?' he repeated several times.

Finally they plugged the damn thing in. Tad and the girl went 'Oh, wow!' when it lit up. Another agent, a balding guy with a full beard, came in smoking a joint. His name was Herbie. He looked at the sign, said 'Oh wow!' and wandered off again. Byron shifted haunches and cleared his throat. He was being patient.

Abruptly, Tad turned to business:

'Okay, man,' — the voice was now officious — 'in twenty-five words or less tell me why we oughta book the Prince Byron Rock 'n' Roll Revue.'

Byron took a deep breath. 'Like I said, the woods are full of Elvis fans that never saw the real Elvis and never will.'

'Not sure.' Tad shrugged. 'He tours — you oughta know he's in Portland this week, man!'

'I know, I'm in touch with his organisation. But that —' Byron paused significantly. 'That ain't the *real* Elvis.'

'Yah. Sharlene, what do you know about Elvis Presley.'

The secretary stopped chewing on her bubble gum for a second. "Hound Dog," right?"

Tad looked back at Byron with a smirk.

'She's nineteen going on sixteen — see what you're up

against? We book mostly schools, Byron. Elvis is out of the past. As we all know, he's fat, he's spilling out of his jumpsuit —'

'That's the whole point of my act,' Byron snapped. 'I do *early* Elvis, like he was fifteen years ago.'

'Byron, it's not our audience. College kids are into what's happening right now. This is nostalgia —'

'This ain't nostalgia.' Byron felt suddenly hot.

Tad looked at him with an incredulous smile.

'Well, it sure smells like it to me, my friend. A novelty — and that's stretching it. How old are you?'

'Thirty-four.'

'Well, I'm twenty-four, and to me early Elvis is memory lane — along with Fabian and Bill Haley and Carl Perkins. It might go over in Vegas with the double-knit crowd, but on the college circuit it's dead meat.'

A red cloud seemed to fall around Byron's eyes. He knew he was losing it with this kid.

'Have you seen me work?' Something in Byron's voice put Tad on guard. His face tightened and he sat up.

'Ah, no — I mean, how could I — ?'

'See me work before you be my judge and goddamn jury.' He could hardly see Tad through the haze of red.

Tad sighed and looked at his watch.

'Byron, where are we going with this? You're not getting the point —'

Unexpectedly, Byron jumped to his feet and took a menacing step toward Tad. His voice was snapping with intensity.

'Shut the fuck up, punk!'

Tad shrunk back in horror. Herbie's face appeared in the doorway. Sharlene swiveled slowly around.

Tad cleared his throat. 'Look, uh, Byron. We've got your picture, got the tape — I'll honestly try to come up with something. We've got your phone number —'

Byron's voice cut like a razor. 'Forget it, man. I don't need you. I don't need your fuckin' double-talk.'

'Byron, I promise you. If something comes up —' Tad

was inching his chair toward Herbie's office. 'Um, Herbie? Could ya come here a second?'

Herbie's face vanished instantly.

'Something comes up, you just suck on it,' Byron muttered, stalking out the front door, slamming it, ferociously.

Tad and Sharlene breathed with relief. Herbie now ventured in from his office. 'Who was that? Who the *hell* was that?

'Just what the world needs,' Tad sneered. 'Another Elvis Presley.'

Byron hit the street like a storm. His mind was reeling. He didn't know where he was going. He didn't care. He had failed. He'd go back to Portland now with nothing. He vaguely hoped nobody crossed him right this moment because he felt dangerous. It was all darkness up ahead.

He bought a half-pint of whiskey and downed it in the street in three or four gulps. He passed through the Public Garden, where he met a ratty-looking hippie who sold him some quaaludes. He wandered on to Charles Street and bought a quart of beer, chugging the ludes down, draining the bottle. Now he was feeling a little better. He wanted to ask where the hell the bus station was, but realised people were crossing the street to stay out of his way.

He rolled into a bar called Fathers and had a few whiskeys with a hoarse, tough-looking kid who claimed to be a boxer. The kid said he'd walk to the bus station with him, but they ended up downtown where the strip clubs were. The kid wanted another drink so they stopped in a joint where the strippers started off in evening gowns and went all the way down to nothing. Byron lost touch with the kid. He remembered sitting heavily at a table watching stripper after stripper till it made no sense, and he saw spangles and body shapes moving around out there with darkness creeping over all of it.

When he woke up, he was in a park somewhere. It was night. As he lay on the ground trying to make sense of just one goddamn thing, the sky began to lighten. It was dawn.

He drew himself into a sitting position. He wiped his face and then the full force of his hangover hit him. His head burned and throbbed. A bolt of nausea sent him to his knees, gagging, but his guts were long since puked out and nothing came up. He had slept in a patch of bare dust, and his clothes were grimy with it. Fighting through the pain, he stood up and made himself walk. He walked toward the nearest street and asked an old bum for directions to the bus station. His pictures were gone, his tapes were gone, he was a mess.

At the Greyhound terminal he cleaned himself up a little. He had been rolled sometime during the night — rolled for an empty — but they missed the return ticket in his shirt pocket. There was a bus leaving for Portland. Scruffy, stinking, moving like an old man, he climbed on board and took a seat back near the toilet.

It was over, for sure. He knew that. He was finished. There was no place down here for a goddamn Prince Byron. He'd never go beyond TR's. He'd never get out of the goddam factories. He was a nobody. A zombie. A walking corpse. He was no more Elvis than he was Jesus Christ! Why not just give it up? Give it up to Elvis. Elvis had him beat out, finessed, dominated, humbled in every possible way.

Then he was in the toilet, retching again. The bus started up. Byron missed the headlines in the row of newspaper machines as the bus rolled out. They all said the same thing: ELVIS PRESLEY DEAD.

Thanks Elvis

She spooned some sugar into her coffee and tried not to hear Marcia gnawing on her Shredded Wheat or Katie blowing her nose while she hoarded the paper. Wendy was close to the end of her string with these ladies. They were too much like her sisters. Marcia was skinny-faced, like a rat, and Katie had a kind of grey blob for a face that shook like Jell-O when she was upset. Why they ever picked Wendy as a roommate was a mystery to her. Everything she did seemed to get their goat. If she had a man in her room, it took them a week to get over that. If she came in late from a gig, she'd hear about that. If she tried to tell them what was going on in her life they'd listen, but as if she were making a slightly sordid confession. She fascinated them and revolted them at the same time. They got the same thrill out of her they got from watching soaps or reading *The Enquirer*.

Take Byron, for example: they were madly curious about the affair but horrified at the thought of this local Elvis-type. Lately she was spending so many nights at Byron's she hardly spoke to them about anything. She knew they were dying to suck up the details, but if they didn't have the balls to inquire it was their own problem.

He had been due back last night. Wendy wondered why she hadn't gotten at least a call from him. Now it was 8 A.M. Marcia was slurping her coffee and working on another bowl of Shredded Wheat. Katie was sitting on the paper. Wendy was just about to give him a call, in case he had over-slept for work, when the kitchen door flew open and he crashed in, looking like an axe-murderer.

Marcia's coffee cup fluttered, spattering brew on her lap. Katie's face jiggled like vanilla pudding.

'Jesus, Byron —' said Wendy. 'What happened?'

'I need some coffee,' he muttered.

Katie and Marcia finished up fast, rattling their cups, and cleared out of the house. Byron slumped at the table, staring at the floor and sipping his coffee. Wendy sat with him in silence, watching, waiting. Suddenly he bolted for the bathroom and puked up the coffee. Wendy followed him to the john and knelt down beside him, holding his head.

'Can't keep anything down,' he whispered harshly. Then he was weeping. He heaved a few times in between waves of sobs and burbled miserably, 'I can't get a goddamn break. Who am I kidding? I'm a fuckin' loser —'

'Stop feeling sorry for yourself,' Wendy said in a voice so steely it surprised even her. 'What happened?'

'Oh, mama,' he moaned, reaching for her, trying to bury his face in her. 'I got shut down. Oh, God, I'm a fuckin' nobody —'

'Stop it, Byron.'

'I'm in a hole and I can't get out. I try one thing, I try another . . . I oughta die and get it over with.'

Wendy kissed him and roughed up his hair.

'Who's your hair stylist? Nice job.'

Byron looked at her with sudden feeling.

'Listen, honey — I want you to live with me. I need you with me all the time. I want you to move in with me —'

'Let's get you to work first.'

'Fuck it. Fuck work. I want you with me.'

Wendy ran a washcloth over his face and combed his hair. The thought of living with Byron had already occurred to her.

Let me think about it. Come on, Byron, let's go.

He was a good hour late for work. Naturally, Turner had to ride his ass about that — that and being absent the day before. But Byron was determined to let it roll off today. He was too weak, he hurt too bad to let Turner's bullshit get him. He settled into the line and struggled to fight off the nausea that was still with him. He was trying to be a good robot. Trying so hard that he didn't see Turner huddling over the paper with old man Timbro. Turner broke away with a laugh and they both sneaked a look at Byron before Timbro headed back to his office.

Then Turner was coming straight at him with a silly grin smeared across his face, holding up the paper so Byron had to see the front page.

'Looky here, Byron.'

It was Portland's version of the headline.

ELVIS PRESLEY DEAD AT 42

Byron stared at the paper, goggle-eyed. The room seemed to go white. A heavy ripple of dizziness rolled over him. He took a deep breath and reeled back several steps. His mouth hung open and his eyes rolled up.

Turner's grin faded. 'What's the matter with you — ?'

'I'm okay.'

'Well, keep working, man. It ain't a national emergency —'

Byron swayed and fell to the floor, out cold.

'Christ —!' sputtered Turner. Then he shouted, 'Get the nurse over here, for God's sake. He's fainted!'

'Wednesday . . . Elvis's body lay in a solid copper casket, wearing a white suit, a light blue shirt, and a dark blue tie. An estimated twenty thousand mourners, many overcome by heat and exhaustion, filed through Graceland Mansion to view the remains in a final tribute to the King of Rock 'n' Roll . . .'

Byron slumped in front of the TV, in his underwear, his eyes hidden behind dark glasses. Since they had brought him home, he had stared hypnotically at whatever flashed across the screen — movies, soaps, game shows, interspersed with the occasional mention of Elvis, a tribute, a flash of old clips, news reports of the funeral, and now, the morning after, a summary news feature. On the screen, Elvis crooned, kicked ass, kissed shyly . . .

Byron had started drinking again as soon as he cold, not explosively this time but steadily, relentlessly, drinking himself into a trance to dull the shock. Wendy had been in and out but she couldn't do anything with him, and something told her to keep her distance — at least for a while.

'The funeral procession was led by eleven white Cadillacs and a full entourage of motorcycle policemen down the three-mile route from Graceland to Forest Hills Cemetery. Along the way eight thousand mourners stood silently, saying their last goodbye to the man who, in life, had meant more to them than politicians, religious leaders, or sports heroes . . .'

It was over. He was gone. Byron felt old. He felt the hands of death that push you into the future, into the dark. He felt those clammy hands closing around him. If Elvis Presley couldn't wiggle through those hands, who the hell could? He felt his own heart beat and seize and rumble and he waited for it to burst like Elvis's. He wanted to die.

Down in Boston, Tad, held the poster up for Herbie's appraisal. It said:

HONOUR ELVIS!
A MEMORIAL CONCERT FOR THE MAN
WHO STARTED IT ALL
HARVARD SQUARE THEATRE — SATURDAY,
AUGUST 20, 7 P.M.

'Wow!' said Herbie, wriggling with glee. 'What a brilliant move!'

'A pre-emptive strike, man — low-cost, to be sure. Like, the local bands we get for nothing, right? Appeal to their sense of history — y'know, the funeral, the emotional outpourings, the tributes and blah, blah —'

'What a coup. The Harvard Square — nobody does concerts there anymore!' Herbie sucked on a joint.

'Hey — just goes to show: You get an option on a date, hang onto it. Something's bound to turn up.' Tad cast an upward glance. 'Thanks, Elvis —'

'A movie theatre — aw, wait a minute, I'm having a vision. We start off with, y'know, *Jailhouse Rock* or something — then the screen rolls back and there's —'

'No movies, man. We're going to off movies in that theatre for good. It's one of the best small concert halls around, and if we don't make a move on it soon the jerks that run it'll break it up into a triplex and that'll be the end of concert rock in Harvard Square.'

'Who cares, though — like ultimately?'

'Who *cares?*' Tad sighted down his nose at Herbie. 'You'd have to be a Harvard man, old boy. Let's just say there's a lot of very old, very hip money out there that would love to see control of that theatre pass to us. Think about *that*, now — the Superstars' Theatre, a mere step away from Harvard Yard!'

Herbie blew his nose. 'Gotcha.'

'Okay: a long-term strategy to gain control over there, right?' Tad stroked the poster lovingly. 'We're opening with knockout force . . . with the ultimate promotional vehicle — death.'

Herbie wailed with delight. 'Wow, death! Oh, wow . . . !' Then a sudden frown — something somber crossing his mind.

'What? What?' Tad's toe tapped nervously.

'Needs something, needs something, one more element.'

Tad leaned back and relaxed, twirling his death's head coke spoon. 'As usual, Herbie-bubby, I'm one step ahead of you,' he said with a smug grin. 'Just guess who's gonna close the show?'

When Byron's phone rang, he was still parked in front of the tube. Wendy had decided enough was enough. She'd clean the place, cook him a healthy breakfast, water his plants — but she was damned if she would answer his phone while he sat there like a zombie. It rang four times without a twitch out of him. Finally she dropped the watering can and rushed to pick up the receiver.

'Don't answer it!' Byron said sharply.

She glanced at him. 'Why not?'

'Just don't. I don't wanna talk to anybody.'

Wendy frowned. 'That's ridiculous. Why have a phone if you're not going to answer it?' But she hesitated.

The phone stopped ringing. With a sigh, Wendy returned to the plants. 'Don't put so much damn water in there.'

'Water 'em yourself if you don't like it,' she snapped back. She stared for a moment, fuming. 'Why don't you get out of that chair? You're not dead. Elvis died, not you — !'

'Just leave me alone,' Byron roared. 'You haven't got the slightest fuckin' idea what's going on here, do you? You just don't fuckin' get it —'

'I guess not.'

The phone rang again. This time Wendy picked it up.

'Hello?' She eyed Byron coolly. 'Just a minute . . .'

Without a word, she dropped the receiver to the floor and left it dangling as she walked out of the room. Byron watched it bounce. He got up and retrieved it, held it in his hand for a moment, finally put it to his ear.

'Yeah.'

The voice dripped honey. 'Byron? Tad at Superstars, man. Hey, I wanna apologise about Monday, about that misunderstanding, y'know — we're just in *shock* over here about Elvis, man, and that's sorta why I'm calling — because we're in the middle of doing something about it and we really, really need your help.'

Tad paused expectantly. There was no response so he plunged on.

'So, ah . . . here's what we're doing man: We're putting on a memorial concert — a big tribute to Elvis — "Honour Elvis", we're calling it. We want you to come down and do a medley for us, man. Early Elvis, late Elvis, whatever it is you do. How about it?'

Byron glanced incredulously at the phone in his hand and hung up with a ferocious slam.

At Superstars everyone heard the slam. Sharlene whistled through her teeth. Tad and Herbie, huddled over the speaker-phone, glanced at each other with mild surprise.

'Hello?' Herbie said loudly. 'Hello, Byron . . . ?'

'Don't worry,' Tad said after considering it for a moment. 'He'll come around. He may be an idiot — but he's not a fool.'

'They want me to rob his grave. They want me to eat his body!' Byron was pacing back and forth desperately. 'I can't do this, I can't smear his memory —'

'But it's a tribute. The whole point is to honour him, isn't it?'

'I don't care what they're callin' it — they're heaping shit on his memory,' Byron raved. 'I don't wanna have anything to do with those agency bastards. I wasn't good enough for 'em three days ago, now they want my ass. How come? I'll tell you fuckin' how come — they want me to help 'em rob his grave!'

The phone rang again. Byron looked toward the living room in stony silence. His jaw set. He waited, indecisive, unable to move — then finally, unable not to move.

Tad spoke to Byron now in a simple, sincere tone.

'Man, these are very difficult days. The King is dead, right? Somebody's gotta carry on . . .'

He winked at Herbie, who made a silent oh-wow. Tad propped his feet up on the desk and leaned into the speaker-phone.

'The way we feel, man, it's like — to honour this man's memory, the man who invented rock 'n' roll — it's just such an *important* thing to do, for all of us . . . I mean, I beg you, man. I'm on my kness. Here's a chance to warm a lot of hearts.'

Tad closed his eyes and waited.

Finally, Byron's voice came back, a tiny rasp over the speaker-phone.

'Yeah . . . all right.'

Tad and Herbie silently slapped hands.

'You won't regret this, man,' Tad purred. 'You won't regret it.'

Respect for the Fuckin' Dead

TO: COL. TOM PARKER
C/O GRACELAND
MEMPHIS, TENNESSEE

APPEARING AS STAR ATTRACTION IN TRIBUTE TO ELVIS.
SATURDAY, 7 PM, HARVARD SQUARE THEATRE, CAM-
BRIDGE, MASSACHUSETTS. VITAL YOU TRY TO COME.
MUST LOOK FORWARD TO FUTURE. NOW MORE THAN
EVER I URGE YOU TO TALK TO ME.

PRINCE BYRON

'SATURDA-A-A-A-A-A-A-A-AY . . . !!'

The Boston stations repeated the ad every ten minutes —
a piece of 'Blue Suede Shoes' banging away in the
background and two blabbering announcers, drag strip-
style.

'*Superstars presents — HONOUR ELVIS DAY, a special
memorial concert at the Harvard Square Theatre Saturday night
at seven, to remember the King of Rock 'n' Roll. Listen to this
incredible line-up- Leather Boys! RatFunk! Greasers Holiday!
Spacemud! Tire Iron! And Special guest Prince Byron IS
ELVIS in a tribute to the man who started it all. The King is
Dead — and what a royal send-off! Tickets at the box office,
first-come first served, so "get down" and honour Elvis
Saturda-a-a-a-ay!*'

They heard it six or eight times on the way down from
Portland. 'Holy shit,' said Larry, 'They must've bought the
station!'

Each time the ad blared on, Byron whitened and took a swallow of whiskey. His fingers shook as he rubbed his lips. *Prince Byron is Elvis*. Actually saying that on the radio. He looked around. Where the hell were they? Was this a fucking sight-seeing tour?

'Back Bay,' Larry said. 'That's M.I.T. over there.'

Byron didn't really care if the Pope was over there. He was a shade this side of head-spinning drunk and trying to keep cool.

'Fuck M.I.T.'

The horrors. *Prince Byron is Elvis* . . . His mind jangled crazily as if there were hamsters inside turning wheels.

He thought: The hole is open, waiting to be filled. Elvis prophesied all this when he gave up his gun. Now, by dying the night before Portland, the very night — he had cleared the path. Open field ahead, all the way . . .

When the thoughts came this way it made sense. It made him strong. *Prince Byron is Elvis* . . . Yes, it was smart to send the wire to Colonel Parker, to remind him. It made sense to be doing this show, even with cannibals like Tad and Herbie — who were on their hands and knees with their teeth in Elvis's heart. This thing could go bigger than those assholes ever dreamed.

Byron kept sipping whiskey — just enough to dampen the horrors lurking behind the thoughts, the buzzing grids at the back of his head. His eyes were glassy with apprehension when they approached the theatre. Wendy snuggled close and shook him gently.

'You're gonna be okay,' she said.

Early in the day, swarms of kids from the suburbs had descended on Harvard Square, forming the beginnings of a mob in front of the theatre. They were scruffy, long-haired 'motor-heads' — the kids Larry called 'the downers and Boone's Farm set' — tough kids with blankets and bottles of wine, fans of the local bands, bikers without bikes, come to blow their heads away on wine, dope and music.

Byron saw the mob in front of the theatre and stopped short. The cops had set up barricades, trying to contain the

61

crowd, which by now spilled over the sidewalk into the street. More kids kept arriving. Bikes roared up as the real bikers crowded in. It was only mid-afternoon, with the concert four hours away.

'They've got trouble here,' Byron said.

In side, Tad was officiating with anxious precision. He unlocked the glass lobby door for Byron and Wendy, then immediately relocked it and rushed off to deal with some crisis in the box office. Herbie escorted them backstage.

'You'll be going on last,' said Herbie, who was talking compulsively to keep his nerves down. 'RatFunk'll back you — they know alla Elvis's shit. Their guitar player, Rooster Van Dyke, he knows all that shit, Elvis, Chuck Berry, Stones, Zeppelin, all that shit. RatFunk. That's Danny Malone's band. I'll introduce ya — oh, shit what a day! I don't know, man — want a joint? There's plenty of booze and stuff backstage. This is gonna be one to remember, man, I'm tellin' you . . .'

Backstage the rockers were milling around in whatever space was available. Roadies hauled equipment in and stowed it in the wings, conferring about staging problems, lighting, the house sound system. A friendly coke dealer spooned his way from band to band. Groupies hovered in the corners and the musicians' girlfriends stuck close, hanging around their men with cool territorial presences.

Herbie introduced Byron to Danny Malone, who responded with elaborate super-jive sweetness.

'My pleasure, man, my pleasure,' he said, clapping Byron with a hearty overhand grip. Herbie smiled benignly and departed, leaving Byron and Danny to work out the mechanics of Byron's medley. Danny summoned Rooster, a tall bony kid with a mop of dirty blond hair.

'Check it out with the Rooster, man. I won't even be on stage.' He bowed out with a sunny grin and drifted toward the coke dealer.

Rooster took it all down on a piece of paper.

' "Hound Dog," sure . . . "Blue Suede Shoes" . . . "Heartbreak Hotel", ah sure . . . "Don't Be Cruel," yah

. . .' He taped the list to his guitar and meandered off to chat with his bass player.

Byron was starting to lose it. This wasn't his crowd. He didn't identify with these flash rock 'n' roll band guys. They were little and skinny and dressed in glittery feminine clothes. They all had hoarse voices and runny noses. Elvis never dug this kind of crowd. He wouldn't be doing a show like this, not even his own memorial; he wouldn't be caught dead in here.

'Are you okay, honey?' Wendy was studying him close up.

'Hell, where's Larry? Let's eat some fuckin' dope.'

By three o'clock there was complete confusion out front. At four a plainclothes cop was inside shouting at Tad.

'You gotta kill those radio ads! You've got a mob out there — it's gonna be another Altamont!'

At five, Tad stood just inside the lobby doors, peering out at the turmoil. Herbie, Sharlene, and several long-haired ushers in 'Superstars' T-shirts stood around nervously awaiting instructions.

'Are the bands all here?' asked Tad.

'Yeah,' said Herbie.

'Sharlene, go get 'em ready.' Tad gritted his teeth and stared grimly ahead. 'We're gonna have to start early.'

Through the heavy glass they faced the crowd. The crush was enormous. People were jammed against the doors like souls churning in hell, pleading through the glass.

'Okay,' Tad snapped, 'Let 'em in.'

The ushers threw open the doors and a roar went up from the street. They stampeded, surging throughout the lobby and into the seats, filling every available inch of space, clogging the aisles.

'It's full, it's full!' Herbie shouted back desperately.

'That's it,' Tad barked at the ushers. 'Lock 'em up!'

They struggled to close the door against the squirming rush of bodies. Finally the pushing waned as, inch by inch, the doors were forced shut. Tad sat heavily on the floor, dripping sweat. 'Good grief,' he wailed. 'We didn't collect a single ticket!'

Out in the street, the rest of the crowd realised they weren't getting in. Fists were raised, rocks and bottles flew. Now it was a genuine riot. In the middle of the mob, a scrawny, wasted kid waved a chrome-plated revolver in the air. Several clean-cut hero types tried to take it away from him. Blasted and incoherent, he shot one of them in the leg. Now the cops moved in, flailing away with nightsticks, bashing up the heroes as the gun-toting kid slipped away.

Inside, the schedule had been changed to let the big crowd-pleaser, RatFunk, open the show. Tad approached the mike, in a terrified sweat, to introduce them. He cleared his throat and tried to sound jaunty and relaxed.

'Hey, welcome everybody! Let's get mellow, okay?'

A cherry bomb exploded right next to him. The crowd roared with delight.

'RatFunk, everybody —' Tad croaked, cutting his speech and clearing out fast, leaving the mike to Danny Malone.

Danny was tough and self-possessed in front of his band. He knew exactly how to handle a crowd like this.

'Shut up, assholes!' he thundered over the PA.

The crowd cheered.

Suddenly two skinny bikers clambered onto the stage, out of their minds, and lurched toward Rooster, grinning absurdly. Danny drove them back with a flurry of karate kicks, then stormed back to the mike.

'What d'ya think this is, the fuckin' zoo?'

More cheers from the crowd.

'Let's get one thing straight,' he bellowed. 'Anybody else comes up here and I'm gonna punch their fuckin' lights out!'

That brought a heavy macho roar.

'This is supposed to be Elvis's night — let's have a little respect for the fuckin' dead! All right!'

The biggest cheers yet broke over the stage. Danny had engineered his opening. He whipped the mike out of its stand, jumped high in the air, and RatFunk exploded.

The show went by in a haze for Byron. The rockers came and went, the music boomed and pulsated, the crowd thundered. The cherry bombs kept on going off and now he was laughing at them. Wendy smiled at him uncertainly — Byron knew she didn't like him doing quaaludes on top of whiskey. But what the hell — finally, he felt his blood running thick and smooth like corn syrup and he knew he was going to be okay. He felt good — as each band whipped the crowd higher and higher he felt better and better. The horrors left. He wasn't afraid anymore. With his head in gear like this he could do anything. Wendy had to notice the sureness surging into his face. She had to see he was strong now.

The groupies saw it, their eyes flickering over his slick polyester slacks, the apricot sport jacket, the purple shirt with the blue suede shoes. The rockers saw it, making way for him now as he paced in wider and wider circles like a wakening tiger. The coke dealer saw it when he came close to snort him up before time to go — the final ingredient, a little nose candy.

'Elvis . . . ?' said the dealer, offering the spoon. And Byron could hear the recognition in his voice. If Colonel Parker was out there, the ball game would simply be over — instant victory.

On stage Tad was back, more confident now, addressing the crowd:

'People! He's here tonight! Elvis Presley is here — !' He waited for the cheers to die down. 'And more than anyplace else, he's in the actual person of a man who's standing behind me right now with the boys from RatFunk. I mean Prince Byron — the New King of Rock 'n' Roll!'

A vast cheer went up as, simultaneously, everyone lit matches and held them aloft, revealing what looked like the youthful Elvis, resurrected, humble and arrogant, shy and cocky, sexy and mean and ready to fly. The crowd, high enough to get behind any hallucination, instantly bought the vision, a miracle, an unforgettable, supreme, majestic goof. Out of their collective mind with delight, they stood up and roared.

And the medley started, big and loud.

Byron was hot and everybody in the theatre knew it: Wendy watching from the wings. The band, jumping, turning, strutting behind Byron's slithery madness. Tad and Herbie, awestruck by the unexpected. And the crowd, who at first hadn't cared one way or another about Elvis Presley — till there he was, the King, alive, smoking with energy, a firestorm blowing out of Graceland. Byron, most of all, knew how hot he was — raging, writhing, skimming the limits of control, giving the old classics firepower on a scale that dwarfed anything Elvis himself had ever produced. The medley steered itself, like a careening beer truck barely holding the road at eighty miles and hour, needing only the slightest touch to send it veering in any direction.

As he brought the show to a climax of leaps, crashes, power chords, the crowd surged forward, past the ushers and onto the stage. Was Colonel Parker seeing this? They got to Byron, lifted him to their shoulders and held him high. The moment went on and on as he turned, turned, and turned in the chaotic jumble of lights, noise, rush and confusion. He was the King. In the flickering of his mind there was one thought: He was *alive*, he was surging with life, his heart was pumping like an oil well. *Beat that, Elvis!* He raised his fists and grinned wildly, eyes flashing with the ecstasy of sheer power.

Vampire Dreams
or
Nothing But A Bare Pecker

Monday morning Byron was back at his place on the line.
Back in Robot City. Little pieces of chrome and steel toilet
pumps went stuttering by and he joined them together with
fingers that were somebody else's fingers. He was in
somebody else's body. The original reason for all of it was
gone, missing, the reason to be in this place. He was
encased in the solid concrete body of a shambling factory
worker named Bluford. Even to be standing here in
Bluford's body was beyond comprehension. A trace of a
laugh shook his face. Unreal. What could surprise him
now? If the line flipped over and rolled backwards? If he
spread his arms and floated up to the ceiling? No, nothing.
Nothing would surprise him. There was no craziness that
wouldn't look sensible after this turnabout.

What in the bloody hell was he doing here? He had blown
the roof off down in Harvard Square, there was no doubt
about that. Tad and Herbie had fallen all over themselves to
promise him work. Why was he here? Why wasn't he there?
Was he such a simpleton? What the *hell* was he doing on this
goddamn line?

'Well, my oh my, royalty is with us today.'

Turner had sauntered up to the line just across from
Byron. What a charmer. He looked like a dumb joke with
his arms across his belly and his face oozing sarcasm.

'Think you could speed things up a little, your royal
highness? Or is it "Your majesty" now — ?'

A fuse lit inside Byron's head.

'Turner!' he said sharply. 'Come here a second.'

Something in the voice alerted Turner. The sarcasm drained away.

'What for?'

Byron grabbed a section of pipe from the moving belt and held it up. His lip curled into the one-sided grin.

'Stick this up your ass,' he said evenly, and then, with quiet emphasis, 'boy'.

Turner's eyes narrowed. He scowled back in frozen silence. Up and down the line all activity ceased as the workers were instantly aware of the face-off.

'Don't push me, Byron,' said Turner in a hoarse whisper.

'Come on — bend over,' Byron pressed, almost playfully. 'Let's see if turkeys have assholes.'

'Stop the line!' Turner roared.

The assembly line suddenly ground to a halt, leaving high-tension silence in the air. The two men stared at each other, motionless. Suddenly Byron flipped the pipe at Turner, just missing his head. Turner stepped closer. They were face-to-face across the stilled assembly line. Deliberately, without taking his eyes off Turner's, Byron swept his arm along the line, scattering parts to the floor.

'Son of a bitch —' Turner growled.

He launched a gob of spit that landed just under Byron's eyes. Blinding white fury flooded Byron's mind. He clambered over the assembly line, punching Turner two, three, four times, till somebody yelled, 'Byron!'

Turner slumped heavily to the floor, bleeding from his nose and mouth.

There was an amazed silence. Finally Ronnie Spaulding broke it by clapping his hands together and whistling loudly. Then there were a few cheers and catcalls and the place broke into general hilarity. Byron was still standing over the foreman when Larry McCann ran up and grabbed his arm.

'You better get out of here. He's got about twenty cops for cousins. You better get out of town.'

Byron thought: *Boston*. A smile crossed his face.

Just then the old man Timbro's office door flew open.

'What the hell's going on?' he shouted

Turner was semi-conscious now, moaning and clutching his face.

'C'mon,' Larry was urging, and Byron let himself be rushed toward the rear exit. Suddenly he swung around and raised his fist.

'TCB, boys,' he bellowed, 'I'm taking a little vacation!'

Outside, Larry hustled him to the parking lot, moaning in despair.

'Aw, Byron, what a damn fool thing. Now you're gonna get hurt, they're gonna ruin your face. You're gonna have to split, I'll never see you again — what a damn fool thing to do, man!'

'Larry! Come with me, okay?'

Larry was shoving him into the truck. 'I can't damn it. Now get out of here — oh shit, the only friend I've got in this hole and they're gonna kill you. Go on, go on, man, go! Just write me, wherever you are — but Byron, *get moving!*'

First stop was TR's. It was early, but Hogan opened at the crack of dawn to serve his small, wasted coterie of nightshift workers and early-drinking sods. This morning there was only one old drunk, a wizened regular, down at the end of the bar. Byron watched impatiently as Hogan pulled a week's pay out of the cash register and counted it three times.

'There you go, Byron,' he said, shoving the wad of bills across the bar. 'Boston, huh?'

'Got to make my move, Mr Hogan,' Byron answered, counting the bills himself. 'Ain't getting any younger.'

Hogan chuckled at that. 'Seen the morning paper?' he said, tossing a copy on the bar. Byron finished counting and glanced at it. *The Boston Globe*. Hogan had it turned to the entertainment page. There was Byron, on stage with RatFunk. Above the photo, a small headline:

PRINCE BYRON SPARKS ELVIS TRIBUTE

Byron gazed at it, breaking into a grin.

'Can I have this?'

'Better'n that,' said Hogan, reaching under the bar. 'I put one in a frame for you.' It was a plastic Woolworth's special, with the clipping inside. Hogan scratched off the price sticker. 'My compliments, son. Good luck to you . . .'

Byron was genuinely touched. 'Thank you, Mr Hogan.'

Hogan waved him off. 'It's nuthin'. Now, I got a piece of advice for you. Forget about Boston.'

Byron's smile faded.

'No sir, I'm gone,' he said firmly. 'I'm on my way and that's it.'

'I don't mean stay here,' said Hogan, raising a hand. 'But Boston — hell, Boston's just another dinky town on down the road. They'll just book you around New England, that's all. You'll be right back up here, workin' little roadhouses up north and so forth. You'll be breakin' down in the snow, staying in shitty motels. I'll tell you where you ought to be heading. Las Vegas.'

'Las Vegas . . .?' Byron stared back at him blankly.

'That's it. I know that town. I go there twice a year. Elvis Presley was the biggest star they ever had there.' Hogan squinted one eye at him. 'He's gone, but he ain't forgotten. Take my word for it. Go to Vegas. They understand entertainment there, the value of a good act and all that.'

Las Vegas . . .

'Whoa, that's some idea!'

As the full force of the notion struck him, Byron made a fist and punched the air. *Of course! Why not think big? Why waste any more time around New England? Go right to the hot spot. Fill the vacuum. Go in there before the cheap imitators, the "impersonators". Show 'em the real Elvis, the rocker, before some idiot starts doing 'rhinestone' Elvis — the fat man, pasteurised, homogenised, safe as milk.*

Hogan poured himself a beer. 'Like I said when I hired you, Byron, you've got something. Hell, they'd eat you up in Vegas now that he's gone. All of a sudden there's a reason for your act, it makes sense.' He sipped his beer. 'You could do real good in that town.'

Down the bar, the solitary old coot raised his glass and flashed his bare gums. 'Go git 'em for us, Byron!' he yapped.

Larry skidded to a stop in Byron's driveway just in time to catch a glimpse of Byron's truck heading down Larch Street. The house was boarded up. After a short, horn-honking chase, Larry pulled even and motioned him off the road. Through the cab window he saw Byron's hand gripping Elvis's .22 Savage.

"Thought you might be Turner for a second,' Byron muttered.

'He's still trying to count to ten. You really popped him.'

Byron nodded without expression.

'Where you going?'

'Las Vegas.'

Larry stared straight ahead. The pickup trucks, side-by-side, seemed to pant and blow like two horses.

'You must be nuts.'

'Wanta come?' Byron's mouth curled into a sly grin.

'How the hell could I pull that off?'

Byron waved the objection aside. 'Just hit the road, man. Ride with me.'

Larry wouldn't look at him. 'You gonna get chewed to pieces if you go there.'

'Not according to Hogan. Look here —' Byron produced a business card and held it up. Larry slid aross the seat and squinted. The card said:

FRANK BRUNO TALENT AGENCY, INC.
LAS VEGAS

'Hogan played poker with the dude. It's a personal connection. C'mon, Larry, go with me.'

Larry's head wagged from side to side. 'Can't. There's Thelma, the kids, my mom, her mom. They stole my balls years ago. I'm totally incapable of making a move like this. I'm a coward, I'm lazy — forget it. You're the hero, man, not me.'

'Larry, I need a friend.'

'I brought you a going-away present,' he said after a moment and tossed a plastic freezer bag across to Byron. Inside were quaaludes, tranquilisers, a clean ounce of pot, and a tiny baggie of cocaine. Byron smiled and nodded thanks. He reached out for the forlorn fat man and they clasped hands from truck to truck.

'We're always gonna be friends, Larry. Right?'

Larry's lower lip was quivering.

'Hey! You gave me that big push in '58, right? I owe you. See you in Vegas, Larry!'

Byron gunned his truck, hit the road on three wheels, and was gone, leaving Larry snuffling, then sneezing and gagging on the road dust.

'Couldn't you knock once in your life, you slob?' Marcia shrieked, spilling half a cup of coffee into her lap. Byron ignored her and sailed through the kitchen to Wendy's room.

'We're going!' he said with a grin. Then, when she just stared back at him: 'Get packed, honey, we're going to Las Vegas!'

'Las Vegas?' A smile flickered across her face.

'That's it — pack your bag.'

'Wait a minute, Byron —'

'Nah, no waiting — you've been wanting to go someplace special — well, today's the day. We're going!'

'Right this second?'

'Gotta fly while the window's open. C'mon, honey, get packed. Fifteen minutes.'

'But why the big rush? Talk to me!'

'I just stirred up a little trouble for myself, that's all. If I hang around too long it's gonna blow up in my face.'

'Byron —'

'Pack up, honey. I'll tell you all about it on the road.'

Wendy looked around, already calculating what she would take, what she would leave. The instant Byron had said 'Las Vegas,' she knew it was the right move, the only move to make. Sureness flooded her. It was irresistible. Her heart pounded and her cheeks were surging with excitement. She and Byron stared crazily at each other in the same split second they both knew that yes, she'd go!

In an hour they were headed south, cruising down I-95 into New Hampshire. In two hours they had circled Boston without even a look. Boston didn't mean anything now. The country was flowing by, thick, green, dry around the edges from the August heat. They kept the windows down and let the hot summer air blow in, full of the thrill of the future.

Byron figured three days for this trip. He spooned some coke out of Larry's goody bag and suddenly every thought was exultant and made him pound with happiness. Prince Byron in Vegas — yahoo!

At a rest stop in Connecticutt they parked off to the side to drink some whiskey and ended up with their clothes half off, making love in whispers with the sound of picnickers all around them and trucks screaming by twenty yards away. Everything was just the way it ought to be. Open field ahead.

In West Viginia the sky darkened up. Byron wanted to keep rolling right on through but around nine it was raining so hard they got off the interstate near Charleston and found a motel. By the time they had dragged the bags out of the rain they were drenched. Wendy kicked off her shoes and danced around the parking lot till her clothes stuck to her and her hair hung down in dripping strings. Byron caught up with her, sloshing in his boots, and tackled her gently, rolling her onto a grass strip an inch or two deep in water. A crack of lightening struck somewhere nearby.

'Shit!' Wendy struggled to her feet. 'Let's get the hell inside!'

They dried each other off on one of the giant double beds, stroking gently with the towels, rubbing, whispering, licking off the rain, giving each other wet, soulful kisses, melting slowly into sleep.

In the middle of the night Byron bolted awake, moaning

and sweating. Wendy cradled him and stroked his hair till he was calm.

'Just a bad dream, honey,' she said.

'I know.'

'Hey, dreams can't hurt you.'

Byron breathed slowly and stared ahead into the dark. He shrugged. He rubbed his lips with a finger. He seemed to be looking backwards into his mind. His voice was thick and sullen.

'Sometimes I just don't get it . . .' He broke off and tapped his head silently.

Wendy kissed him around his forehead and kept smoothing his hair. He parked his head between her breasts. Like an infant gorilla, she thought. After a while his breathing evened out and little bubbles popped at his lips.

'Mr Bruno, I'm Byron Bluford from Portland, Maine . . .' Byron gripped the steering wheel and stared blankly down the highway. 'Since the death of Elvis Presley I'm the only Authentic practitioner of Elvis's tradition, the early Elvis, that is, the youthful Elvis that took the nation by storm —' His eyes flicked back and forth as he ran through the speech. 'What do you think?'

'So far, so good.'

'Mr Bruno, I'm Byron Bluford from Portland Maine . . . d'you think I ought to just say Maine? Or cut it altogether? I mean, who cares if I'm from Maine?'

'Try to make it sound like you're just saying it — sounds like you're reading.'

'Aw, Jesus!'

'Keep at it, honey. You'll get it after a while.'

'Shit,' Byron wailed. 'What am I doin', anyway? This whole goddamn thing is insane.'

'Do the second part.'

'There's . . . there's a hole in —'

'In the sky —'

'— in the sky where Elvis was, and I'm here . . . I'm here . . .'

'— to fill it.'

'To fill it. Jesus Christ, my mind is like sieve!'

In Memphis, Byron wanted to stop and see Graceland. It was late afternoon and stormclouds hid the sun. As they approached he fell silent and broke into beads of sweat. Lightening streaked across the night-grey sky.

'There it is,' he said.

The mansion's entrance was still thronged with Elvis's mourners — unreal, like Disneyland. They pulled into a parking lot across the highway from the main gate. Byron sat for a minute with a stunned look.

'What's the matter?' said Wendy.

He shook his head and stared at the dashboard.

'C'mon', he muttered suddenly and started the truck.

They were halfway to Little Rock before his mood began to break. They checked into a motel and slept till nightfall. Byron woke up slowly, watching Wendy make peanut butter and jelly sandwiches.

'Wanta hear what I dreamed last night?' he said after a while. 'It all came back when I saw Graceland.'

Wendy sat by him on the bed and waited.

'It was like this: I was hangin' around Graceland. Somebody came running out and says . . . Elvis is inside, with his heart pulled out! And I thought right away, I'm gonna eat that goddamn heart.' His voice had faded to a whisper.

'Eat it?'

'Yep. So I go in and I'm inside a dark room and Elvis is laid out in his coffin and the heart's on a plate beside him. It's sizzling, like a steak. And there'a A-1 Steak Sauce and stuff to eat it with so I sit down and start carving this . . . heart or whatever it is. And I'm eating it, till all of a sudden I see Elvis rising up in his coffin like a vampire and I'm trapped — I can't move — my muscles won't work — all I can do is chew.'

Suddenly Wendy burst out laughing. 'A-1 Steak Sauce . . . oh, boy!'

Byron's eyes widened. His hair seemed to stand up like an angry cat's. He fell into a confused silence. Immediately Wendy realised she had blundered.

'Byron, I'm sorry. I'm sorry, honey —'

It was as if she had tossed him a snoutful of ammonia. With a touch of desperation she watched him receding from her, down a long cavern. Suddenly she wanted to pull him back. She went after him and clung to him, murmuring sweet little whimpers of apology, kissing him until his lips answered just a little. Her hands raced anxiously over his body, stroking and kneading until the Little Prince stood up hard. When he wouldn't come to her, she opened her bathrobe and pressed against him, spreading herself, sliding onto him, straddling and riding him slowly. 'C'mon, baby,' she whispered. 'Don't go away from me.' Finally he rose to her and they rode together.

'Come for me,' she hissed, and shuddered once when she heard him groan — then again when it struck her what things she did to please this dream-ridden lunkhead maniac lover of hers! She shook her head, half expecting to hear marbles rattling inside.

I damn sure must love you, Byron, she thought.

In the morning Byron wolfed down a huge breakfast — including a sizzling steak — and was ready to go. There was no more talk of nightmares. Now it was Destination Vegas, pure and simple. There would be no stops now, except for gas and food. The great middle of the country flowed by and turned slowly into the dusty burning Southwest, so hot sometimes it made them want to drink radiator water.

Byron had loosened up again.

'I tell ya, man — Elvis and me were sent here from a different planet. Krypton or someplace. We both came into the world with nothing but a bare pecker. That's about as fundamental as it gets! If you come from nowhere you have to fire yourself out of a cannon just to get in the game. But I'm in it now, just like Elvis. And honey, let me tell you, it ain't easy! An ordinary person can't just get up and do what

Elvis Presley did — it's impossible if you're ordinary. Impossible!'

Finally, in the cool of the desert night, with the darkness giving way to purple dawn behind them, they saw Vegas twinkling up ahead like a carpet shimmering in the air.

'Well, holy shit!' said Wendy. 'Look at that!'

'I've had dreams about this, too,' Byron said. 'I just didn't know what it was.'

And then they were in the midst of it, the night-jungle of casinos and hotels, cruising downtown and along the Strip — through the wild profusion of lights and colours, with the sky turning quietly from purple to blue.

The big names went by: The Sahara, The Desert Inn, The Sands. The marquees offered up performers like grocery specials. 'Liberace! $12.95 with dinner' . . . 'Charo' . . . 'Danny Thomas' . . . 'Tom Jones' . . . 'Wayne Newton.' A supermarket of stars — all breathing the same air as Byron. Amazing!

Coming back down Paradise Road he saw the Hilton rising out of the desert like a giant rocket. He pulled in.

'We can't stay here,' Wendy protested, but Byron waved her off.

'This was where he worked . . .'

The casino was vast and quiet, the sound of the morning slot machine action dulled by lush carpeting and upholstery. At the door of the showroom, the hotel had erected a little memorial display to Elvis — a protrait, flowers, a guitar. Byron paused, glared oddly at it, then lowered his head. He tugged at the showroom door. It was unlocked.

Inside, the theatre was cool, dark. They could barely see the vast empty stage. Wendy stood a few paces back from Byron, watching him closely. She saw him begin to sway, then stagger. Then he was almost falling toward her, into her arms.

'Byron — ?' His skin was clammy and moist. 'What's wrong, honey?'

'Dizzy.'

She led him back into the casino. He stood and watched

the bacarat players till his skin lost the sweaty whiteness that had come over it.

Out side, the sun was up full. Morning in Vegas. Byron pressed his arms suddenly around Wendy. They held each other in the baking sunlight. Wendy didn't want to talk.

'Let's go to one of those chapels and get married,' Byron said.

'Are you nuts?' said Wendy. She squinted at him in despair. 'Yeah, you are nuts.'

Byron drew back half playfully.

'Well, fuck you, girl —'

'Don't play games with me Byron, okay?' She could almost feel tears. She knew she was tired. 'C'mon, let's get some breakfast.'

Byron watched her climb into the truck. He shrugged, then he laughed. 'Just an idea, honey. You can't kill a guy for having an idea.'

Alive and Well in Las Vegas

At nine o'clock they went looking for Frank Bruno, the agent. The address on the business card led them to a side street motel, The Royal Flush, a blue stucco double-decker with several apartment units. On the door of one, a fake walnut plaque read:

FRANK BRUNO TALENT AGENCY

Byron knocked on the door and waited. No answer. He knocked again and they could hear someone scuffling around inside. Then the door opened a crack and Frank Bruno poked his pudgy, sleepy face out into the sunlight. He was about fifty-five, an elderly beatnik with a paunch, a ratty goatee, and an undershirt that looked like he had tie-dyed it in coffee. He had to clear his throat a few times before he could talk.

'What's this?'

'Mr Bruno?' Byron spoke up brightly. 'My name's Byron Bluford, from Portland, Maine —'

'This about the midgets?'

Byron faltered. 'Midgets? Ah, no. It's about . . . it's about Elvis Presley.'

Bruno relaxed slightly.

'Well — I believe Elvis don't live here anymore.' There was a twinkle in his eye, even though he was squinting. He cocked his head to one side, as if now he had heard everything.

Byron scratched his nose, confused.

'You *are* Frank Bruno, the talent agent?'

'Well, you done your homework.' Bruno's eyes narrowed. 'You ain't a process-server, are you?'

'Hell, no man.'

'I've been expecting a few unauthorised visits. A magician's tryin' to drag me into court on some damn ridiculous beef —' He spat and checked out the parking lot with a glance. 'Well — come on in. I'm getting a headache from this glare.'

Bruno waved them in.

'Sit down, I ain't awake yet. Lemme put some coffee on.' He puttered around the kitchenette while Byron and Wendy looked the place over.

It was a mess. Empty food cans, helf-empty coffee cups, tattered milk cartons lay scattered on the floor next to yellowing stacks of show business papers. Pictures of clients hung at crazy angles on the walls — hypnotists, animal trainers, showgirls, Hammond organists, all signed, 'To my good friend, Frank Bruno.' Byron sniffed: The air smelled like dirty laundry mixed with old garbage.

'Nothing worse than a disgruntled magician,' Bruno muttered, turning the burner up under a kettle of water. 'You can imagine — rabbits in your soup, shit like that.' He sighed. 'Ah, they come and they go, it don't bother me. I been in the same motel for five years — that's something, ain't it?' He turned to Byron and looked him over, tugging on one earlobe. 'Now, er . . . ah —'

'— Byron.'

'I know yer name,' he said with a touch of irritation. 'What's the lady's name?'

Wendy spoke for herself. 'Wendy,' she said, rather cool.

Bruno picked up her vibes and chuckled to himself.

'Very pleased, dear. How 'bout you rustling up this coffee for us so Byron and I can talk. I'm a little short of breath this morning —'

Wendy almost told him what he could do with his coffee, but Byron nudged her firmly toward the kitchenette. Bruno lowered himself into his easy chair, puffing and grunting. He cleared his throat and gave Byron a brand new look.

Time for business.

'Now then — you got an act.'

'Yes, sir. I do Elvis Presley.'

Bruno's expression didn't change, but Byron could see wheels start to revolve. 'You do Elvis?' He nodded. 'Mmhm. Well, ah, tell me — exactly *how* do you do Elvis?'

Byron simply handed him the framed newspaper clipping. Let the world do the talking. Bruno read it silently, moving his lips. After a few minutes, during which Wendy rattled around the kitchenette making as much noise as she could, he looked up.

'Sounds like you tore the place up,' he said with a warm smile.

'I did.'

'Prince Byron, huh. Didn't think you boys'd be here so soon.'

Byron's face went blank.

'You're here for the competition, ain't ya?'

'What competition?'

Bruno squinted at him. 'At the Roman Garden . . . the Battle of the Elvises.'

Byron didn't know what he was talking about. To keep from looking stupid, he raced ahead: 'Mr Bruno, you're looking at the only authentic practitioner of the Elvis Presley tradition. There's a hole in this town where Elvis used to be and I'm here to fill it. What I say is, watch me work in front of a crowd and then make your own decision as to whether the King is dead and gone — or alive and well in Las Vegas!'

Bruno's eyes lit up.

'Well, well, well!' He smiled and his head bounced up and down. Now the wheels were spinning. 'You do look like him. You got a band?'

'I work exclusively with house bands.'

'Smart.' Bruno closed his eyes. 'Well, I'm having a flash of inspiration. How 'bout this — could you work tonight?'

Byron couldn't believe what he was hearing. He broke into a laugh.

'Tonight — ?'

'Bring that phone over here, honey,' Bruno said to Wendy, pointing toward a pile of rubble near his bed. Wendy dug it out and handed it to him.

It rang in his hand.

'Oh shit,' groaned Bruno. 'Hello? Huh . . . ? You're funnin' me!' He clapped a hand over the phone. 'Byron, look out there and tell me if a limo just pulled up.'

Byron nodded. Sure enough, a long silver-grey Cadillac was sitting in the parking lot.

Bruno arched his eyebrows. 'All right, bring 'em in,' he said into the phone and hung up. 'How do ya like that — they called me from their goddamn car!'

Byron watched as three midgets in cowboy hats emerged from the limousine and ambled up the stairs followed by their manager, a shifty-looking old bag of bones in an electric blue suit. They were an act — they juggled and did rope tricks while singing pop classics like 'Yesterday' in three-part munchkin harmony. Halfway through the audition, Bruno withdrew to the kitchenette with the phone.

As the midgets swung into a Hank Williams medley, Bruno finished his call and whispered gruffly into Byron's ear. 'Got ya an audition for tonight!' He was pleased with himself. 'You tell me, does Frank Bruno operate in the fast lane or not? Hell, let's get these nitwits outa here and have breakfast.'

As the morning ripened, Bruno put on a great show of handling every detail. He booked Byron and Wendy into the Royal Flush, a few doors down from his 'office' and put downa week's rent in advance. He gave them a spin around the town, took them grocery shopping, and staked them to the $1.95 breakfast buffet at Circus Circus. In the evening, he drove them to the club, a mangy-looking dive called Lords 'n' Ladies, grabbed a prime booth for himself and Wendy, and made sure 'the boy' had all he wanted to drink. Then he dragged the ravaged old club owner out of his office to shake the boy's hand.

'Great little joint!' said Bruno, rubbing his teeth.

'They're gonna love you.'

Lords 'n' Ladies was a roadhouse hangout for local blue-collars. Inside it smelled like dead cigarettes, piss, and sweat burned dry by the desert sun. A clump of slot machines whirred and jingled continuously. The waitresses wore blond pile wigs. The parking lot was full of pickup trucks belonging to the regulars, plus a smattering of vans and tourist campers lured by the marquee, which read:

PRINCE BYRON IS ELVIS — TONIGHT!

Creamery Butter, the house band, was a standard country-rockguitar group — basic Southern-style rowdies. Their heads were a little scrambled on reefer, but they were friendly enough and told Byron they sure's hell *could* get off behind a set of pure old-fashioned Elvis.

Byron felt at home. This was his kind of briar patch. He knew the moves to make here. He knew he could blow this place away — just like TR's. Up in smoke. Except this was Las Vegas, entertainment capital of the goddamn world — slight difference there! His throat swelled into an exultant gufaw each time the thought went through his head. What a blitz — his first day in Vegas and they'd put his name in lights! *Prince Byron Is Elvis*. What an unbelievable turn of events!

Byron threw down a few bourbons, compliments of the bar. No heavy downs, just a Valium or two. He was fresh. His head was clear. Not a trace of horror. By the time he stepped on the stage, the room was thick with smoke and noise. He tapped his mike to make sure it was on.

'Test . . . test . . .'

A Merle Haggard ballad boomed out of the jukebox. Byron leaned into the mike.

'Let's kill the jukebox, please.'

Bruno, almost unrecognisable in mirrored shades and a ten-gallon hat, scurried over to the big Wurlitzer and yanked the plug, grinding Merle to a halt.

A fat-faced cowboy swivelled around on his bar stool.

'Plug that motherfucker back in — !' he bellowed.

83

Byron's eyes seemed to darken a shade.

'Nope. We're not gonna plug that motherfucker back in,' he drawled, his lip curling, Elvis-style. 'This is where the show is at, right here.'

The TV above the bar was playing a baseball game.

'Bartender,' Byron added, 'let's turn that tube off, okay?'

A handful of baseball fans put up a fuss. The bartender threw up his hands and looked back toward Byron with a shrug. They were regulars.

'I don't work with a TV goin' . . .' said Byron, building the pressure a notch.

Now the bartender shook his head in a firm no — it damned well wouldn't be him that turned it off.

For a second, Byron went blind as a wave of rage broke inside his head. He clenched his teeth and hung on until the wave subsided, then he was cool again, knowing exactly what he had to do. He jumped from the stage, strode across the room, vaulted the bar, shoved the bartender aside, and snapped off the TV. He turned to the astonished baseball fans and faced them with an icy grin.

'You got TV sets all over town, boys,' he said smoothly, 'But I'm live — and there's only one of me.'

The moment froze into silence as the sporting crowd glared across the bar at this outrage. The bartender edged toward the cash register where his shotgun was stashed.

All at once, down the bar, two pairs of hands began to clap ridiculously.

'Atta boy, Elvis!' drawled a voice so countrified that the tension in the room suddenly dissolved in laughter.

Byron wheeled around and saw two tough-looking hippie-cowboys with droopy moustaches, grinning 500-watt grins at him and bobbing their heads up and down in encouragement. Beneath a touch of menace, something about them was so goofy that laughter spread through the bar and the crowd was clapping along with them and cheering Byron on as he walked back to the stage.

' "Hound Dog",' he hissed at the band.

Frank Bruno, who had risen half out of his seat, relaxed

and settled back with an occasional glance at the room to check reaction as the boy got underway. With the first rush of music, Byron was in control, leading Creamery Butter through a set that brought the club owner stumbling out of his office to break up what he thought was a riot.

Frank Bruno grinned like a fat, pampered cat and licked his dry lips. Wendy's face remained set, like a mask, but her eyes had turned into pools of admiration as she watched the new fans pounding Byron on the back and pumping his hands.

'Let's have a bottle of Jack Daniel's,' Bruno said to the waitress. He glanced back toward the bar. 'And get those two boys whatever they want!'

The two grinning dudes immediately rambled over to introduce themselves — Buddy, a fat talky extrovert with a Texas accent, and Junior, a wiry inarticulate kid with big hands and a nervous manner. They had been great fans of Elvis.

'We loved that man like Jesus Christ!' said Buddy, picking at his teeth.

When Bruno went off to the men's room they coaxed Byron and Wendy out to their van for a snort of coke.

'Good Lord — !' Byron exclaimed as they walked toward the glittery, plexiglassed van. Inside, it was all indirect lighting, lush burgundy carpeting, easy chair, stereo, a bar and a gleaming marble tabletop on which Buddy started chopping a small pile of coke and separating it into lines.

'We never did get Elvis into this van,' Buddy said. 'I kept tryin' but you couldn't make Elvis do nothin' without fifteen or twenty other people.

Byron looked at him, astonished. 'You knew Elvis?'

'Oh, hell yeah,' said Junior casually.

'We saw everything Elvis ever did in Vegas,' said Buddy. 'Elvis was sort of a hobby for us. Still is.'

Buddy rolled a hundred-dollar bill into a tube and handed it to Byron, who snorted up two lines and passed it on to Wendy.

'No thanks,' said Wendy.

'What's the matter with you?' Byron snapped.

She shook her head and cast a single icy glare at Buddy. It was as if she had caught the scent of a natural enemy.

Buddy smiled at her.

'What does your lady do with herself?' he asked Byron.

'I'm a musician,' Wendy answered quickly, before Byron said anything. 'And you can ask questions directly to me.'

Buddy blinked and then broke into a laugh.

'Well, hey!' he exclaimed. 'We're musicians, too, y'know. Junior plays guitar.'

'I do.'

'He does, he does!' Buddy hooted. He leaned over and snorted Wendy's lines. Junior broke into a small fit of giggles. Byron smiled Wendy didn't.

People think dealers can't do nothin' else but deal that dope — but we got music in the blood.' He fixed an eye on Byron and got serious. 'You're real good, man. Ain't he, Junior?'

'Yup. Real good.'

'Thank you,' said Byron graciously. Buddy pulled a cigarette out and lit it.

'But . . . you could be a lot better.'

Byron looked at him sharply.

'Now don't take me wrong,' said Buddy, holding up a hand. 'You're damned good — I done said that. It's just — see, Elvis was sonething *else*. You'd have to go a ways further to do what Elvis was doing.'

Byron felt his neck stiffen. He was used to praise. He could handle being told he was good — but nobody had ever said anything like this to him. Hell, was knowing Elvis supposed to make you a goddamn expert? He knew Elvis, too. Elvis had given him a fucking gun. These bozos couldn't even get Elvis to stick his nose in their swishy van — and now they were passing judgement? Byron struggled to get hold of himself.

'Exactly what is it I don't do good enough?' he said deliberately.

Buddy looked to Junior for support, then turned back.

'Aw, it's just . . . little things. Little gestures. Just a few things you don't do quite right.'

'Also — you don't wear that white jumpsuit,' said Junior.

'I don't need it. I do early Elvis.'

Buddy smiled, uncovering a row of brown-stained teeth. 'But in Vegas . . .' he paused significantly, 'that ain't Elvis.'

'Most of the impersonators wear the jumpsuit —' Junior nodded.

'Fuck 'em!' Byron snapped in a flash of anger. 'Who said I was an *impersonator* anyway?'

Buddy and Junior just blinked and waited, unable to fathom that remark, but impressed just the same.

Byron cooled down. 'I do early Elvis because it's pure. I don't need a thousand-piece orchestra, I can work with any house band. The Vegas shows — that's pretentious bullshit. I don't need it.'

'But see,' Junior persisted carefully, 'that white suit, with the jewels and all — that's where it's at. That's Elvis.'

Byron fixed him with a tight-lipped stare.

'Listen, man,' said Buddy, putting his hand on Byron's shoulder, 'we got a garage full of videotapes of Elvis. Interviews, tour films, all kinds of stuff. We collect 'em. Come on by the house anytime and take a look.'

Byron had to struggle not to flash out again and blast these baboons. What the hell did they know about being Elvis — even if they'd seen every show the sucker ever gave? But something told him to keep quiet. They were on his side. They could help him.

'You're good, man, really,' Buddy reassured. 'You could just be better, that's all . . . better.'

After a long pause, Byron gave a stiff nod. Without a word Wendy stepped out of the van and headed back toward the club.

Rubber Duckies

The next morning, Frank Bruno opened his door and stepped out into the sun, blinking and scratching his stomach. He spat. He yawned. Then he ambled several doors down to Byron and Wendy's room and knocked.

'Up and at 'em, Byron!' he shouted, knocking again. 'We got business in this town.'

Inside, Wendy covered her head with a pillow and turned over in the dark. Byron felt his way to the door and cracked it just wide enough to see Bruno's pudgy, grinning face.

'Meet me downstairs, son, just yourself, okay? Hurry up, now, we got a lotta ground to cover. And bring yer PR kit — we're gonna make a business call.'

Bruno twirled his navel hairs into a tight little ringlet as he strode back to his room. On a normal morning, he would have brewed himself a pot of coffee and taken it back to bed, thumbed through *Daily Variety* and dozed till afternoon. Today, however, he had bedecked himself in turquoise and laid out a clean T-shirt ('Mahoney's Drive-thru Funeral Home, Dallas Texas') and a slick pair of expandable slacks. Frank Bruno was a never-say-die old gambler, and it was the kind of morning that keeps a gambler's heart singing. Mysterious promises were hanging in the desert air. Re-emerging from his room, he shuffled his feet in an imaginary little dance step. A rare goddamn morning! With his beard freshly trimmed and a new pair of sunglasses wrapped around his eyes, Bruno strode off to meet the boy.

Byron also emerged dressed to kill. From now on, every

time he went out he would be a walking advertisement for Prince Byron. He wore the vintage apricot sport jacket that hung smoothly almost to mid-thigh, the shiny indigo slacks, slightly pegged, and a clean pair of white bucks. Downstairs he got the nod of approval from Bruno and they climbed into the fat man's car and rolled off toward the Strip, top down.

'Not too fast, man. I don't want my hair blowing all over the place.'

Bruno sent up a cloud of cigar smoke.

'I never drive fast, son.'

Byron leaned back and sniffed at the desert air. Dry as a bone — Western air, not like the kind you got back in Maine where there were five damn kinds of weather a day. Nothing here was like Maine. When you raised your eyes above the casino signs there was nothing but clear light and sky and dusty moon-mountains in the distance. This was another damn planet for sure. Unreal.

'Radio work?'

'Nope.' Bruno shifted one haunch slightly and cut a fart. 'Radios are a dime a dozen. Listen to the engine. Runs like Timex. You can't beat the sound of a good American car.'

Byron laughed. Some character, this Bruno, with his busted radio. They cruised by Lords 'n' Ladies and Byron almost died young when he saw the marquee again: PRINCE BYRON IS ELVIS. In daylight it looked like all the other stars' signs. Frank Sinatra's . . . Johnny Carson's . . . Dean Martin's. Jesus Christ, his own sign in Las Vegas! Damned if this Bruno wasn't a fox.

'Lemme tell you about this town,' Bruno was saying as he yanked at a slot machine. 'You got fifty million Elvis fans, something like that — that's a conservative estimate. Now most of 'em try to come down here once a year. You can do the arithmetic yourself. This town was Elvis Presley's bathtub. Still is. All his rubber duckies are still here, waiting for somebody to step in the tub and play with them. I'd say you're in the right place at the right time.'

A shower of quarters cascaded out of the slot — a small jackpot. Bruno whooped with delight.

'Lookit that! Breakfast!'

Breakfast was at the Casino Royale. Eggs, Canadian bacon, pancakes, juice, toast, sausage, and coffee — and over the third or fourth cup, Bruno got around to explaining the Battle of the Elvises, which was a kind of contest for impersonators. At first Byron felt his neck tighten at the thought of an amateur night for some scroungy bunch of Elvis drag queens. But then he re-thought the situation: This was Las Vegas. Maybe he ought to play according to house rules, at least until the town realised that there was no real competition. In due time it would be his game, his rules. He listened.

'This Elvis competition, it's gonna be big. It's international, and there's big bucks involved. The nostalgia merchants got a shot in the arm when Elvis passed on, see. So they're throwin' a giant Fan Fair at the Roman Garden. The Battle of the Elvises is the big event that goes with it. It'll be taped for network TV. Then the whole Fan Fair goes on tour, worldwide, and the winner goes with it as featured entertainer — the world's champion Elvis impersonator. Next thing to being Elvis himself. It's a real plum.'

Byron's eyes had widened as Bruno talked. This was bigger than any amateur night. This was major. His palms went slick with excitement. Network TV — that might just be the ticket! The straightest route to Colonel Parker, the way to being Prince Byron to the Colonel in one sweeping blow.

One thing was crucial: The Colonel had to be shown that living Elvis was early Elvis, that Prince Byron was Elvis alive and well in Vegas. What better way to do it all than to humble a bunch of jumpsuit Elvises on national TV?

'Do you think — ?' he began.

'I'll tell you what I think,' Bruno continued, leaning across the table. Last night I couldn't sleep, I was so excited. There's a man named Jerry Margolis who's producing the whole package for the Roman Garden and soon's we finish up here we're gonna pay him a visit and get you entered, one hundred percent official.'

'What the hell are we waiting for?' Byron shot back.

Byron smiled. 'That's the spirit! You want it, don't you? You're ambitious —'

'What do you think, man?' Byron laughed.

'I think you better be hungry for it,' Bruno said with an even stare. 'If you ain't — then hell, don't waste your time in this town, because the hungry ones'll eat you alive.'

Byron stood suddenly and looked down at Frank Bruno with a commanding glint.

I'm hungry enough. Finish your coffee, man. Let's get moving.'

Bruno beamed and drained his cup with a loud slurp.

Jerry Margolis Productions was five floors up in a glass- and- concrete tower on Ogden. The inner office was dominated by a slab of a desk scattered with pictures of Jerry Margolis's grandchildren. Margolis himself, a bald, swallow-faced producer-promoter, sat sunk behind it, grunting as he skimmed Byron's clipping and glanced at his pictures. He looked up at Bruno, not impressed.

'This picture supposed to be Elvis?'

'Early Elvis, Jerry,' Bruno emphasised.

'Well, it doesn't look like Elvis. Looks more like Sha-Na-Na or something. Where you working, kid?'

'Lords 'n' Ladies.'

'In Vegas?' Margolis waved it off. 'I never heard of it.'

'Well, ah —' Bruno coughed. 'I think they changed the name from, ah . . .'

Margolis shook his head.

'Look, Frank, lemme be honest with you. This event is for professionals. We got NBC, we got the best Elvis impersonators from all over. Might even get Colonel Parker involved, which we're in negotiations now. I'm talking about an international event with international exposure.' He turned to Byron. 'Now from what I gather, you don't have a band, even a jumpsuit. What kind of show could you possibly do that'd compete with these pros — ?'

Margolis had reached into a file and was dealing out 8 x 10 glossies of Elvis impersonators.

'Look at this — big Elmo, Vester Pressler, Johnny Lipsky — these guys are big time out in the sticks, as big as you can get with this kind of thing, look at 'em. Those suits cost thousands of dollars. You got here a five-dollar Salvation Army sport jacket —'

Byron exploded. 'It cost fifty bucks!'

Bruno reached out to restrain him. Margolis shrugged and looked at his watch.

'I'm sorry, kid.'

But Byron was rising out of his chair, blowing and seething.

'You're sorry — you're sorry?' He jabbed a finger at Margolis. 'I'm sorry for *you*, man. Because you're making a fuckin' dumb mistake!'

Margolis controlled himself. 'Frank, get the kid out of here,' he breathed, averting his eyes.

'Hey —!' Byron hooted. 'He doesn't pull my strings and neither do you, man. I'll walk outo here when I'm good and ready. I just got to this damn town and I ain't about to slink around with my tail between my legs —'

Bruno rested a hand over his eyes and waited. Margolis drummed the desk several times with his fingertips. Then there was only the sound of Byron's heavy breathing.

'I'll see you outside, Frank,' said Byron suddenly and stalked out, leaving a wake of awkward silence behind him.

'Some boy you got there, Frank,' said Margolis after a moment. 'Touchy, I'd say — kind of kid that comes back with a gasoline can and burns the place down, y'know? You oughta stick with the midgets.'

'He's for real, Jerry.'

An alarm went off in Margolis's wrist watch.

'Time for my medication,' he mumbled. 'I got high blood pressure thanks to real people like that.'

As they drove slowly along the Strip, Byron's anger had

turned into a dark, lurking sulk.

'We'll get you in, don't worry,' Bruno was saying. 'Jerry's just a little slow — he's gotta have his nose rubbed in it.'

'He's a sonofabitch. He oughta have his nose punched flat —'

'Forget it. Time's on our side. We've got almost two months to show him something.'

'I don't have to show him nothing!' Byron shot back. 'He's nowhere. Did you see those pictures he was flashing at us? Fuckin' drag queens —'

Bruno looked puzzled.

'Lemme ask you — when you do Elvis . . . how's yours different from the, ah, drag queens? I mean, you ain't the only one who does Elvis.'

Byron raised one eyebrow and gazed at him steadily.

'Look, man, you either *are* Elvis or you're an imposter. If you're the King, you sit on a throne, if you're a fake you get dumped in the alley. And when the King dies, there's only one possible man to replace him. It's that simple. I've got it straight since he died: I'm that man. I'm not faking anything. I'm just swimming in the river of history. I use to imitate Elvis. Now I am Elvis. You saw me —'

He waited for an answer. After a moment, Bruno nodded, blinking heavily.

'You know it's true,' Byron went on. 'Now it's a matter of spreading the news. And that's your job, right? I'll go among the imposters. I'm not afraid to dirty myself with those freaks. I understand it's all part of a purpose. So go to it, man, get me in — I'll humble the motherfuckers — they'll be on their knees to me y'know?' He smacked the side of the car with his palm. 'Jesus! When a sonofabitch like Margolis tells me I'm small time because I don't have a fuckin' jumpsuit —' He shook his head furiously.

'But, but, *but* . . .!' Bruno raised a finger. 'He's got a shred of a point, you have to admit. It's not a *Vegas* act. It needs more. Needs strings and brass, choreography, chicks — you know, Byron? You know what I'm talkin about?'

'I don't need that bullshit,' Byron snorted.

'Wrong. You can impress a few cowboys with that early Elvis rockabilly shit, but to make it with the real nuts, you've got to do the Big Show. This is Vegas! Remember — Elvis himself bombed here doing 'early Elvis' in the fifties. They don't wanna see a greaser in a zoot suit. They wanna see God!'

Bruno turned off the Strip and nosed into a parking spot at the Roman Garden.

'C'mon,' he said. 'I'm gonna take you somewhere.'

Attached to one side of the hotel's sprawling ground floor was a small modern chapel. A dignified sign over the door read:

ELVIS PRESLEY MEMORIAL MUSEUM

Byron's mood shifted to uneasy reverence and they entered. He was on holy ground. He realised his mouth had gone dry.

'Only took 'em a week to throw this shed up,' said Bruno ironically. 'Thay were busting ground the day of the funeral.'

The place was darkly lit, with oil portraits of Elvis in different moods, classic poses — some copies of famous photographs that Byron recognised. Behind glass, in a display case, were mementos of Elvis's Las Vegas years. A coat he once wore, a glittery guitar he once used, a lock of his hair. Several families of tourists cruised around in polite silence, shushing their kids.

'You've gotta see this,' said Bruno, moving Byron along.

At the back of the museum was a full-size statue of Elvis eerie and lifelike, in a fancy jewel-studded white jumpsuit. Byron's heart began to pound.

A little boy trotted up to the statue and pushed a button in the base. There was a click, then the voice of Elvis, coming from the statue, sang 'Hound Dog.'

Byron broke into a sweat. For a moment his vision dimmed and he had to grab the base for support. Through splotchy grey he seemed to be face-to-face with the final suffering of Elvis — the stinking, dying flesh turned to plastic. It was too real, too ghastly, like an accident victim, still alive but bubbling into death in front of your eyes. Byron reeled. For a second he thought he was in Elvis's dressing room again, watching the bulging jumpsuit stick to the King's flesh while it poisoned his body. Bruno's voice droned on as Byron tried to get hold of himself.

'That's the secret — that white jumpsuit. Once you put it on in this town, you don't have to tell 'em who you are, they know. You're starting at the top. You're a god — an automatic god!'

No Geniuses Here

From the first moment Frank Bruno poked his head out of that motel room, Wendy's doubts had grown. How could such a slob do any kind of serious business? Worse than that, at the end of a full week at Lords 'n' Ladies, where was the money? Maybe the guy had a few expenses — but *fifty dollars* for Byron? Ridiculous. And the Royal Flush made you pay up a week in advance. At this rate they'd be camping in the alley by Labour Day.

Then there was the gig itself. Not that it should be the Sands Hotel or anything, but what a godawful dive! Here they had driven almost three thousand miles, left their whole lives behind, and where did this slob book Byron? A Las Vegas version of TR's. A local scene for bikers and rednecks like Buddy and Junior. A slum bar where the off-duty keno girls watched Byron like sleek weasels eyeing lunch.

Wendy had plenty to say about the situation, but Byron didn't want to hear it. His brains were fried by too many bright lights and famous names. He was so high on simply 'working Vegas' that he could have been doing Elvis in a manhole, for all it seemed to matter. So they didn't talk much for a few days, which was fine by Wendy — she knew how to go her own way. She put Bruno on the back burner and hatched her own plan.

Early Monday she slipped into a nice dress, gathered up her guitar and drove off in the truck looking for places to audition. She had a happy-hour set, ten originals for afternoon in a quiet lounge. She had seen *Alice Doesn't Live*

Here Anymore. If that lady could get auditions, she could sure as hell get auditions!

But right away she started learning what kind of Town Las Vegas was. For starters, the toughest job was to walk in and convince the bartender that she wasn't just a goofball or a hooker. That was s tricky little tapdance: Be cute, be eager, be innocent. She had to go through this bullshit at four or five lounges before she got a simple break.

The Mainsail was part of a new motel-casino out near the airport. It had a nautical theme: oars, fishnets, framed photos of famous shipwrecks. The waitresses wore little calico mini-dresses with pinafores and scooped necklines. There were only two drinkers at the bar, a middle-aged couple who watched with boozy concentration as Wendy stepped onto the small stage and tuned up, smiling out at the lights.

The club manager, a portly, sour-faced mafia-type, slid behind a small ringside table and checked his watch.

'Okay, honey, you got five minutes.'

Something about his abruptness soured Wendy's confidence.

' "Proud Mary!" ' yelled the man at the bar, with a rakish wink at his lady friend. She giggled hoarsely and made a big show of shushing him. 'We're from Ohio,' she chirped to the empty room. Wendy began to sing one of her songs, 'Sleepy Heart,' in a light throaty voice. A few tourists wandered in and rattled the slots. Several times the antique cash register clanged loudly.

In the darkness down front the manager puffed on a cigar and listened, patting his bald head. Wendy finished, smiled, and started the intro to something else.

'Who does that song?' interrupted the manager.

Wendy stopped. 'It's original.'

'D'you know any Dolly Parton songs, Anne Murray, stuff like that? "Snow Bird". You know "Snow Bird"?'

'Yeah . . . I guess.'

'What do you mean, you guess?' His voice roughened a shade.

97

'I don't usually do those,' she said soberly. 'I do my own songs.'

'Not here, gal. No geniuses here.' Wendy heard his chair scrape. The bastard was going to walk away, just like that. But first he gave a long stare. 'You've got nice looks, you know. You could make something of yourself, even without a voice. How come you wanna be a genius?'

Wendy wanted to tell him to stuff some mixed nuts up his ass, but instead she let her gaze drop. He grunted, and turned on his heel. Gone.

The couple from Ohio broke the silence with a burst of uneven clapping and ordered a Manhatten 'for the little lady.'

'I remember what it was like to be your age,' said the woman four or five times. Then came her punchline. through a burst of giggles: 'Jeez, was I a horny broad!'

Wendy sipped her drink politely and tried to hold back the desolation that was creeping over her. The couple from Ohio drank up and made an unsteady exit, leaving a black hole of silence behind them.

'This isn't the town for you,' said the bartender from down the bar. Wendy looked at him for the first time. He was grinning gently at her, a thin, angelic-looking guy with a rim of surfer-blond hair. A kid, Wendy thought — then she realised he was a lot older than he looked. He was pretty, but age had hardened the prettiness and etched it into permanent lines in his face. A boy, going straight into middle-age.

'You ought to be in Austin or someplace.' He polished a glass and held it up in the dim bar light. 'Take my word for it, Vegas is not your town.'

'Oh really, whose is it, then? It's your town or something?'

He smiled and shook his head. 'Nope. I'm adaptable. I can live anywhere.'

'You think I can't?'

'That's right.' He put the glass away. 'I think you can't.'

Bar talk. Wendy could spin it out forever.

'Austin, huh,' she said with a sigh that was almost a shudder. 'You know Austin?'

He nodded. 'I lived there for a while.'

'So tell me about it.'

'Low key and funky.'

'Sure. Great people too, I bet, huh?' She drained her drink.

'Naturally.'

'Anything else?'

'Your kind of music.'

'Mm.' She squinted one eye at him. 'Okay. We're wasting time, let's go.'

'Can't. Too many glasses to wash.'

Wendy laughed. 'Well hell, pal — what're you good for anyway? Forget the whole thing.' She sat back and cast a bleak look around. 'What I really need . . . is a job.'

'Easily done. Guess who does the hiring here?'

'Burt Reynolds.'

'We had to let him go.'

'Well, I tell you, after meeting your charming boss, I just don't know if this is the right career path for me, y'know?'

'Ah, don't worry about him, he got your message. When the girls don't fall right down, he leaves 'em alone.'

She realised she was starting to like this guy; he had a gentle way about him.

'Austin, huh?' she mused.

A silence broadened between then.

'Gotta go,' she said abruptly and started off.

'Don't forget,' he called. 'If you want a job.'

She smiled back over her shoulder and headed out into the blinding sun.

Television City

Byron nosed Frank Bruno's ramshackle Caddy to a stop in front of Buddy and Junior's. He leaned and stretched in the noonday heat. Their place looked like a stucco chicken shack. No signs of life behind the windows. What were the bozos up to? Most likely out back running a cockfight. They made him laugh, these two, with their grease-monkey version of Vegas funtime: dune buggies, hookers, craps and roulette, overnight jaunts to Hollywood — bachelor heaven.

Okay, they had wanted him to drop by — here he was.

Byron got out of the car and walked toward the bungalow. From behind the house came the sound of a car revving, minus muffler. He circled around to the backyard.

They might have had grass at one time, but now the yard was all dust, with dark brease patches left by oil spills and leaks. Cans and bottles and old auto parts lay scattered about, rusting. A flashy red dune buggy was half stripped and up on blocks. Behind the wheel was Buddy. A pair of legs, Junior's, extended from underneath. As Byron approached, Buddy gave him a sharp, suspicious glance, which warmed immediately as recognition poured into his face.

'Well!' he squawked, turning off the engine. A grin split his face open like a dropped watermelon. He gave a kick at Junior's leg. 'Git up, Junior. We got company!'

What they had behind the house was a converted garage, a private theatre for looking at tapes of Elvis. A TV with a six-foot projection screen dominated the place like a blank shrine. A video-cassette recorder sat on a low table next to a long, plush sofa. Junior pushed the start button. On screen appeared a woman, squirming and moaning as she caressed herself to orgasm.

'Get rid of that,' ordered Buddy.

Along one entire wall was a shelf of cassettes — the Elvis feature films and road documentaries, the TV specials, the early newsclips and live TV appearances, bootleg tour films and tapes, press conferences. The room was designed for dreamy comfort, with cork panelling, a Naugahyde bar, and wall-to-wall carpeting that matched the opulence of the van. A shotgun leaned against the sofa ('Got a criminal element around here!'). A video camera stood off in the corner.

'Goddamn Television City!' said Byron. 'This is some damn establishment you got here!'

Buddy jabbed a finger at Junior. 'Put Elvis on there. Show him *That's the Way It Is.*'

Junior pulled a cassette off the shelf, clunked it into the deck and punched Play. On the big screen, instantly, was Elvis, somewhere in the middle of the film, toiling, leaping, spinning through one of the Vegas Shows. The jumpsuit was simple. Not the gold-encrusted white balloon of the final years. Elvis was slim.

Byron felt the skin on his back crawl. He had seen the movie four or five times when it first came out — but that was before Prince Byron. Everything had changed since then. Now he realised he was seeing things he hadn't seen before, ever.

'We got tapes and tapes, man,' Buddy droned. 'Elvis is alive in this place. We keep him alive.'

'Does this thing stop, go forward and back and all?'

'Sure does, man.' Buddy reached for the controls. 'Got freeze frame, instant replay, mud flaps, continental kit and wet bar! This is the state-of-the-art. You can't even buy these yet!' He punched *Pause*, halting Elvis in mid-gesture.

Byron's face was tense with excitement.

'You can come here any old time,' Buddy drawled. 'We got a complete set of records, too, everything he ever put on wax. Just make it your place, man. Sleep here if you want

101

to. This is your place to study Elvis. Any old time —'

'How about right now?'

Buddy's face beamed. 'Hell yeah, Boss — go to it!'

Buddy and Junior withdrew to the yard, leaving Byron alone with the tape. He let it run on for a while, hypnotised by the moves, one flowing into another, stunned by the feeling he had stumbled into a tomb, a burial chamber filled with secret treasure. These guys didn't know what they had here — how could they? They were tools, nobodies. As he watched Elvis covering the stage in great sweeps, an amazing thought grew and reverberated inside his head like a gong: Prince Byron was *meant* to come to this place and uncover these secrets.

But how? How could that be true? Yet it had to be. Because now, what he started to see was a series of intimate messages in every gesture, signs from Elvis he had never understood before. They must have been embedded there, always, like a code waiting to be broken. Somehow this moment, the awakening of Prince Byron, had to have been the ultimate reason for *That's the Way It Is!*

He stopped Elvis in the middle of a leap and rolled him back. He made him repeat a waving motion two, three times. He went to the full-length mirror beside the bar and tried the move, awkwardly at first, then with more assurance. It was a mature man's motion: commanding but full of ease. He went back to the cassette and watched the move again. With a jumpsuit on, he realised, he could get it letter perfect. He made a correction, smoothed it, then let the tape move on until another gesture caught his eye.

Several times Junior appeared with a tall beer. Byron drained it in a few gulps and kept working. Things were making sense. Larger patterns were coming together into statements. Snatches of choreography. Sweeping, running, kneeling sequences. Karate kick-punch patterns. Watching this Elvis was like witnessing an event of extreme import-ance. Like the day Pop took him to Fenway Park and showed him a *real* baseball game. There was endless work ahead. He would have to learn every last lesson Elvis had left for him.

The day got hotter. Slowly the heat overpowered the garage's small air conditioner, but Byron worked on, sweaty, dishevelled, concentrating so intensely that the edge of his vision began to dim.

Eventually the tape ran on, unwatched, as he collapsed across the sofa, lost in exhaustion.

Up front, two hookers had dropped by, a ratty-blonde and a Mexican girl, in their running shorts and I LOVE NY T-shirts.

'Out in the garage,' Junior pointed with his thumb. 'Got a client needs an oil change and lubrication.'

'Crystal' pouted her lips and glanced at 'Brooke.' Since Brooke didn't speak much English, Crystal raised her voice: 'Fuck?' she said and motioned toward the rear. Brooke shrugged and patted her fanny.

'Give us a free pop,' said Crystal. 'Both of us.'

'You got it.'

Buddy broke out a clean syringe and the girls tugged at the side of their running shorts, exposing two shiny mountains of flesh.

'Who eez guy?' said Brooke, looking toward the garage. She and Crystal blinked heavily at each other.

'Elvis Presley', Buddy pronounced solemnly.

'Run that by me again?' said Crystal, thick-tongued as the smack spread out.

'Elvis Presley.'

Brooke stuck her tongue out at him. *'Cabron!'*

'It's the damn truth,' Junior whined. 'He's back in town. Now y'all go give him a little thrill. Go on.

'No weird shit, man. This is my day off —'

'Hey!' Buddy's eyes were popping. 'Scouts honour. Elvis is here. Now get on back there and grease his front end.'

Byron's gaze barely picked them up as they entered the garage. He lay with his legs apart, sprawled across the couch.

'Elvis . . . ?'

'Elvees . . . ?'

The girls broke into a giggling fit as they came close to him.

'Get fuckin' serious,' Byron mumbled without opening his eyes.

They knelt on either side of him. Shaking with laughter, Brooke raised her T-shirt and flared her breasts. Crystal massaged his groin and mockingly ran her tongue back and forth across her lips. After a while she stopped to rest her hand.

' 'Sis guy a stiff or what, man?'

With his eyes half open, his mouth sagging, Byron had slipped into a dark, bottomless stupor.

Some Damn Crazy Ride

When Wendy heard him come in she was soaking in the bathtub.

'Byron?'

He stumped around for a minute and then hit the bed. Something told her he wasn't quite right.

'You okay, Byron?'

He grunted. 'Why wouldn't I be okay? You okay?'

She splashed water on her face and climbed out of the tub.

'Oh, I dunno . . . this town. I can tell already, it's gonna burn me out. There's nothing for me here. Not unless I start falling over for the club owners.' She waited for Byron's reaction. There wasn't any.

She shrugged at herself in the mirror and left the bathroom, wrapping a towel around just her hair. But Byron lay face down on the bed, so rather than risk a chill from the air conditioner, she gave up on enticing him and slipped into her bathrobe.

'Maybe I'll check out the hair salons. We've got to start pulling in some money somehow,' she muttered, opening a beer.

'I'm making money —'

'At Lords 'n' Ladies? Show me. Frank Bruno's taking it all.' She felt a quick surge of anger.

'He got the gig.' Byron hadn't moved or looked up.

'He got the gig,' she mimicked. 'Well, I never heard of a manager with so many expenses in one week that nothing was left for the artist. He's a parasite. He's sleazy, man — I can't believe you don't see how sleazy he is. He's into midgets and dog acts, probably hookers, too —'

Byron looked up with a sly grin. 'I oughta ask him about that.'

'Aw, to hell with you!' snapped Wendy, ripping the towel away from her hair and throwing it at him.

They looked at each other. Byron's grin turned into a radiant choir-boy smile. Wendy tossed her hair and glared back at him. She couldn't think with Byron flashing his lights at her like that.

'Byron, you're so weird,' she blurted finally. 'How can I be involved with such a weird person?'

His eyes shifted away from hers, following the curve of her hips.

'C'mere. I'll show you,' he said with a teasing jerk of his head.

She realised her anger was draining away. He could still dominate her with a simple shift of mood. What an array of effects he could produce! With a little sigh, she let herself be coaxed to the bed. Byron pressed her against him and kissed her tenderly until she pulled her lips away.

'This whole thing is crazy,' she said. She felt herself wanting to open to him, but something was making her tense. 'I'm miserable here, Byron.'

Byron raised himself on one elbow. Instantly, his eyes took on a dark brilliance that came up out of nowhere. The change startled her. He was Prince Byron now — about to make a great declaration, a burst of passion.

'Listen, honey. Something amazing is happening to me. I don't know exactly what, but it's big. Things are coming together from all over. I can feel it. I'm on some kind of special trip, that's all I know. Stick with me, just stick with me.'

She cradled him against her. By now she knew the speech by heart, but it never failed to excite her.

'Byron . . .' she whispered. 'If we could only be like this all the time . . .'

'Mama,' he said in a little boy's voice, 'be good to me.

Don't leave me. I need you.'

'I'm not going anywhere, honey,' she said, rocking gently back and forth, feeling herself want to encircle him. 'I don't have to get gigs here. I can write . . . I can work on my songs. I'm gonna look for a day job. I'm not going to leave you, Byron —'

A helpless emotion had rolled suddenly through her, a sweetness that flowed like milk to her nipples. The thought of loving him that way, at her breast, produced a flood of desire.

'Oh, Byron,' she whispered, amazed at the force of it. She lay back. She wanted him inside her. He unzipped his pants and settled between her legs and she knew she would be coming fast, even before he did, out of sheer craziness for him.

Then, in the middle of it all he laughed, a harsh guffaw.

'What's so funny?'

'Those two . . .' he said.

'What two?' She could hardly form a thought.

'You know what they call me? *Boss*.' He laughed again, in two separate spasms.

Wendy's hands and feet went cold. She felt a tightening in her stomach. For a split-second she was looking down from the ceiling, watching herself jammed mindlessly against the headboard. She held on tighter, her desire curdling like bad cream. Buddy and Junior. Those two. Byron came suddenly, then relaxed, falling instantly asleep.

Jesus. Numb anxiety ran down her spine like ice water. Oh Jesus, this was some damn crazy ride, all right.

Earthquake
and Screech

'Assholes . . . !'

Byron slipped out of the garage in a slow-burning rage. Here it was Saturday, two shows to do, and these damn fools were galloping around the yard like a couple of drooling idiots, blazing away at a lizard with their .38 Magnums.

'Yee-hah!' Buddy yipped.

The lizard slithered down his hole, safe, but Buddy and Junior were too far gone to stop now. Byron watched them reload and start blasting beer bottles, a Castrol oil can, a hub cap, anything, until he just couldn't stand it anymore —

WHOMP!

An ear-shattering blast froze the dumb bozos like a pair of trapped rats. Byron glared at them from the garage door, the shotgun smoking in his hand.

'Cut that goddamn racket!'

'S-Sorry . . . sorry, Boss,' said Buddy, guilt spreading across his fat smear of a face. Byron let them hang for a moment.

'Somebody get me a beer,' he said finally, going back inside the garage.

In a few seconds, Junior was cowering at the door with a tall Bud. His hand shook slightly.

'Boss . . . ?'

Byron stared off in the other direction. 'What.'

'Your beer.'

'Pour it.'

Byron had caught on to their game the moment they

started calling him 'Boss'. Service was their bag: they took to it like ducks to a pond. He had them in his pocket — bodyguards, slaves, partners, all rolled together. Of course, half the time they were too goddamn whacked out to get it right: Almost every day now Byron was at the garage, stripped to the waist in the heat of the afternoon, working himself into a lather — and every day they came up with something to blow his concentration away.

So he laid down rules? There had to be absolute quiet. No damn dune buggies revving in the backyard — take 'em around the front. If they had to enter the garage for some reason, knock first and wait for an answer. They should appear only when he needed food or beer — in other words, treat him like an artist. But he had to laugh sometimes, watching them bend every which way to get it all together.

At 285 pounds, Buddy was known around town as 'Earthquake'. He had amiable fat lips, a hoarse voice, and a soft chuckle in the back of his throat. Junior, his reverse image, was nicknamed 'Screech', a skinny desperado — always squinting, as into the sun or the wind, his face always burning with an angry fever.

According to Frank Bruno, Buddy and Junior had drifted into town about five years back hoping to land jobs in the Elvis Presley organisation. Even though they mouthed off about ten years of road experience with the Allman Brothers, Willie Nelson, Charlie Daniels and so on, no one in those organisations had ever heard of them. Whatever the truth was, the Presley people treated them like a case of rabies and they never got near anybody important, much less the King himself.

But Buddy and Junior liked Vegas, it was their kind of town. Buddy landed work as a bouncer in a downtown casino (cheaters were dragged to the change room, pictures snapped for the record, then Buddy worked over them with a bag of quarters). Junior couldn't hold a job: He was 'warped by the State', as Buddy put it, with a criminal record that started at age fourteen with assaults on officers, went on through 7-11 store heists, break-ins, more assaults, and climaxed with a botched bank hold-up. He would have earned a slab in the Vegas morgue if it hadn't been for Buddy, who sheltered him like an emotionally disturbed dog.

Neither of them ever got to first base with Elvis. Not even the converted garage, with the most complete collection of Elvis records and videotapes anywhere, not even that pure act of worship attracted as much as a scrap of attention from the Presley people. So the boys just caught Elvis's shows as often as they could and kept sending little invitations to 'E' himself ('We hope you will visit our priceless tribute to you and your career . . .').

Now, as minor drug dealers (under Vito 'The Barber' Piccolito, a semi-retired mobster who took a grandfatherly shine to Buddy), they managed to live their own version of the Elvis Presley Lifestyle — mostly dune-buggying, whoring, getting high and hanging out along the Strip, where they were a familiar sight to the pit bosses and croupiers.

Like all dealers, however, they hankered to be doing something 'real'. The notion that someday they might really work for Elvis had sustained them, given life a heart that beat. Now with Elvis suddenly removed from the face of the earth, they went from shock to drift. What next? Another star wouldn't do. When you had experienced Elvis, how could you settle for Tom Jones?

They were stunned with grief. For a few days following the funeral, they worked on a vague plan to steal Elvis's body from Memphis and truck it home to Vegas, to bury the King in their own garage, the place made sacred to Him. They were lost.

Then came Byron. And they were found. Instinctively they realised: *Elvis was back*. But this time around, an Elvis that could be theirs . . .

They were certainly good for Byron, all right, handy in all sorts of ways. They ran errands for him, made his phone calls, kept undesirables away from the back room at Lords, made sure no jealous nut broke his nose with a sucker punch. They could also 'negotiate': like the time they sat down with Frank Bruno to talk money. Bruno never mentioned the discussion, but the same week, Byron began taking home a larger share of the gross.

The crowd at Lords had changed. Women now packed the tables and fought for snapshots and kisses from the stage. The chaos, the air, the noise were terrible. Wendy had given up on the place after the first week, and in the vacuum of her absence, Byron found himself encountering new faces in the cozy darkness of the back room. It was too easy — a knock . . . Junior's voice over the shout-level din of the crowd outside:

'Boss?'

'Huh.'

'Girl out here says she used to do stuff for Elvis.'

'What kind of stuff?'

'Y'know . . . personal services.'

'Send her in.'

Not that he was looking for love — he had *love*. Just something unusual, some girl who made a move he just couldn't let pass.

'I wanted to see your sneaky lips up close,' said this girl, eyeing him from the door. 'You're almost as pretty as Elvis was. But not as cosmic.'

Byron stared back at her evenly. The girl broke into a half-smile and leaned against the door frame. She closed the door behind her. She sighed.

'I'm not really into this,' she said, 'this back-room kind of thing.' She spoke quickly and with a cultivated sort of lisp, like a prep-school girl. 'I hate Vegas. I'm just driving through to Tahoe. I never stop in Vegas, never ever — only I saw your sign. Elvis . . .' She laughed to herself and looked him over boldly. 'You've got a lot of nerve, man . . .'

Byron waited for the move. She fidgeted for a moment and tugged at her blouse, which fell open to the waist. The move.

'Actually, Elvis wasn't *really* such a great guy, you know. He was a sort of a slut. Someday some asshole'll write a book about what a stoned hillbilly slut Elvis was . . .' If she could just stop running her mouth for half a second. She came closer to Byron and her eyes warmed. 'Like, if you tried real hard, you could even be a better human being than Elvis, you know?' She bit lightly at the tip of her tongue and let her body move in until it touched his lightly, chest to chest. Slowly she began to sway, caressing him, caressing herself. Her voice dropped to a whisper.

'Let's go, Elvis. I've gotta get to Tahoe.'

Cheap thrills.

Wendy was wide awake when he got to the motel, sitting in her bathrobe smoking a cigarette. The guitar was on the bed with her. Sheets of paper were all around her. She was working on another masterpiece. Byron figured there was no way she could know about the Tahoe girl, but she must have suspected; it was written all over her face. Her eyes were little black holes as they followed him around the room. He didn't want to look.

'Hi, Prince.' She blew a cloud of smoke toward the ceiling and started banging away at the guitar.

'Put that damn thing down for a minute.'

Was she determined to drive him up a wall? It seemed like she never put the goddamned thing down anymore. Either she was out trying to crack into the hair salons or she was home being a pain in the ass — whacking the guitar, going over and over and over the same piece of a line until Byron thought the top of his head was going to blow off.

'You're beatin' the shit out of that thing!'

'How the hell do you think you write a song?' she said, tight-lipped.

Byron looked down at her. 'Why are you trying to drive me crazy?'

'Drive *you* crazy?' She stopped strumming and started sniveling. 'I've got a right to have a life, too, you know. This is a free country. I don't have to sit for four hours at Lords every night like I was your grandma or something, keeping the girls off your body. Ah, yeah, smile — how many blowjobs did you get tonight?' Byron's smile vanished. Wendy watched him closely and began to nod. 'Yeah. That's right, isn't it. Don't bullshit me, I can smell it.'

She went back to the guitar, back to her masterpiece.

C'mon, lay off the guitar —'

'Fuck you, pal! D'you think you're the only scene in this town?'

She kept at the same three chords, trying the same dopey words in her whiney little voice. Byron's head was throbbing. He felt like shaking her teeth out.'

'Cut it or I'm gonna break that goddamn thing over your head!'

Wendy stopped short. Her face seemed to dry up and fall apart. She was trembling suddenly, trying to keep herself together.

'I'm sorry, baby,' he muttered.

She scambled off the bed, looking for some clothes to put on. Byron watched her dress.

Well, damn it, she could have a little more consideration. He was struggling with big pressure now. If he played it right, he could lever himself right from Lords into The Battle of the Elvises, but he had to play it right. He was walking on the edge; he could fall either way. Didn't she understand he had to keep his concentration sharp, keep his mind focused on that one goal? What the hell was she thinking, anyway? Why the hell had they come to Vegas in the first place? So that she could whine herself into some third-rate Joni Mitchell imitation?

'Where're you going?'

'Don't worry about it, man.'

She threw on her jeans and a T-shirt and grabbed her purse. Then she was out the door. He heard her clattering down the stairs and listened to her footsteps fade off into the street.

Well. To hell with her. He would have made it up to her if she had just stuck around. In the mirror his peach sport jacket was beginning to look grey around the cuffs. He took it off and hung it in top of the lavender rayon special that he saved for Saturdays. Back to the mirror, checking the lines of muscle that rippled under the yellow shirt sleeves, the defined chest that peeked through the open collar.

Youth. It just wouldn't go away. What he saw when he looked at himself, what he had always seen, was fifteen-year-old Byron Bluford. The kid was still there, But lately he was also seeing something new — something heavier, tougher, more commanding in the face. There was a full-grown man there now. Wendy ought to realise this was no punk she was riding with. This was a phenomenon, happening right in front of her very eyes, if she could just put down that lame guitar and watch it happen.

At moments like this, he knew clearly what was in progress: he was changing, caterpillar into butterfly. Prince Byron's cocoon was breaking up and a mature new Elvis was about to emerge. She just didn't recognise how laborious it was, how exhausting; that it meant he had to turn himself inch by inch into a whole other performer — not the kid who burst out of nowhere, but the man who came back, with everything to lose, who brought the town to its knees, dominated it, humbled it. That's what maturity was all about. That kind of power. The gun. The jumpsuit. The sheer mastery of Elvis-in-Vegas. He ripped his shirt off and killed the air conditioner. Let the hot air in. He turned the TV on, some dipshit Western. Come on back, baby, don't be a fool. Don't run away from the main feature. Across Vegas he heard some loser somewhere howling like a stricken wolf in the night.

It Ain't All Tears

She walked to the Strip and turned left. Far away, around the mountains, the sky was pink, shading off into purple, but in the street it was still dark night. She didn't know where she was going. She didn't care. The big casino lights looked crazy against the faint dawn. The more she walked, the more night turned into morning. Men called to her outside the hotels, thinking she was a hooker, but she looked straight ahead and kept walking. Her legs moved like a machine. She didn't let herself think, she just walked. Past the Sands . . . past the MGM . . . past the airport. A thought burst into her head: If she wanted to, couldn't she simply walk into the desert, forever? She saw the Mainsail. Maybe what she needed was a drink.

Inside she forgot about the desert. A blading, middle-aged guy was tending the bar, not Eddie, her friend. She ordered a double bourbon. The bartender slid the drink toward her and leaned casually against the bar. She knew he was about to sprout a line.

'Where's Eddie?' she said quickly to unbalance him. A trace of a frown flickered across his face.

'What do you want Eddie for?'

Wendy took a long sip of bourbon. 'Sex.'

The bartender chuckled. He had a sense of humour anyway, even if he was a little slow.

'El Dorado Apartments, honey. The other side of the strip. Number Fifteen, by the pool.' His eyes narrowed. 'And if Eddie's asleep, you just come on back here and let Daddy do it.'

'Sure thing, Daddy.' She gulped the rest of her drink and slid off the stool.

Outside, the morning had broken and it was already bright and hot. Across the Strip the El Dorado Apartments complex sat by itself in a patch of desert. It was like a lot of things in Vegas: brand new and rising out of nothing. People were already hanging around the pool. She saw Eddie sunning himself in a beach chair. A radio somewhere was playing 'Stairway to Heaven.' She wondered for a moment what the hell she was doing here. Then Eddie spotted her.

'I know you.' He sat up and took his shades off. His face wrinkled into a smile. 'The girl with the songs. The genius.'

He wasn't mocking her. Something in the way he said it was sweet. Almost adoring. 'What in the world are you doing here?'

Wendy shrugged helplessly.

'I don't know, man. I just don't know . . .'

Eddie was easy to be with. The morning crept along lazily and he didn't push her at all. The girls he shared the place with were both away, so he dug out one of their swimsuits and left Wendy alone in the pool for almost an hour. She took a long shower and found new towels and a terrycloth robe waiting when she stepped out. Meanwhile Eddie had whipped up a Spanish omelette for breakfast. He sat her back in the soft chaise longue on his patio and brought coffee. The sun fell directly on her. She felt herself relaxing. Eddie poured his own coffee and sat at her feet like dog.

'You're nice,' she said to him.

Eddie shrugged. 'I was wondering what had happened to you.'

'Not a hell of a lot.'

'Remember what I told you?'

'Wrong town.'

He nodded. 'Figured it out, huh?'

'Unfortunately, I can't do much about it right now. It just seems to be my destiny or something — I mean, everybody's got to be someplace, right? Guess I've got to be in Vegas. Tough, huh?'

'Relax.' He moved closer and took her hand. 'I'm glad you came to see me.'

Wendy shook her head. 'Don't be too glad. There's not much in it for you.'

She felt him recoil.

'Hey, I didn't mean that like it sounded —' She reached out and roughened his hair, then caressed it. 'Just that . . . we oughta be friends, you know?'

He nodded once and kept his eyes on her.

'See, it doesn't make much sense, but . . . I'm in love with this guy.' She had put off thinking about Byron until this instant. 'I can't explain it.' She shook her head. 'Since we got to Vegas, we haven't . . . taken care of each other.'

'It happens.'

Eddie fell silent. They listened to the sound for a while, the splashing from the pool, the radio, the clear sound of hammering from miles away in the crystal desert air.

Wendy felt herself saddening. Something was about to make her cry and she didn't know what. What the hell was wrong with her? Emotions whipsawing her like this — She swallowed hard and then began to sob. She shook her head and tried to smile at poor Eddie through the sobs.

He stretched out next to her on the chaise, holding her gently, cradling her hot, wet face in the hollow of his neck. She let herself reach for him. His skin was warm. He felt nice against her. Amazingly, she felt herself pull close against him. She kissed him. His lips were cool and thin. He lay very still and finally turned his face away.

'No,' he said. 'You were right. Let's be friends and not mess it up.'

Right. What the hell was she doing? She pulled back and let the momentary surge of stray feeling fall apart. Just wait. Everything falls apart if you wait long enough. Nothing really changes. The same radio was going. The same backyard carpenter was still hammering in the distance.

'I feel old,' she said after a while. 'Funny, huh? Twenty

117

years old and I feel like I'm over the hill. My career's a big fat nothing. Sometimes I just want to lie down and never get up.'

'Don't say stupid things like that —'

She hardly noticed him. 'But I'm a woman, right, so why don't I just settle down and get into some nice regular guy, right?' She shook her head desolately. 'And I almost *could* trade off for that sometimes — a guy like that. Almost. Then Byron turned sweet on me and I forget all about it. I forget about everything.'

Eddie listened, all stern and angry-looking.

'Hey, Eddie,' she said, feeling better all of a sudden, 'It ain't all tears. When he's good, it's good.'

Eddie shrugged.

'I'm sorry, man. I'm just dragging you along, aren't I.'

'So?'

'But I need a friend, I really do.'

Eddie's face relaxed a little. He smiled.

'Listen, you've got a friend,' he said. 'Whatever kind of friend you want me to be . . . you've got it.'

From the Grave

Estelle, 'Tailor to the Stars', was a shy, plump, near-sighted lady who lived in a bungalow on Wayne Newton Lane. She had designed one of Elvis's last jumpsuits — designed it to contain him at over 250 pounds, a bloated seal. He died before he could wear it.

'She's also a psychic,' Bruno said as they pulled up to her bungalow. 'Y'know, gets in touch with spirits and such. Elvis came back the other day, gave some reporter an interview through Estelle. For *The Star* or something.'

'What —?'

'I'm not shittin' you guy. Watch the grocery stores, you can read it yourself . . .'

Byron stopped halfway up the walk. His face turned serious. He reached out and halted Bruno.

'Wait a minute, man. If this lady can talk to Elvis —'

'— no, no. She doesn't talk to Elvis, she lets Elvis take over. He does the talking himself — using her voice, like she's an amplifier.'

'Can you set it up?'

'If she's in the mood.'

It had begun to haunt him, that jumpsuit, visions of a new, mature Prince Byron glowing in white. He knew it could never be a simple matter; the jumpsuit wasn't just a costume. There were sinister possibilities — Elvis had fattened in it, putrefied and died. There was danger attached to it.

But where there's danger, Byron realised, there's also power, and he had come to recognise that late Elvis was full

119

of the most majestic sort of power. He had raised his sights. Now he was aiming for all-out splendour: the imperial grown-up Elvis — solid class. This would be Byron Bluford's ultimate achievement. And as for history — with Elvis dead, wasn't late just as 'historical' as early? Well, hell, of course it was!

After three weeks he dropped 'Prince Byron' from the Lords 'n' Ladies marquee and had it replaced with the grander-sounding 'King Byron'. Now he had to have the jumpsuit. And he had to have it fancy — festooned with glittery hangings and patches of brocade and macramé. He wanted a high gold collar and American eagle designs in studs and rhinestones. It had to be magnificent — it had to shimmer.

Estelle had seen Byron at Lords 'n' Ladies. Halfway through his first break she had agreed to make him a suit at a fraction of her price. She was tiny and round, and padded around the house in rhinestone slippers and a satin tent dress. Her face was even rounder than the rest of her and her eyes were hardly visible behind giant garnet-studded shades with thick, purple lenses. She served tea with her head averted either out of shyness of because she thought her blond beehive was slipping off to one side. She made small talk in a high baby's voice about some brownies she was about to send her sister. Then she gulped her tea and pulled out a tape measure.

'First,' she said, 'I want you to close your eyes and describe it to me.'

'It shines. It's as white as you can get.' Byron had given it a lot of thought. 'It's got things that reflect the lights different ways, like prisms. The collar's tall but loose, and I want my chest to show. There ought to be pine trees, for the state of Maine, and some Indian signs — America before the white man — I'm part Indian y'know. The American eagle on the back, of course, and I want him clutching the four seasons in his claws and the four directions of the earth, North, South, East, West. There ought to be dollar signs and signs for Cadillac and the words *Elvis* and *Byron* woven together with *TCB* and stuff like that. And pictures of things that were sacred to Elvis . . . the Cross, the face of Jesus, Colonel Parker with a cigar, stuff like that. You know?'

Estelle nodded.

'He wants to talk to Elvis, honey,' Bruno interjected, clearing his throat. 'Is that possible today?'

Estelle fixed him with a faint smile and immediately bowed her head. Bruno shot a glance at Byron and nodded. When Estelle's face reappeared it was transformed: her lip curled into a sneer, her chubby roundness seemed to have slimmed into a sculpted triangle. She shoved her glasses above her forehead, revealing a pair of bright liquid eyes.

'Elvis?' Bruno said.

'Huh,' Estelle grunted, from deep in her gut.

'Will you talk to Byron here?'

'Does a bear shit black?' said Estelle — or Elvis.

Bruno leaned back and crossed his legs.

Byron's eyes were blinking with amazement. His mouth fell open. He laughed once, then turned to Bruno in confusion.

'Ask him a question,' Bruno prompted.

'Elvis, ah . . . ' He laughed and shook his head. 'This is ridiculous —'

'Byron don't waste my time, son! The voice came from inside Estelle, a powerful command. Byron snapped to attention in his chair. 'C'mon ask me.'

'Ask him what it's like to be dead,' Bruno whispered.

'What's it like, Elvis? To be dead?'

'Awful, man. Nothin's happening here. It's awful.'

'Do you . . . remember me?'

'Remember you . . .' Estelle was rocked by a single chuckle. 'I never forgot you, brother. I think about you all the time. I'm with you every day. You're my unfinished business. My last link with life is you, man, just you.'

Byron's mouth had gone dry. His eyes rolled as a ripple of dizziness flowed past his head. He leaned toward Estelle.

'Colonel Parker — does the Colonel know about me? Is

he gonna help our chances to stay alive?'

'Yes. But you've got to earn it. The world's got to see you earn it. They've got to see the miracle before they believe. Once you've earned it, he'll step forward and claim you. There will be a great meeting. A great public event. In the meantime, he'll be guiding you along with his unseen hand. He'll be making things happen for you because you're my main man and we all know it.'

'The Battle of the Elvises —'

'You're in, man. Once you've got a real Vegas act, you're in. Listen to Frank Bruno.'

Bruno nodded in agreement and peeled out a fresh cigar.

'The Colonel's gonna make sure I win? I mean, if something went wrong there —'

'You're the winner, man. We're takin care of business. It's all foreknown . . .' Estelle's eyes fluttered and closed. She slumped in her chair.

Byron swiped the air with a triumphant fist. Bruno's eyes sparkled as he lit his cigar.

Within days the suit was finished, and the final fitting held in candlelight. Byron stood on a pedestal surrounded by mirrors. Estelle, her mouth full of pins, knelt before him, going over every inch of her creation. She was wearing a priestly black mu-mu. She rose and stepped back. Bruno started a record, Elvis's signature theme '2001'. In the multiple mirror, hundreds of Byrons raised their arms, letting the matching cape spread and fall. The music thundered through the room. Bruno and Estelle watched, awestruck. In the semi-darkness, as the little bungalow shook with the climax of the music, Byron was the image of the resurrected King.

King Byron *was* Elvis.

A Dime-Store God

Saturday night was a sensation at Lords 'n' Ladies. People reached out to touch him as he walked on, slow and dignified, a shimmering white presence. Elvis the zoot-suit kid was gone. Tonight it was all Vegas material — 'See See Rider', the Vegas opener, and straight into the rap intro of 'Polk Salad Annie', word for word.

'Let's go down to Louisiana. Some of y'all never been down South too much. I wanna tell you a little story so you'll understan' what I'm talkin' about . . .'

Before dawn, in the darkened garage, Buddy and Junior sat with Byron, watching a video replay of the evening.

' . . . Down there we have a plant that grows out in the woods and fields, and looks somethin' like a turnip green. Everybody calls it polk salad. That's *polk*' — bumping one hip, as Elvis always did right there — 'salad!' and two hips.

'Incredible!' Junior said under his breath.

'If you ain't ninety-nine percent Elvis,' said Buddy, 'I'll eat a goddamn alligator!'

Byron kept his eyes on the big screen.

'I gotta get the scarves going,' he said, half to himself. They were at the end of a long day and coming down, but he didn't want to stop. There was more work to do. He told them to throw on *Elvis in Hawaii*. While it rolled he sniffed water to loosen the coke residue in his nostrils and give him one more hit before daylight.

'Why don't you get some sleep, Boss?' said Buddy.

Byron shook his head. On screen Elvis whipped off his guitar and tossed it over his head. Behind him, one of the

123

musicians caught it.

'Right there —' said Byron suddenly. 'That's what I need, someone to catch the guitar and bring me water and feed the scarves to me, all that shit —'

Junior jotted it down on a note pad.

They ran the tape forward. Now the women had pushed their way down to the stage.. Elvis was tossing scarves. Another ritual. It had to be done right. Byron watched, bleary-eyed, a sheaf of scarves hanging loosely from his neck.

As Elvis grabbed each scarf and tossed it, Byron carefully duplicated the motion. He threw scarf after scarf, studying the screen, making Buddy and Junior reverse the tape and gather up the scarves, throwing them again, until they were so dead tired their eyes were rolling, and it was dawn.

Wendy was lying awake when Byron stomped into the motel room and sat heavily on the bed. She looked at him for a minute, wondering how far gone he was.

'What've you been doing?' she said.

'Working.'

'Working, huh.' Her voice had a dull edge. 'How about that. Well, guess what — I'm working, too. Ain't that a coincidence?'

Byron's lips hardly moved as he simply repeated the word tonelessly. 'Working . . .'

'Yeah. I got a job.' She turned away from him bitterly. 'I'm a waitress now. Fabulous, huh?'

'Yeah. Great', he mumbled.

What she had waited up to tell him, but didn't now, was that her period was late, over two weeks late. She faced him. Her lips were trembling.

'Listen, Byron. I've gotta say this. I don't have any purpose here beyond you. But I've just got to have more. Everything's gonna dry up otherwise. You've got to love me a little more. I mean, talk to me sometimes. Or just —'

She broke off suddenly as Byron slid to the floor, landing in an unconscious heap.

'Oh, fuck . . .' she whispered, turning her face away.

Byron felt terrific after some sleep. Bruno had set up a picture taking session in the afternoon, with the new jumpsuit and all. Byron got a facial and a hair set so he'd be looking just right. Then he went off with Buddy and Junior, trying on rings and pendants and picking up a pair of purple-tinted aviator shades. At the photographer's he checked himself out in a mirror till there wasn't any doubt: it all pulled together.

As the camera clicked, Bruno stood to the side, satisfied with what he saw. Elvis — studlike, ornate, sure of himself. The King of Rock 'n' Roll.

'A dime-store god', he said to himself, chewing on a toothpick.

Room to Move

Dear Larry,
Here's a plane ticket. I can't describe what's going on out here! You've got to see for yourself. Get your ass on the plane, man! You've got no excuse now.

Byron

Dear Mr Margolis:
As you have heard, I am drawing record crowds with my shows at Lords 'n' Ladies, 'King Byron and the Eternal Flames', featuring Creamery Butter, now my exclusive backup ensemble. It should interest you to see me perform this vintage combination of Elvis's greatest Vegas shows, in a custom-ornate white jumpsuit designed by Estelle, Tailor to the Stars. We have added keyboards, synthesiser, another guitar player and backup singers. We now exactly duplicate the actual sound of Elvis Presley's giant stage orchestra. Since his death, there is no doubt I am the premier historical preservationist of Elvis's late Vegas years. Once again I extend you my personal invitation to attend any show free of charge (your name is permanently on our guest list). I can confidently say we are ready in every way for the 'Battle of the Elvises.' What I do is unique in Vegas. Come to Lords and prove it to your own satisfaction.

'King' Byron Bluford

There was one nagging problem: Lords 'n' Ladies was just

too small. Byron's crowd consistently jammed the place, threatening to spill over into the band. The stage had been a postage stamp to begin with, but now, with the added musicians, Byron had less than no room to move. The dance floor was right under his nose; more than once he had eaten a piece of the mike as some asshole reeled into the stand. He had to be ready at any time to shove a boot into someone's butt if they veered too close.

Standing in one spot was sheer humiliation, the exact opposite of everything Elvis's Vegas shows ever stood for. It drove Byron nuts to come sweeping out like royalty in a jewelled American eagle jumpsuit — then do the whole goddamn show from one spot, like a cheap bar singer. After his face suffered a head-on collision with the new guitar player's Telecaster, he took it up with Bruno.

'I can't work any more under these conditions!'

The old guy watched him pace the back room, blood still streaming from his nostrils.

'This is the fuckin' end. Get me a real room, man. Get me a showroom!'

'I'm workin on it —'

'I don't wanna hear that,' Byron railed. 'Don't tell me you're fuckin workin' on it. I'm turning myself into Elvis Presley atom by atom, I don't stop for one second — and you tell me you're *workin'* on it. What's the point if I can't move on stage? Do I have to die standing in one spot in this dive? Hey — I gotta go from A to B to C to pull this thing off — I'm still human like everybody else, right? Do you think Jerry Margolis is gonna fuckin' *drop by* Lords 'n' Ladies? How in the name of Christ am I supposed to get to that man? I mean, shit — an Elvis that stands in one spot — where's that at? You told me yourself I've gotta prove I'm valid — well c'mon, let's go! I've gotta have a showroom. And I've gotta live somewhere that ain't a stinkhole motel. I've gotta drive something that looks right. You're the fuckin manager — get me something! Do I have to parade down the Strip on a flatbed truck like a goddam Okie? I want out of here! I want action!'

Bruno's eyes flashed, the only sign of anger he ever showed. 'Don't worry, kid,' he said after a moment. 'You'll get it.'

The next day Frank Bruno gambled and won. The Paradise Motor Inn was a new hotel-casino without a personality. It had been built in the no-man's land between downtown and uptown, and in its short, checkered history had changed hands a half-dozen times, owned by several conglomerates, a hotel chain, a TV star, and most recently, a New York group fronting for a Rhode Island crime family. It had a showroom, Paradise Alley, that had never been properly booked. It became a well-known dumping ground for booking agents, and the new manager, a tough roly-poly Italian named Mike Porco, was trying to do something about it.

But not only was Porco a hick from Pawtucket, Rhode Island, he was also a complete amateur in entertainment. After a number of rough experiences in life, the first question on his checklist was always, 'Who do you trust?' And in this case, in this town full of sharks, he trusted himself and no one else — with the possible exception of one marginal figure, an old drinking pal from Fall River, and reputedly his third cousin, one Frank Bruno. What he liked about Frank was he could call him for advice and get an honest opinion. (even though he always did what he wanted anyway). Frank knew the town, but he was easygoing, didn't try to put a load of crap down your throat.

Bruno knew what Porco thought of him. He had carefully cultivated trust, knowing that someday, some way, he would score behind it. He had watched the Paradise Alley go to waste as Porco and the others made mistake after mistake. Dinner Theatre! That was Porco's latest bomb. It might have worked at that — with the New York cast of *Hello Dolly* or something. But Mike insisted on bringing in some weird original musical from L.A. and it was garbage from Day One. Now he was so desperate that he was dealing with agents again, trying to save the room by putting a star attraction in, something that would be surefire. Only he couldn't afford the real stars, and the marginal names were too risky. Bruno knew the situation. He knew the cards were in his own hands. And he knew one other factor: Mike Porco had loved Elvis Presley.

Bruno did most of his business from the motel by phone. He seldom had to put on a suit, but today he dressed to the nines — electric blue polyester double-breasted suit, yellow silk shirt, string tie with turquoise clasp, Tony Lama boots and an immaculate white Stetson with a silver hatband. He dropped into Porco's office smoking cigarillos through a silver holder and flashing a Pearldrops grin. He was beautiful.

Porco was in a fit over his latest headliner, a French pop star who was supposed to have a following over here, but where the hell were they — French Lick, Indiana? It was a good time for Frank to show up, with Porco fuming, slamming phones down, needing to see someone he could believe in. Frank's gamble was to put every ounce of trust he had carefully built up in Porco right on the table — and to risk it all on Byron. For the first time ever he came on strong to Porco, he pressured, he wheedled, he sang.

'I'm not gonna give you some two-bit dead dog act. I'm not even talkin' about an ordinary attraction. What I'm offering you — and Mike, think about this, think about it — is Elvis Presley. Outa the grave and into the Paradise!'

Bruno was over his head and he knew it. He had never placed a headline act in a room like Paradise Alley. He was pulling strong now that he had never even touched before. There had been Elvis impersonators in Vegas before, but with Elvis on ice the potential for such an act was now boundless — and Bruno's boy seemed to be in on the ground floor. Slowly Porco's face lit up. He was laughing like a kid as he riffled through the glossies. He was banging his desk with a fist and, finally, pouring booze to drink to it. Elvis Presley in his club!

Back at the Royal Flush, Frank Bruno popped himself a beer and stripped off his meeting suit. Settling into an easy chair in his underwear he felt satisfaction spread through him like rippling waves. Finally, at this late date in his life, he might just have a tiger by the tail. So what if there was some weird shit going down? Let the kid think he was that much closer to Colonel Parker, it wouldn't kill him. The important thing was momentum — he had it, nothing could disturb it. Whatever force of destiny had steered Byron Bluford to his motel door had dropped the goddamn tiger in his lap and the trick was to handle with care. So far so good. The sky was the limit. With God's help he'd be up to the rest of it.

During Wendy's first week on the job, the Mainsail was the prime watering spot for a convention of software sales reps who kept the lounge hopping every afternoon. She wore a thin little calico uniform that showed her off nicely, and the software boys couldn't keep from gawking whenever she headed for the bar with a load of dirty glasses.

'Scuse me, honey,' said one fatso, trying to sound suave. 'Got my Seagram's yet?'

'Coming up,' Wendy sang out, forcing a smile.

She set her tray down at the service area and waited for Eddie to make up the order. Byron had drifted in and was leaning against the bar with a flushed face. His eyes sagged. Quaaludes, she figured, and a few beers. His speech was slow and thick.

'So anyway, the old coot did it.'

'Did what?' She was irritated that he would come in here and demand attention in the busiest part of her day.

'Got me a supperclub. It ain't exactly on the Strip, but it's a real showroom, the real goddamn thing. And he's got a whole damn warehouse to rehearse in — can ya believe that?'

Byron leaned across the bar and poked Eddie's shoulder. 'C'mon man — get us a shot of something.'

Wendy blew her stack. 'Listen, asshole, I've got to get this order to that table, and five other orders as well, or I'm gonna get fired. You know what fired is?'

'Hell, all I want is a little drink with you,' he whined with exaggerated humility. 'T' celebrate —'

'No!' she snapped. Eddie finished filling up her tray and she headed for the table with the order.

Byron shrugged. He was too loaded to let it get to him.

'Well, *get* fired,' he bellowed after her. 'It doesn't make any damn difference. You won't need this fuckin' job anyway — not with the kind of money I'll be making!'

Wendy winced as she served the order. The men swivelled around to look at Byron, then glanced at Wendy.

'Too much cough syrup, I guess,' she said, trying to laugh it off. The men blinked.

Byron swung back around to the bar. 'All right . . . gotta go take a look at this club,' he muttered. 'Gimme a shot of Jack there, sonny.'

Eddie poured a shot of Jack Daniel's and shoved it at Byron with a silent stare.

'What you lookin' at asshole?' There was bemused challenge in his voice. Eddie continued to look for a moment, then dropped his eyes.

'Nothing.'

Byron gulped the shot of whiskey. He pointed across the room at Wendy.

'Put it on her tab, Babycakes.' And he was gone.

Gone — like a cool breeze. Down to Fremont Street, drawing glances like he always did these days, and humming with a good, slow, hazy buzz on. Like old wine. And there was Bruno, puffing away on a stogie in the Cadillac, top down, right where he said he'd be and what a choice day this was! Clear blue cool desert air. A damn fine day. They parked after a short ride and walked into the Paradise Motor Inn like they were going to buy the damn place.

There was nothing particular about the lobby — it could have been a Ramada Inn. The action was in the casino. The showroom, Paradise Alley, was dark. Byron and Bruno turned a corner and there it was — like coming onto a hidden cavern, subdued, spacious, lush. A couple of cleaning ladies were vacuuming the place, but otherwise it was deserted. The broad stage thrust forward into arc after arc of tables and so much space that Byron lost equilibrium for a moment and staggered.

'Big, huh?' said Bruno proudly.

The room was bigger than anything Byron had imagined. His eyes widened and a sudden rumble of nausea weakened his legs. He went white with the horrors and his eyes darted back and forth, trying to focus on something nearby. He put his hand on a table to steady himself. A cold sweat was bursting all over his face. This was bad. Like a beast raging through his mind.

'You okay —?' said Bruno, his eyes narrowing as he watched Byron carefully.

'Yeah,' Byron whispered, waiting for the beast to pass. 'Yeah, I'm okay . . .'

But he wasn't okay. The room was like the flaming mouth of Godzilla. He knew it could swallow him without a trace. Just the sight of it made him want to lie down and die.

'Lemme drive you home,' said Bruno.

'I'll walk. I gotta get some air.'

Later, when Wendy came off her shift, he was outside the Mainsail, leaning unsteadily against a parked car.

'Baby, I'm sorry,' he was saying, 'I'm sorry, I'm sorry . . .'

All the way to the truck his hands were groping at fenders and walls for support. When Wendy got him to the motel his skin was slick and clammy. He shook like he had caught malaria. She stripped off his clothes and made him sit in a hot tub until his colour returned.

'What drugs did you do —?' she began.

'It ain't that.'

He was silent for a while. Then he looked up at her.

'It's sickness. Some kind of sickness. It makes me afraid.'

'Well, hell, Byron — it's natural to be afraid.'

He dropped his gaze, shaking his head mournfully, muttering to himself. 'Got two weeks. Two weeks to take a major show into that room.'

'What happened today?'

'I saw it. The room. I . . . couldn't even walk in there.' His voice trailed off into a whisper. He swallowed hard and moved his head back and forth.

Wendy's eyes narrowed with determination. 'Well, you *can*, damn it! You *can* walk in there.'

He looked at her with surprise.

'We'll go back there together — I'll go with you.'

Slowly the pain that lined his face broke up and was replaced by a tired, sheepish grin.

'Jesus!' He spewed out a long, shuddering sigh. 'Sure is lots of people running around inside my head!'

She looked at him hard. 'Well, which one am I talking to? Who's talking to me now?'

'Now?' He waved one hand vaguely. 'Blue-Suede Bluford, a coward, a fool. A nobody. A nothing. A dumb shit we're trying to leave behind.'

'Stop it.'

Wendy jumped into the silence that followed. 'Well, you know something? I'm gonna miss him.' Her voice roughened with emotion. 'Because I like him a hell of a lot better than I like some of those other bastards you carry around inside that head!'

Byron searched her face in confusion.

She sighed. 'Ah, don't worry about it, Byron. Don't worry about the things I say.'

Byron sat up in the tub. There was a dangerous fierceness in his eyes, but suddenly he reached for her and kissed her so tenderly it made her want to swoon.

'Keep loving me,' she whispered. 'You — this one right here. Let this one come to me more often.'

He drew her close. 'I can't take ten steps without you honey, you know that. Down the line, when there's time, I'm gonna turn things around, I'm gonna dress you in white —'

Byron, don't play with me.'

'Play, hell —!' He rose up dripping. 'You want me to

prove it? You want to go right down to one of them marriage chapels? Let's go. Let's do it now. Hell, I don't need my clothes.'

He stepped out of the tub and strode toward the front door. Wendy ran after him and held him from behind, letting his wetness soak her. They stood for a long time without saying anything.

Finally, Byron spoke: 'It just gets kind of tricky sometimes, keeping it all straight, you know . . .'

But his mind kept on moving. He pulled away from her and seemed to look at the room for the first time. His smile vanished. The dizziness came roaring back like hungry beast . . .

'Jesus,' he whispered, 'If this would only pass . . .'

All the Way

It passed. But now he had given it a name. For two weeks, the Beast came and went every few hours, ravaging his head. He couldn't drink it away, eat it away, fuck it away, or drug it away — and he tried them all. He'd had nerves before — he'd been afraid, but this was something else. It came on suddenly, anywhere — the back room at Lords 'n' Ladies, the warehouse in the middle of a rehearsal, at night, at dawn, at high noon. It drained the blood from his soul, left him grabbing at the walls, shaking like a sick dog. It came whenever it wanted — and whenever it wanted, it was gone. Like a cool breeze.

'No needles,' he kept telling the boys.

But he was doing heavier and heavier drugs — barbiturates, pain killers, super tranquilizers. He spread his head like a pharmaceutical sandwich and swilled down quarts of beer whenever he felt rough edges. When he got hungry, he pigged whole cakes and pies. If he went too far down, there was always a ready supply of cocaine and standard uppers. Eventually he had worked it out, a way of tiptoeing around the Beast, playing hide-and-seek with it, staying on his feet, functioning, working. He was able to make it through the final week at Lords 'n' Ladies, able to plough his way through rehearsals at the warehouse, and finally, with his head thick as cheese, he was able to walk calmly into Paradise Alley and get himself through a three-hour, full-dress run-through.

But opening night the Beast came back and wrapped him up like a baby in a shroud. Backstage, he was in a panic. Sweat drenched him. He heaved until there was nothing left to heave. Wendy held a cold washcloth to his forehead. Buddy and Junior kept the dressing room cleared and sent for a Dr Feelgood.

'Oh, God —' Byron moaned, and hung on to Wendy like she was the Holy Mother. 'I'm dying. Just let me die.'

Out front the marquee read:

ALL-ELVIS SPECTACULAR!
THE KING RETURNS
****

KING BYRON AND THE ETERNAL FLAMES

The magic of Elvis's name, and the novelty of what was promised, had pulled in a sea of Wonderbread-fed Elvis fans. The regulars from Lords 'n' Ladies made it a sellout, and the crowd was mostly seated now, eating and drinking, as Morty Zack, a middle-aged stand-up comic, worked the opening set. Morty Zack was a favourite of Mike Porco's and did jokes like this:

'Yeah, they got Polish muggers — I was over there. Guy said, "Stick 'em up", threw me his wallet and ran off!' A solid laugh.

At the rear of the house, Bruno and Porco stood watching the show. Porco was enjoying Morty Zack.

'He's a gem, Frank. Another Jackie Kahane, don'tcha think?'

'Could be,' Bruno shrugged.

'I'm lookin forward to this, Frankie. I was a big fan of Elvis's. I cried when he passed away, I kid you not — like a baby. This is very special for me, very special.'

'For all of us, Mike.'

'Of course, if he bombs . . .' Porco rolled his eyes. 'We'll all go sky diving without parachutes.'

Bruno answered with a pale grin.

Backstage, Byron tried again to struggle to his feet.

'Where's that doctor?'

'Be here any minute,' said Buddy.

Wendy supported him till he staggered back into a corner and squatted.

'I can't even stand up. My head spins —'

'Just relax,' she whispered firmly. 'Remember, you've done this before. You've never failed. It's just nerves.'

'But I can't even fuckin' walk!'

Frank Bruno walked in and Byron turned on him with desperate fury. 'There y'are. Jesus, I want you to stay with me, not go wandering all the hell over!'

'Just checkin' the house,' Bruno replied evenly.

'Well, what about the billing out there on that marquee? Makes me look like an opening act to Elvis or something.'

'We're fixin' that.'

'Margolis out there?'

'Yah.'

'Colonel Parker?'

'Ah . . . didn't see him.'

Byron suddenly grabbed Bruno's shoulder and pulled him close, his face rippling with anxiety.

'Jesus, Frank, I'm so scared. I've never been scared like this.'

The door opened and in walked a young black dude with an Afro like a basketball. He broke into a grin and held up his doctor's bag, dangling it from one finger.

'There's my man!' crowed Buddy in pseudo-jive. 'What's happenin', Doc?'

'S'happenin',' the doctor replied as they slapped hands.

'The King needs a little help, Doc.' Buddy steered him over to Byron.

Byron recited his symptoms. 'My head's spinning. I can't breathe . . .'

The Doc took a syringe out of his bag and filled it with amber fluid. Wendy watched tensely.

'No problem, your majesty — this'll smooth you right out.'

'What the hell is that?' said Wendy.

'Vitamins A through Z, baby —'

'He doesn't need that shit,' she protested.

'Shut up!' Byron cut her off. He nodded to the Doc. 'Go ahead.'

The needle plunked into Byron's forearm like a dart. Almost immediately, he was relaxing. He took several deep breaths. He stood up and walked around. Suddenly confidence was flowing back into his face. He looked at himself in the mirror.

'All right,' he said with authority. 'Time to take care of business.'

When the showroom stage went dark, the crowd rustled and buzzed with anticipation. There were a few whoops and whistles. In the near-darkness, the musicians could be seen as dim moving silhouettes. Then came the restrained, foreboding first notes of the signature theme. The crowd hushed.

The announcer's voice boomed through the PA with awe-struck solemnity: 'Ladies and gentlemen, Paradise Alley and the Paradise Motor Inn are proud to bring you . . . the King of the Elvis Illusionists, King Byron and the Eternal Flames!'

Out of the climatic symphonic chord burst the band, vamping the intro to 'See See Rider,' and the stage suddenly flashed into light as Byron bounded on, moving gracefully through the expanded space like a buck deer. There was not a trace of nerves now. The horror was gone, he was free.

The show rolled forward like a new Cadillac. Byron tossed off a brief early Elvis medley and moved smoothly to the later stuff: 'Proud Mary', 'Love Me', 'Bridge Over Troubled Waters', 'Polk Salad Annie'. His voice quivered like a hummingbird, between high tenor and throaty baritone, encompassing every nuance Elvis had possessed. He swept across the floor like a karate fighter, leaping, turning, kicking, drawing huge circles with his arm, pointing toward heaven, humping the mike stand, cradling the hand mike. He flipped the guitar over his head, Elvis-style. He let the women come forward with their snapshot cameras. He tossed them scarves in flurries and knelt at the edge of the stage to bestow ritual kisses. Gone was the scruffy, punky, early Elvis. What Byron had mastered in the last few weeks, what the crowd now saw, was the smooth, mature dynamism of Elvis the legend, the King.

'Polk Salad Annie' brought the room to a plateau of amiable hysteria. Dripping with sweat, Byron motioned for a flunky to bring him water. Now he played with the crowd the way Elvis always had, flashing one-sided grins into the darkness, reacting spontaneously to whatever craziness bubbled up from the house, sipping water, rapping.

'Whew! I bet you're sayin' . . . he ain't tired, he's faking!'

A ripple of laughter went through the crowd as they recognised the quote from Elvis. This was a gathering of the faithful. Aging high school queens and would-have-been queens grown plump with children, and their husbands, the old greasers of yesteryear, hair now sprayed into freeze-dried clumps. Jewish and Italian couples from Long Island. Leisure-suited union officers. Young local cowboys and their mamas from Lords 'n' Ladies.

And women — sad, fat, yearning women, flashy young-ish women looking for adventure, hungry-eyed bounty-hunters with Elvis in their hearts.

One of these threw a hotel key on stage.

'Huh? Wha'sis?' said Byron, picking it up. He pretended to read the plastic tag. 'Lemme see . . . SPCA Kennel Number Five. Must be a dog. Anybody want a dog? I tell ya, it's a dog's life — I may be movin' in there myself . . .' Laughs from the crowd. 'Nah. Just kiddin' — thanks honey, let's, ah, get together later and talk about the first thing that comes up . . .'

A pair of panties sailed out of the crowd and landed on stage. Byron picked them up and dangled them from his fingertips.

'Must be the same dog.' He howled over the laughter. 'Ah-ooooo! Growf! Just don't bite too hard, baby, that's all I ask.'

A little girl in a Hawaiian grass skirt came forward shyly with a lei of flowers. The crowd dissolved into 'aww's and 'coo's.' Byron bent down and let her slip the lei over his head. Her mom, who had trailed her down to the stage, lifted her up to Byron. He pecked her on the cheek. The crowd applauded warmly as Mom led the little sweetheart back to her seat.

'Thank ya, honey,' Byron called after them. 'That was sweet. She gave me a lei. First time I ever got 'lei-d' by an eight-year old —' More laughs mixed with mock outrage. 'I better shut up and sing — or whatever it is I'm s'posed to be doin'.'

From a booth near ringside, Wendy and Bruno watched fascinated, as Byron pulled the show along with supreme control. The eclectic late Elvis — singing anything that caught his fancy, any style, any artist — flowed by as Byron delivered the heroic ballads, the heavy rockers, the sentimental laments, the grandiose pop arias — 'Sweet Caroline', 'Hello, Mary Lou', 'If I can Dream,' working up to the melodramatic 'American Trilogy', and finally, Elvis's traditional closing number, 'Can't Help Falling in Love.'

The crowd spilled out of their seats, wild with applause. Wendy smiled in grudging admiration, tears clouding her eyes. He had brought it off. He had sold the illusion and the crowd had bought it. For the first time, she realised that it was a great accomplishment, this long, tricky, demanding performance. Like an athlete, Byron had trained for it and come home with a victory.

Backstage was complete chaos. Wendy had to push and claw her way through a throng of fans, mostly women, to get to the dressing room door.

'Well, 'scuse me, honey, I'm sure,' snipped a tough-looking groupie.

'Who's that one think she is, Priscilla or somethin'?' whined another.

Wendy beat on the door till Buddy pushed it open just far enough to squeeze her in. Byron was receiving fans. He was so high his face seemed to give off light. The whites of his eyes showed as he threw back his head to laugh. His attention jerked back and forth from face to face, acknowledging Wendy for only a split second, then moving on, his eyes briming with power.

A man and woman in their thirties stood close to him. The woman was very pregnant. Her husband rocked from one foot to the other uncomfortably.

'Feel him,' the woman urged Byron. 'Put your hand there —'

Byron rested his hand on her abdomen. Her husband grinned affably.

'I can feel him dancin',' Byron said. 'He's gonna be a rocker.'

'I just want your blessing,' said the woman. 'If he's a boy, we're namin' him Byron Elvis Whipple.'

'Well, that's nice, darlin' —' Byron began.

The woman reached for him compusively and hissed into his ear, 'Last night I dreamed that you made him!' She kissed him on the lips, lightly at first, then escalated to open-mouthed passion. Her husband held on to his grin and waited.

At the door, Jerry Margolis squeezed through and caught Frank Bruno's attention with a wave and a chummy nod. His entire manner was transformed: Now he was buying.

'Okay, Frank — your boy made a believer outa me.'

Byron let Margolis pump his hand. 'What'd I tell ya, Jerry?'

'Call me tomorrow and let's schmooz. I wanna start some promotion around the kid.'

'We're ready, my friend.'

'It's a hell of a show — I want it.' Margolis winked broadly. 'Tomorrow,' he emphasised, ducking out as Buddy held the door for him.

Bruno turned to Byron in triumph.

'We're in,' he shouted across the room. 'We're in the competition!'

Byron raised both fists and whooped ecstatically. Bruno

fought his way through the hangers-on and embraced his boy, laying a kiss on each cheek. Wendy put her hand on Byron's arm and started to say something sweet, when the door suddenly shoved open and an apparition blew in: an Elvis Woman, dressed in a jewelled white jumpsuit slashed to the waist so that her breasts heaved and bounced freely in the bare cleft of the V. Her hair was swept back into a version of Elvis's and her eyes were hidden behind purple-tinted aviator shades. Ignoring everyone else, she rushed straight at Byron, throwing him off balance as she pressed against him and kissed hard.

Wendy staggered back a step, the breath taken out of her — first by the woman's sheer boldness, then by Byron's response, as she saw his hands grasp her butt. Then by a larger, more sickening vision of the whole thing: Byron locked with Elvis in a hungry mutual embrace.

Later, in the dark of the motel room, Wendy made love to Byron desperately, as if to reclaim him, pull him back from some lost place where she could never go. 'Jesus, baby!' he said finally as her hunger surged back again and again. 'Let's rest it a minute.'

Neither of them could sleep, so they lay in bed watching dawn colour the outside. Byron's eyes were shining. His mind was racing. Wendy was quiet.

'Do you believe me now?' Byron said. 'God, did I blow 'em away?'

'Yes, you did.'

'I just can't stop thinking and thinking. I don't ever wanna sleep again. I won't ever be afraid again either. Just let that sun come up, I wanna celebrate!'

'Byron.'

'Huh?'

'Tell me something. Where's all this going? Where are we going to end up?'

Byron propped himself up on one elbow. His eyes were lit up with confidence.

'You know anything about Colonel Tom Parker?'

'A little.'

'He's the world's greatest manager. He built Elvis's career from the ground up, block by block. Then — all of a sudden he lost him.'

Byron waited for Wendy to react.

'Well?' she said after a moment.

'Well, hey — put two and two together! Parker's no fool, he needs another Elvis. He needs me. That's how the music business works. Me and Frank have been talkin' about it —'

'What does Frank say?'

Byron broke into a grin. 'All the way baby! All the way to the Colonel! That's what this is all about.'

Wendy watched him for a moment, silently. Byron. Prince Byron, King Byron, Elvis.

'Look, honey, I'm closer to one hundred percent Elvis than anybody in the world. Winning this goddamn competition'll be just a way of showing it — it ain't nothin' by itself. Just a signal to Colonel Parker, that's all. Then you watch — history's gonna take care of itself.'

'How?'

'How?' Byron spoke to her as if she were a three year old. 'I'll be doin' whatever Colonel had in mind for Elvis, that's how. Things Elvis would have done. He was gonna tour Europe — he was goin' to Japan. There was more movies to make, more records, more tours . . .'

A flicker of excitement crossed Wendy's face. 'You think . . . it really could happen?'

'My time is comin', honey. I've been getting ready for this all my life. I've got the inside track now. There's no way to stop me. No way . . .'

The Brown Circle

Why not? she could almost believe it. Why couldn't his lunatic dream become real? Sheer possibility was the fuel they were both running on. What made Byron still irresistible to her, even now, was the cloud of possibility that hung around him like a mist. Opening night had been no fluke. Byron's fans from Lords came over to the Paradise and packed it for a solid week. Tourists from up and down the Strip were standing in line. Jerry Margolis seemed to have fallen head-over-heels in love.

When she saw momentum like this Wendy could imagine almost anything for Byron. But for herself . . . when she tried to write, no songs would come. The moments when she felt the starry ambition and drive of Wendy Wayne hardly seemed to exist anymore. Playing with visions of her own success simply pulled her spirit down. Something inside refused to go along — a heaviness that nailed her to the earth, like a living presence that just wasn't interested.

She was sluggish, squeamish in the morning. It had been all she could do to roll out of bed and get herself to the Mainsail by noon. One day she vomited, just barely inside the ladies room. Her period had never come.

'Better get you a test kit,' said one of the waitresses. Wendy's knees weakened. 'Hey, six weeks — you're knocked up, hon.'

Not just late. Knocked up.

She got one. She watched the test tube for two endless, nail biting hours, watched the brown circle form — firm, round, unmistakeable. Yeah, she was gone all right. And weeping and shaking as the future broke against her like surf on a rock. Byron's baby — Byron and Wendy's baby! — conceived in the weird magical city of Las Vegas, in the middle of a dream of greatness.

'I'm quitting,' she said to Eddie. 'Can you do without me after Friday?'

His eyes flickered with disappointment. The bar was empty except for a few slot players quietly working their lucky machines.

'I guess. But why?'

'We're finally making money, Eddie. Believe it or not. He spends it like water and we still come out ahead.'

'Terrific.'

'This week — he ordered a new jumpsuit, he bought out a whole rack of sportshirts and some silk underwear for me —'

'He told you to quit, didn't he?'

She spoke gently: 'Look, Eddie, next Monday we're moving up to a penthouse suite on top of the Paradise. You can see the whole city from the balcony. We're making it, Eddie.'

'I'm very happy for you.' His mouth formed a thin line.

Wendy hesitated for a minute, then broke into a sunny grin.

'And I'm pregnant.'

'Sorry to hear that,' said Eddie after a pause.

'Well, I'm not.'

Eddie's face paled. 'Don't tell me you're going to have it?'

'Oh, c'mon, Eddie. Give me a break. Of course I'm going to have it.'

His voice was suddenly laced with icy contempt. 'I can't believe you.' He wagged his head slowly. 'You let yourself get knocked up by the world's crudest asshole and you act like I ought to be cheering —'

Wendy looked back, defying him quietly. 'I guess you'd just have to be me, wouldn't you?'

'I guess you'd have to be as stupid as you, maybe —'

'C'mon, man.'

'You c'mon — I can't rejoice over this. I think it's terrible.'

'You just don't accept one big thing: I love Byron, as stupid as that may seem to you — as much grief as it's causing me — I love the guy, and when he loves me back he knocks me off my feet. If you understood that, Eddie, you might not be so horrified to see me carry his baby.'

'If I understood,' he echoed, looking away with a humourless little grin, then back. 'Don't be an idiot. Get an abortion.'

Eddie sometimes had a way of making you feel really dumb. She felt anger and tears swelling in her throat as she watched him, his own anger draining his face and giving it a flinty sharpness.

'I can't help it,' he said, 'I hate the guy's guts. I hate everything he stands for. I've been in Vegas too long. I've seen too many flamboyant losers flaming out and taking everybody with them.'

Wendy's anger cooled and toughened. Her tears dried up. She wanted to hurt Eddie back.

'Don't call him a loser, man. He's up there, doing something extraordinary and making a success out of it. What are you doing that's so terrific, anyway? I've seen where he came from — I've been with him all the way from nowhere. He's worked and sweated his way out of the pump factory all the way to a showroom gig in Las Vegas — all on the strength of a vision of himself. What kind of vision have you got? Byron's about to do something that you couldn't even conceive of.'

'What's that?'

'He's gonna fill Elvis Presley's shoes. He's going all the way to Colonel Parker —'

'Ah, come on,' said Eddie with a desolate laugh. 'Don't insult my intelligence — or your own either. What kind of bullshit is that? Who's putting ideas like that into your head?'

Wendy didn't answer.

146

'Listen: I know where he's at. Guys like him get so involved in emulating a monster like Elvis Presley that their own personality disappears. They think they're some kind of American hero like Johnny Appleseed, but it's all haywire. You get these crackbrains running around thinking the Great Spirit has descended on them and now they're semi-devine, with a cosmic role to fulfil. With him it's Elvis. It might as well be Napoleon or Jesus Christ. He's a nut. He's not normal up there —' Eddie tapped his head. His contempt had softened into a tone of deliberate pleading. 'He's going to crash one of these days, Wendy, and you'll go down with him.'

'He's not crazy —'

'He is. It's like people who think the radio is telling them what to do, or they're hearing voices that tell them the Russians are poisoning the water —'

'You don't know him. You think you do but you don't. You just see him strutting around acting outrageous. You don't see him when he's tender or when he's frightened. When he's just Byron —'

'I don't have to. I know the whole story, honey. He's got your spirit captured.' Eddie's eyes widened with a new thought. He came closer and grasped her shoulders. 'Wendy, listen: Let's get out of here. This town is poison — I've been here too long. There's something evil about this place and it's prehistoric. I've been planning to go back to Austin for months but I haven't been able to move. Let's go. Come with me. Let's just get on the road and get out of the way of all this.'

Wendy shook her head and pulled away.

'No, Eddie. I'm having a baby —'

'You can have it. I'll take care of you. I'll help you through it. But, honey, you've got to get away from here, away from him —'

'No! How do I get it across to you — I love him. I even love his weird trip. If he's crazy I'm crazy because I've got dreams too. Eddie, Jesus man, I'm not going to leave him — we've got some problems, but deep down at the basic level we're a team, we come together and give each other courage and energy. He's not a bad person. He's not insane. He's fucked up, but the more he achieves, the less fucked-up he's gonna be. And I want to be around to enjoy that.'

Eddie had drawn back. His face had settled back into its normal mask of coolness. But Wendy could see the hurt behind the mask. She went toward him impulsively and threw her arms around him.

'Eddie, Eddie — you're so sweet, I know you want to make me happy and safe, but you've got to let me live my life, and you've got to live your own, and we've both got to let Byron live his. It's just got to be that way —'

'He'll hurt you,' Eddie said, letting his arms dangle stiffly. 'He's going to hurt you bad. You won't know what I'm talking about until it happens. Then it'll be too late.

'So be it, man, so be it.'

Doodly-Squat

Friday afternoon, Eddie sent her home early, as a going-away gesture. She kissed him on the forehead, told him goodbye, and went straight to the grocery story to get something special for Byron — a steak, something extravagant. Tonight they really would celebrate. She picked up two luscious-looking fillets and let herself buy the fanciest, most expensive of anything else that caught her eye. Tonight there would be no skimping — it would be steak, silk underwear, and caviar!

Frank Bruno was lounging beside the motel pool in his white Stetson and a long bathrobe. He was smoking a cigar and listening to jazz on his pocket radio. Wendy noticed him as she entered the patio and for a split second, the things Eddie had said flitted across her mind. Instead of going straight upstairs she turned toward the pool and approached him.

'Sit down, dear,' said Bruno, smiling. 'You're home early. Workin' new hours?'

'I'm not working anymore.'

He took that in with a casual bow of the head. Suddenly Wendy remembered how little she trusted him.

'I want to talk to you. About Byron.'

'By all means, dear, what's up?' He was smiling like a Buddha, his eyes hidden behind mirror shades.

'Is he going to win that thing?'

'I believe that's the plan.'

'Then what?'

'Well.' He smiled even wider. 'This is Las Vegas — I

always say the sky's the limit!'

Wendy looked at him for a minute and then tossed a little bomb.

'And when does Colonel Parker step in and take over?'

Bruno's smile faded slightly. She had set him up and now he knew it. His voice dropped almost to a whisper.

'Y'never know,' he said.

And now Wendy knew it was all hollow talk. In a flash she saw the whole thing: he was a bullshit artist — and she had known it from the start. He was telling Byron whatever would keep him stuck in the fantasy of becoming Elvis. Like feeding sugar to a diabetic.

'You're lying, aren't you? Why don't you tell me the truth?'

Bruno puffed sloppily on his stogie.

'What's the truth?' he said finally.

Wendy struggled to pull her thoughts together. What was the truth?

'Maybe he's not . . . normal,' she heard herself say.

'Sure he is.'

'Take off those shades, man, and look me in the eye and tell me you think he's completely sane.'

Bruno looked away. He pulled on the cigar, not noticing it had gone out.

'Look, kid, everybody's a little crazy. This is his way. I'm not gonna take it away from him —'

'Oh, how thoughtful,' Wendy muttered. 'You're such a great guy.'

Bruno stared back at her for a moment.

'Don't expect fuckin' miracles from me, girlie. I'm doin' what I can —'

'I've got to put the milk away,' she cut him off, gathering up the groceries. Without looking at him, she climbed the stairway and walked briskly along the balcony walkway. Bruno watched her from the pool.

At the door, she fumbled for the key, thrust it into the lock and turned it. The door opened six inches and then clunked to a stop. It was chained from the inside.

'Byron — ?' Wendy listened for a moment. 'Byron . . .' Silence.

She called down to Bruno. 'Frank? Is Byron —'

Abruptly, the door closed from the inside. Then came the sound of the chain lock being removed. Wendy waited for something to happen.

The door opened again and there, spilling out of her ridiculous white jumpsuit, was the Elvis Woman, trying to slither past like a creamy big-nippled lizard.

'Sorry, honey,' she drawled. 'Guess there's just more than enough Byron to go 'round.'

She eased by and started down the walkway. Wendy caught a glimpse of Byron inside the room, half-dressed. She began to growl deep in her throat. Still clutching the grocery bag, she darted after the retreating Elvis Woman, catching up with her on the stairs.

' "Sorry — ?" I'll make you sorry you ever crawled out of your own stinking slime!' she screamed, pelting her with groceries — gobs of meat, jars of fancy fruit, ripe tomatoes, eggs — driving her toward the car. Halfway down the stairs her hand pulled out a jar of caviar. Looking at it, she stopped and let the pain break out on her face. She slumped down on the steps, sobbing inconsolably.

The Elvis Woman halted, dabbing at the smears of beef and tomato innards that dripped from her face and hair.

'Be a big girl, now honey,' she cooed softly, as to a baby. 'You just have to get past this.'

Wendy looked up at her with stupefied amazement — which the Elvis Woman misread as submission. She came close and touched Wendy's cheek. Her voice turned sultry and low.

'Lord, you're a pretty thing. I see why he wanted you.'

She grinned up at Byron who was peering anxiously over the banister. Her fingers brushed Wendy's lips. She moved her face very close to Wendy's.

'Let me in baby,' she whispered. 'Let's be sisters. I can help you with him —'

The smell of Juicy Fruit on her breath made Wendy want

to throw up. Somehow, her hand found its way to another
tomato. With a blind thrust she smashed it into the bitch's
face.

'Go!' she screamed, 'Get your foul ass out of my sight!'

This time the Elvis Woman didn't look back. As if
propelled by her undulating butt, she sprinted to her
Corvette and screeched the lavender monster back and forth
furiously, burning a pound or two of rubber on her way out
of the parking lot.

Suddenly Wendy looked up and saw Byron watching her
from the landing. With a howl of anger she threw the caviar
straight at his head and charged blindly up the stairs, flying
at him and flailing him with her fists.

'Okay, enough!' he said grabbing her wrists. 'You made
your point.'

Her point! She couldn't believe her ears. Byron held on
till she gave up and slumped against him, trembling with
exhaustion. When she spoke, her voice had a harsh
deadness that seemed to come all the way from hell.

'You're just lucky I don't have something to kill you
with!'

She wrenched past him and went into the room,
slamming the door in his face.

Byron came within a gnat's hair of following her in, then
he thought better of it. Something in her fury turned him
around and he decided to mosey on down and visit with old
Bruno.

'Out of control!'

Bruno shrugged and blew a ragged smoke ring. 'Jealousy
thy name is woman . . .'

'I fucked up, didn't I?'

'Comes with the territory. Who does she think you are —
Mary Tyler Moore? She'll get over it.' He turned to Byron
and watched him for a moment. 'Shook you up a little,
huh?'

'I feel like . . . like I just kicked a dog or something.'

Bruno reached for him, put one pudgy hand on his
shoulder. When Byron didn't respond, he shook him a

couple of times. Byron grinned half-heartedly.

'Don't take it so hard, guy. The world's still turnin'.'

'Suppose . . . suppose she cuts her wrists or something. Maybe I better go up.'

.'She ain't gonna cut her wrists. She'll cut your throat first. Give her some time. She's no fool, she'll figure it out.'

Byron bobbed his head to one side.

'Hey, hey.' Bruno gave him another shake. 'This ain't what's important. None of it. You know what's important, don't you?'

'Winning. Gettin' there. All the way to the Colonel.' Byron was mumbling absentmindedly.

'That's right. The women have to realise that. A blowjob here or there don't mean doodly-squat.'

'Mm.' Byron stared heavily into the pool. After a while he looked up with a glint in his eyes. 'Well, I tell you one thing — you have to be prepared for the unexpected around here. One minute you're doing a crossword puzzle, next minute somebody in a jumpsuit has your pants down, next minute your girlfriend's gone berserk and throwing food all over the place —'

'Why don't you pick that mess up,' Bruno said. 'If she don't come out we can cook it up in my place.'

'Maybe I'll get her — some flowers.'

Roses. If that didn't do it, nothing would. He bought a dozen American beauties from Jackpot Florists at the corner. Wendy had left the chain off, so he just sauntered on in — but slowly, in case she had a ball-peen hammer aimed at his head. She was lying motionless across the bed. After a minute he could see that her back was rising and falling in rhythm. Still alive, anyway.

'Wendy, honey?'

No answer.

He went outside and gathered up the food, brushing dust off the steaks, cradling the champagne and caviar in his arms, walking it all back to the room. She hadn't moved yet. He grabbed the roses and knelt beside the bed.

'I got something for you, baby.'

She shook her head without looking up.

Slowly, Byron began to pluck at the bouquet, dismantling it, dropping it on the bed, bloom by bloom, encircling her with roses. After a while he got to his feet. He watched her for a full minute, his head cocked to one side. With a shrug, he went to the kitchenette and started rattling the pots and pans. He cooked dinner with fastidious care, whistling and humming, glancing at Wendy from time to time. When the steaks were ready, he set the table and served their plates.

'Dinner honey.'

He popped champagne and poured two glasses. He lit a candle and sat, waiting for her, knowing something had to happen, something . . .

'C'mon, baby.'

Damn it — was she going to lie there forever? His eyes widened; his face turned dark. Suddenly he threw back his chair and stood up. He reached for the carving knife and rushed to the bed, crashing to his knees again. Wendy looked up as he placed the knife in her hand.

'Go on,' he said, his voice shaking. 'You've got something to kill me with now, go on and do what you want.'

She blinked at him and held the knife up, as if to protect herself.

'Do it. I deserve it. Whatever you want to do.'

She rose on her side and Byron watched a flow of bitterness rush to her face as she levelled the knife at him. My God, he thought, she's gonna do it. Then the knife clattered to the floor. She began to weep with a desolate weariness, trembling, gagging on her sobs as if they were craggy chunks of misery.

Byron pressed close to her and finally, in her exhaustion, she let herself cling to him, to the muscles in his neck and shoulders, to his smell, to the tenderness of his lips. She couldn't break it, the bond that held her spirit to him. She didn't want to break it. She knew, with a forlorn certainty, that underneath her fury there was always hope; that in her most desolate moments, she wanted him, she desired him, she wouldn't give him up.

Byron felt her push away from him. Now she was looking at him with wonder.

'I can't break it,' she said. 'Whatever it is that ties me to you —'

Byron grabbed her by the shoulders. His voice was hoarse with eagerness.

'Don't try honey. Just give me a chance. Listen: I'll die for you, I'll die anytime you say. Things just get weird. Sometimes I don't even know why I did something I just did. But when it's all over, when all the smoke blows away, Byron's gonna be somebody — it's all gonna add up to something. And then we'll be together till it's just rockin' chairs and gravestones and beyond — you and me, dancing off into the dark.'

Wendy's eyes had softened and now a new expression came into her face. It was a haziness, a languid flush, full of body heat and desire. Her eyes flickered across his face. She moved a little closer to him and her fingers played shyly with his sleeve. When she spoke her voice had gone small, like a little girl's, but there was a tension in it that made her seem almost haggard with age.

'Touch me,' she said. 'Give me what I need. Please, please, please . . .

Please Pull My Strings

Dear Col. Parker:

As you know I am now beyond all doubt the inheritor of Elvis's final performing style. I realise you stay on top of these things, but you may not have noticed that my following at the Paradise has increased till we have standing-room-only twice a night. Six times a week. The 'Battle of the Elvises' is over. It has been won. Jerry Margolis has as much as promised me that — and the winner is me (as I'm sure you've probably been informed). Thus, all is in readiness to move quickly to the final phase where I should be introduced to the public side-by-side with you in a press conference or something like it, maybe connected with a movie or a tour. I mention this only because I think it's important not to lose any time between the 'Battle' victory and going public. We will have the strongest momentum then and should use it. I look forward to the day when you and I can finally come face-to-face and talk about these things. Until then, Frank and I are proceeding according to plan.

Sincerely,
Byron

As the competition date approached, Byron's organisation went through a distinct transformation. A 'Lord-Byron-Is-Elvis Fan Club' sprang up, spearheaded by Hazel Hadley, who ran the Paradise Gift Shop and who had been active in the International Elvis Presley Club, Las Vegas

Chapter. Hazel knew her stuff. Almost overnight she slapped together a load of 'Byron' merchandise — signed photos, ashtrays, pictures, badges, T-shirts — and had them on sale at a booth near the showroom entrance.

Business was brisk. Once a night either Buddy or Junior who now wore dark pinstriped suits and black snap-brim hats, would arrive with briefcases and shovel in the concession money.

Frank Bruno, who had taken to wearing a white linen suit and blue suede shoes, added 'Colonel' to his name and made his presence known around the Paradise Casino, where he gambled, looking like a Turkish banker, and chatted with the interviewers sent by Jerry Margolis.

'So, you're an actual colonel, Colonel Bruno?'

'Yas, yas — a full colonel in the, ah . . . Tennessee whadyacallit, the ah . . .

'Militia?'

'Right. That's it.'

Larry McCann had flown in from Portland and couldn't seem to take it all in. They met him at the airport in the block-long 'Byronmobile'. Frank Bruno had leased the black monster so that Byron could be seen around town, like the other stars, stepping in and out of his own stretch limo.

'Jesus,' Larry said. He was white and pasty and he couldn't seem to keep his mouth from flapping open. 'I can't believe it. I can't believe it.'

'Boys, this is my old friend Larry, who pushed me on the stage back in 1958.'

Buddy and Junior smirked and nodded politely.

Byron wasn't a gambling man, but he had fun leading Larry on a tour of the casino, where nowadays he made quite a stir in his purple velvet leisure suit with mirror-spangles and four-inch fringe. He now wore Elvis's .22 Savage both on and off stage. With a gun dangling from his hip he parted the Red Sea wherever he went, swaggering through the gamblers, letting the fans come to him, talk to him, touch him. 'There's my Colonel,' he shouted, pointing toward Bruno at the roulette table across the room. 'Break the bank, hoss!'

Bruno acknowledged him with a wave of a finger. As far as Larry could see, they had all died and gone to Elvis Presley Heaven.

'I hardly sleep these days, Larry, there's so goddman much to do — massages and hot tubs, racquetball, interviews — hell, I got print reporters coming from all over — Vegas, L.A., Phoenix — TV crews too.'

They were cruising slowly down the Strip in the Byronmobile. Larry seemed to be in shock, meek and permanently amazed, as Byron rambled on.

'This guy Margolis really knows how to whip the cream — although I draw the line on certain things. Merv Griffin, for instance, wanted me on there with four or five impersonators — well, hell's bells, there was no way I was about to be seen with four or five Elvis Presley drag queens, you know what I mean?'

'You turned down the Merv Griffin Show?'

Byron smiled patiently. 'Hey, Larry, I don't have to scrounge my PR hits cheap, y'know. I'm accepted around town as a legitimate star. I make the rounds, I visit with the other stars in their dressing rooms — Liberace, Charo, Wayne Newton — they're always glad to see me.'

As they doubled back, Byron pointed to the Paradise marquee. 'Look at that, Larry.' The sign read:

KING BYRON
EMPEROR OF ALL ELVIS ILLUSIONISTS!!

'That about says it, Larry, doesn't it?'
'That does say it, all right,' Larry echoed.

Jerry Margolis was picking up reports of unusually odd behaviour from Byron. He expected a certain amount of static from these Elvis clones, all of whom seemed to have toys in the attic, but with less than two weeks till the Battle of the Elvises, what he had heard was doubly disturbing. Whoever 'won' (a decision entirely up to Jerry) would represent the Fan Fair organisation everywhere it went. If Byron was going to remain a contender, he'd have to know how to handle himself.

Margolis dropped in at the Paradise to have a look-see. The first thing he noticed was Byron's appearance. He was heavier and puffy around the eyes. Margolis wondered what kind of drugs he was taking. It was near the middle of the show and the women were coming forward for snapshots, scarves, kisses. Byron was loose and confident, but rambling, and occasionally slurred his words.

'Oops — hey, hey!' He looked at his watch. 'Almost time to punch out and go home! Hah, just kiddin' — Mike Porco's back there, aintcha, Mike? I can't run out on ol' Porky, can I?' He let loose a hog-call. 'Pig — sew-www! Hah, just kiddin', Mike. Whew . . .! Oh, Lord, I'm outa my mind up here, will somebody please pull my string?'

He fingered the .22 Savage, strapped into its tooled leather holster. A woman down front pointed to it and called out something.

'Huh? Naw, honey, that ain't a gun, I'm just glad to see you.' The crowd tittered. 'Yeah? You think that's funny? I do carry a gun. Lemme tell you somethin' — this ain't a world for gentle people.'

There was a smattering of restless applause and some whistles. The crowd seemed to be on hold, waiting for the show to move on.

'Hey, you don't believe me? There's two sides, darkness and light,' Byron went on. 'And they're ready for war. Gonna be all-out war . . .

At the back of the house, Margolis found Mike Porco.

'What does he think this is, "The Hour of Decision?" '.

Porco shrugged in silence. What he saw was a full house.

'Hey —' Byron shouted, pointing suddenly. 'Is somebody gonna turn off that goddamn box or not?'

Porco looked over his shoulder and realised a TV was running silently above one of the side bars. Where was the bartender? He moved, as quickly as you can push 270 pounds of lard, to turn it off himself.

'I'm countin' ta five —' Byron said, in a John Wayne drawl. 'One . . . two . . . three . . .' He drew the revolver. 'Four . . .'

Porco scrambled around the bar. Byron aimed.

'Five!'

He fired off several shots, blowing up the TV as Porco dove beneath the bar. The crowd was half-stunned, half-delighted. Porco's face reappeared from behind the bar, twitching with fury.

'Remote control,' said Byron, blowing smoke from the gunbarrel.

Margolis's mouth set and his eyes hardened.

Security for the grand exit was tricky, but Buddy and Junior had devised an escape route. Elvis never gave an encore. Neither did Byron. At the show's end, a guitar player draped him in a white satin cape and he stretched his arms toward the fans. 'You're beautiful — every one of you! Goodnight, now! Goodnight!' He swept off stage, flanked by Buddy and Junior. With Bruno leading the way, they picked up Larry and ploughed through the lobby, past bunches of curious gamblers and tourists, into a waiting elevator.

Buddy pushed P.

'Goddamn I'm hungry!' said Byron, rubbing his hands together. 'I could eat a beaver!'

The doors opened on the penthouse foyer, a marbled hallway area with painted clouds on the walls and ceiling. Ivy climbed up the sides of a noisy plaster fountain with regurgitating cherubs. This was the Paradise's idea of heaven and it suited Byron just fine.

Buddy and Junior unlocked the penthouse door and entered, scanning the room. Byron followed grandly, leading Larry by the elbow. Bruno trailed in last, absorbed in his scheduling book. Inside, the paradise motif continued with white, cloudlike furniture, walls in white fur, a dark, opulent bedroom with star-dot lights twinkling in the ceiling. There were several other rooms in heavenly style. Byron dropped his cape on the sofa.

'Put this away, Junior. Buddy, get on the horn and order some food. Where's Wendy?'

He spread himself out on the sofa and took a swallow of bourbon.

'Wendy?' he called.

Out on the open terrace, Wendy was sitting in the dark. She didn't move. She didn't answer.

'Wendy, what do you want to eat?'

Wendy looked away, through the city lights, into the desert. She didn't turn around.

'Larry, go out there and see what her highness wants to eat.'

'Hello, lady,' said Larry. 'Remember me?'

Wendy smiled softly. 'Hi, Larry.'

'Byron wants to know what you're eating.'

'Nothing.'

'Nothing'. He came closer and lowered his voice. 'How'd all this happen so quick? I mean, not just all this here, but . . . the show, the jumpsuit?'

She turned toward him. Her eyes were rimmed with weariness.

'You like the new show, Larry?'

'Well, ah —'

'You're among friends.'

'It's . . . scary. He's turning scary.'

'Mm-hm.'

'Like his brain's burning up or something, you know what I mean?'

Buddy had room service on the phone and was ordering hamburgers, pizza, chocolate cake, beer. Byron paced back and forth, still fired with energy.

'Damn! Elvis blew out some TV's in his day — but from on stage? Not on your life!'

Bruno looked up from his notebook.

'You could've killed somebody with a ricochet, I hope you know that —'

'Aw, fuck it,' said Byron, waving him off. 'Look on that thing and tell me what's happening tomorrow.'

161

Bruno glanced at his schedule.

'Lady from *Personality*. The one that's been sniffin' around all day.'

Byron grinned and winked at Junior. 'Let's do it in the limo.'

Junior was the Byronmobile's official chauffeur. He drove it like an elongated dune buggy, screeching around corners, dragging the Strip before dawn the nights Byron refused to sleep. The interviewer was a pretty lady in her forties, a touch overweight, but heroically built. She made it clear from the moment she stepped aboard that, given a shred of a chance, she would eat Byron alive. 'I *loved* Elvis,' she breathed, making the words smoke. She produced a mini-cassette recorder and flicked it on.

'Byron, why do you call yourself an illusionist?' She crossed her legs and flicked the top button on her blouse.

'Because it's magic,' said Byron, leaning close. 'These guys they call 'impersonators', they do about thirty-five or forty percent Elvis. But when I go on, I do one hundred percent Elvis, guaranteed. You don't see me workin' at it either. It's magic — as far as a spectator is concerned, I *am* Elvis.'

He caught Junior's eye in the rearview mirror and gave him a slight nod. Immediately the limo swerved and threw the lady against Byron. Her hand fell across his crotch. She left it there.

'Not even Elvis was one hundred percent as often as I am,' he said, with the Little Prince rising under her hand. 'See what I mean?'

The recorder dropped to the floor, still runing.

Junior drove around a little, then parked in some shade and settled back, with Buddy, to catch the action in the rearview mirror.

There was the sound of a zipper — Byron's jumpsuit coming off. Then the lady's breathless voice: 'No — no, leave it on! That's it . . .'

The lady began to moan rhythmically and the limo

rocked slowly to the same tempo.

'Elvis!' she hissed, her fingers caressing and clawing at the jumpsuit. 'Oh, Elvis!'

Buddy and Junior, their eyes glued to the mirror, bore witness.

That night, from the stage, Byron gave the lady a wink and then forgot about her. The Rockin' Doc had shot him up with something heavier than usual and his moves were wobbly and sluggish. Going without sleep was taking something out of him. But not a hell of a lot, nothing to worry about really — things were happening too fast to get all bent out of shape over it. He knew what he was doing; he wasn't addicted to anything. Between Buddy and Junior and the Doc, he could keep himself in high gear, and with the competition less than a week away (he was already seeing some of these 'impersonator' assholes walking around town) that was all he needed.

Still, there were occasional shows like this one, when the energy ran slow, like treacle. But even Elvis had had his weird shows — it was just a different shade. The fans always got behind it.

Tonight, to pick things up a little, he focused on Larry, suddenly ordering a spotlight in his face at ringside.

'Stand up, Larry, that's right —'

Larry squirmed and shuffled to is feet, blushing unbearably.

'I want everybody to meet my oldest buddy on this earth, the man that put me on the path, almost twenty years ago, give 'em a hand — Colonel Larry MCann! Girls, it's his last night in town!' Catcalls and squeals. 'Okay, you can sit down Larry — we're gonna get you laid, I promise.'

Larry broke into a sweat and sat, grinning helplessly.

Jerry Margolis had come back to take another look and this time he brought somebody with him — Ed Gallagher, a top executive of the Roman Garden Hotel, principal backer of the Fan Fair and Battle of the Elvises. They watched without a sign of reaction.

'Hi, Jerry. Zat your dad?' Byron cracked from the stage.

There was the slightest flicker of a grim smile from Gallagher.

'Don't get him drunk now, Girls — Jerry's old dad. Go to work!'

When the women came down, crowding to the edge of the stage for snapshots, kisses scarves, Byron toyed unmercifully with them making faces, dangling scarves and snatching them away at the last moment. A scarf floated through the air and was grabbed by two women simultaneously. A tug-of-war broke out, trapping a third woman in a choke-hold. Onstage, Byron broke into a full-scale laughing fit. Tears were flowing down his cheeks. The laughs came over him in shattering waves. He could hardly stand up. Then, Buddy and Junior were wading into the mess, pulling the women apart.

Ed Gallagher stared at the spectacle with undisguised distaste. He leaned over to Margolis and whispered something. They rose and walked out.

Onstage, Byron fought for breath, still unable to control the silliness that was drowning him. The crowd laughed along with him, thrilled at the unexpected display of spontaneity King Byron wasn't just a performer — he was real, a good ole boy, a real man. Just like Elvis.

Larry took the red-eye flight home that night. The Byronmobile was ordered up and goodbyes were said in the dressing room just before the second show. Larry's amazement had not worn away, but now there was an unsettled, probing look in his eyes that hadn't been there when he arrived.

'Hey, old pal, did ya lose some money? You look like a fish in a bucket.

'I'm worried about you, Byron. I can't help it.'

'Are you crazy? I'm halfway home, man. You saw the gig. Look at these rings, Larry — look at this suit.'

'That's what I'm talking about. Don't you remember what we used to say about that suit? Byron, you put it on and you're out of control, you're a floating balloon, it can kill you — it's —'

'Let's go, boy,' Buddy growled, pulling at Larry.

Byron shoved Buddy back and slapped him twice across the face.

'Don't touch my friend, asshole, y'understand? He can say anything he damn well wants' — he turned back to Larry and clasped him a long embrace — 'even if he's full of shit.'

'We're going all the way, Larry,' Byron whispered. 'Just bring Thelma out here and your Ma and the girls and we're all gonna set up in Palm Springs or Bel Air, someplace like that, 'cause the big wave is about to roll!'

Larry shook his head and stared at the floor. 'Yeah,' he said, 'I guess you're right, man.'

The next afternoon, Byron was watching 'Eyewitness News' and polishing off a chocolate cake. He called room service and ordered a pizza and some dark beer. Wendy had been up for hours and was sipping quietly at a bottle of Jack Daniel's. Suddenly Byron's attention snapped to the screen as the anchorman finished off a four-alarm fire story and shifted gears.

'Well, with the opening of the International Elvis Presley Fan Fair and "Battle of the Elvises" Competition at the Roman Garden this week, Elvis impersonators are pouring in from all over the world to compete for the title of World's Greatest Elvis —'

Byron snorted. 'Assholes —'

'The producer of the event, Jerry Margolis' was at the Roman Garden Convention Centre today and our man Barry Hartz spoke to him — and to one of his "Elvises", a fellow named Big Elmo, the Crown Prince of Rock 'n' Roll . . .'

Byron stopped chewing in mid-bite and craned forward. 'Who the hell — ?'

Margolis was standing next to some turkey in a jumpsuit.

'Barry, this is the biggest Elvis fan event ever held, certainly since the King's death. We've got more Elvis Presley memorabilia and merchandise than anyone's ever seen under one

roof. We're an international event with participants from Europe, Asia, you name it. And even though you can't bring back Elvis, we're looking to the fans to help us crown a successor to the King.'

The reporter turned to Big Elmo. *'Elmo, ain't this an unusual way to make a living?'*

Elmo sneered amiably. He was smooth as a snake. The perfect corporate Elvis.

'Well, Barry, I don't do it primarily for the money. I've had two saviours in my life — Elvis and Jesus Christ — and I ain't about to make a livin' imitatin' Jesus.'

Elmo and Barry chuckled together.

'Who is this bozo?' Byron yelled at the screen, appalled. 'Margolis didn't tell me about this interview — I could've done it.'

'What's the difference?' Wendy murmured.

'The difference is between that wimp and me! D'you want a hot dog or a steak? I don't understand it. Why's Margolis wasting his time?'

Elmo continued under Byron's tirade:

'Barry, I've been doin' this act, out of my great respect for Elvis, since long before he passed away. He and I were friends. He wanted me to take over for him. I'm not one of them 'Elvis-come-lately's that you're seein' a lot of now that he's gone —'

Byron reached for his .22 Savage. Wendy's voice rang out like cold steel.

'Don't do it! Don't you dare do it!'

Byron put the pistol down and gaped at the TV screen in bewilderment.

'Damn . . . goddamn!'

Next morning, Byron, Buddy and Junior took a ride down to Margolis's office. After a dead silent elevator ride, Buddy and Junior took up position at the door, arms folded, and Byron marched straight to the receptionist's desk.

'May I help you?' said the receptionist, very frosty.

'Yeah,' Byron growled. 'I wanna see Jerry. I've called him eight times already.'

'Do you have an appointment?'

'Hell, no — !'

'Well, I'm afraid Mr Margolis has meetings scheduled all day —'

'Tell him it's King Byron,' he interrupted.

With a look that would freeze a fish, she picked up the phone and dialled Margolis's extension.

'King Byron is here,' she said flatly. Then, after a slight pause, 'I'll tell them.'

She hung up. 'He can't see you.'

Byron glared at her for a moment, his eyes bulging in fury.

'Okay, you tell him something for me, bitch,' he spat, 'I want equal time. You tell him that — exactly like I said it. I *want equal time!*'

He turned and swept out of the reception area, into a miraculously waiting elevator, Buddy and Junior two steps behind.

That night the Beast came on like gangbusters. The Doc wasn't around, so Byron did the best he could with booze and some tranquillisers from Buddy and Junior. He was stumbling drunk on stage, but nobody out front seemed to care.

Each time his eyes closed he could hardly open them again. Snatches of dreams fought to run away with his consciousness. A deserted boat sailed right into the Paradise, carrying invisible death gas. 'Oh, God no,' he whimpered, grabbing his head with both hands. He sat on the edge of the stage, dangling his feet.

The women come rushing down then, pawing over him, grabbing him everywhere and somebody from the band had to pull him back on stage and get him to his feet again.

He had known he was in trouble tonight — he'd seen it in the mirror: hollow around his eyes, his face looking fat and pasty — but the fans brought him through it. They loved him. They desired him. He felt it come across the stage and wash over him. A wave of love. It washed the horror away.

But he couldn't do the competition like this. He'd have to

get straight. Margolis might well be flirting with this other asshole, but Byron knew Colonel Parker pulled the real strings. And as long as Colonel Parker saw him at his best there would be no problem.

Byron had a lot to say tonight:

'There just ain't room for two Elvises in the world,' he rambled. 'Hell, Elvis himself had a twin brother in the womb — and he choked the little sucker off. No way could there be more than one Elvis! So . . . it's hard to take this 'Elmo' character seriously — or any of these punks walkin' around in their jumpsuits. Wind-up Elvises! Like what else did Santy Claus give you, punk — y'know?'

'Fuck 'em in the butt, Byron!' a man yelled suddenly, sending an embarrassed gasp through the crowd. A wave of laughter followed immediately, ripening into applause.

'I feel sorry for 'em,' Byron went on hoarsely. 'I do. The poor jerks — here they come all the way to my town for the competition — and hell, we all know how that's gonna turn out, don't we now? Don't we —?'

A round of solid applause answered the question. Byron motioned for more. 'Tell me again! Who's gonna win?'

Cheers and whistles broke out. Colour raced to Byron's face for the first time tonight. He seemed to inflate and grow taller.

'Show me how much noise you're gonna make for me on Saturday!'

Some of the crowd was rising to their feet, delirious with excitement — stomping, shouting, carried away by the moment. Byron couldn't get enough. He raised both arms to them, drunk with rapture, luxuriating in the tide of love as if it were a shower of warm milk.

A Little Drive to Texas

The pool held her, just as, inside, she held the tiny beginnings of the future. Whatever it might be, the possibility in that future made the present look old and strained. Maybe inside her was the real Wendy Wayne, the real Byron Bluford. Maybe the entire point of all this scuffling and craziness had been to make this child of the future.

She watched Eddie's cigarette glowing in the night. She felt tired. The water could dissolve her.

'Look, can't we wait till it's all over?'

'No.' The cigarette tip brightened, then dimmed.

'It's just so backhanded. I'm running away.'

'Listen — whether he wins or loses, either way he'll be insufferable.'

'He'll need me,' she said, almost to herself.

'He's always going to need you.' Eddie crushed his cigarette. 'That's precisely where he's at — he's either needing you or he's stepping on you.'

As usual he was right. She dipped her head under water to blot out his voice.

At dawn she returned to the Paradise. Byron was sleeping in his clothes. She sat beside him for a while and stroked his hair. As she watched him he seemed to change moment-by-moment. He was a child. He was a dark angel. He was a murderer. He was a child again. The child's eyes popped open and looked up at her. The eyes had love in them. The head moved to her lap. For a split second she almost did the one thing Eddie had told her not to do under any circumstances: tell him about the baby.

'Hold me, honey?' His voice was hoarse and had the sing-song quality of half-sleep. 'Let's just . . . hold on . . .' Then he was gone again. What if she had told him, what if?

Eddie had never seen those eyes.

'I love you, Byron,' she whispered. This would be her goodbye, right now. This would be the moment she would remember when everything else was gone.

She stroked him and let the tears fall.

Friday morning the International Elvis Presley Fan Fair opened its doors. By the afternoon, over 10,000 fans had poured through the Roman Garden Convention centre, where the main floor was crowded with booths and displays of relics and merchandise. Dealers from the booming Elvis nostalgia industry were hawking Elvis dolls, memorial plates, figurines, medallions, ashtrays, mugs, buttons, ties, T-shirts, framed portraits, old fan magazines, collector's LP's, and fan photos — every object endorsed with the King's image.

Elvis picture banners hung from the rafters. Huge posters of his grinning face were mounted on the walls. Photo booths with lifesize cardboard Elvises offered a chance to 'Take Your Picture with Elvis.' There were racks of headphones for listening to rare Elvis tapes. A multi-image slide show, 'Elvis: One Man's Story', ran continuously in a specially built screening theatre. All through the arena, giant video screens featured tapes of Elvis in action. Clashing sound sources, mixed with the chatter of the opening-day crowd, kept the noise at chaos-level.

Through all of this, Byron, Buddy and Junior wandered, dazed, transfixed, their circuits overloaded on Elvis. Byron had a shivery feeling, like walking through his own funeral. Something about the sheer volume of Elvis's presence made him uneasy. The air was heavy with it. It was hard to breathe.

'Let's take a break,' he said.

Then they rounded a corner and Byron halted as if he had

been hit by a brick: There, off by itself, was a 'Big Elmo' booth, featuring Elmo's line of fan merchandise. A girl was handing out free 8 x 10 glossies and the rear of the booth was plastered with a giant head-and-shoulder portrait of Elmo that leered down at Byron. He went pale and steadied himself against Buddy's shoulder.

'How come *he's* got a damn booth?' said Junior, taking a photo from the girl and staring at it dumbly.

Jerry Margolis and Elmo were strolling toward the booth from another direction, like a couple of high school sweethearts. Elmo paused at the jewellery display and fingered an expensive Elvis pendant-necklace.

'Like it?' said Margolis with a smile. 'Take it, kid. On the house.'

Elmo grinned and hung it around the already jangling neck of his jumpsuit. Margolis paid for it and they resumed walking.

Byron spotted them from fifty feet away. His eyes narrowed as if he were watching a coiled rattlesnake.

As the two groups came together, Elmo greeted Byron with a relaxed smile. Byron ignored him and spoke directly to Margolis.

'Did you get the message?'

'Equal time? Yeah. What the hell was that all about?'

Byron motioned roughly at Elmo without looking at him. 'Him.'

'Don't worry about it,' said Margolis, his lips forming a tight line. 'Everybody's gonna get equal time — tomorrow. Including you.'

'Good luck, Byron,' said Elmo affably.

Byron looked at him for the first time.

'I won't need it, son,' he said, breaking into a smirk. He gestured to his entourage and they moved on, leaving Margolis and Elmo staring after them.

'I've seen 'em like that,' said Elmo quietly. 'They get carried away — it ain't like an act anymore. They think they been resurrected.'

He pointed at one of the giant Elvis posters. 'There's

Elvis' — then to his own — 'and there's Elmo. I never get confused about that.'

Margolis smiled with satisfaction and patted him on the shoulder.

After nightfall Buddy and Junior pinned Elmo's 8 x 10 to the garage door and watched, giggling, as Byron filled it full of darts. Then they all had a turn, striking Elmo in the face, the chest, the groin. Byron had done some quaaludes and drunk a few quarts of beer. It had cut the edge of blind hysteria he brought away from the Fan Fair, but the frenzy began to surface again in violent spasms of laughter. He ripped the picture down, stumbled to the middle of the yard and pissed on it, laughing till he fell into the dust, still unzipped.

They wrapped what was left of the photo around an empty oil can and the three of them advanced on it, pistols blazing. Byron took the shotgun from the garage and blasted the remainder into tatters. They rolled on the ground, helpless with glee.

All at once, Buddy and Junior stopped laughing as they realised Byron was out of control, doubling up in painful contractions, gasping for breath, unable to stop.

Frank Bruno was lying in bed, smoking, when his phone rang.

'Yah,' he grunted.

'It's Buddy. You better get over here.'

'What's wrong?' Bruno let his cigar go out.

'Byron's askin' for you. Just come on over.' A click, as Buddy hung up.

Bruno replaced the phone in it's cradle. After a few minutes he relit the cigar. He didn't want to go over there. He didn't have the stomach for this ordeal anymore. Things were out of control. He knew Margolis had cooled off — so what was left? Paradise Alley, a good gig, but Byron was about to blow that one, too.

Maybe the girl was right — he shouldn't have spoon-fed Byron with the Colonel Parker bullshit. But on the other hand, the boy wanted to hear it, he demanded it — he'd already made it up on his own, the whole damn fantasy. And hell, stranger things had happened . . .

What the girl could never have understood was how close Bruno came to believing it himself, even now. If you want to believe, you believe, that's all. And Bruno had believed in Byron all the way. Still did, in some small part of his soul. Crazy. A man his age ought to be getting right with God, getting his soul in shape for the Big Trip, and he believed in *what?* King Byron and the Eternal Flames.

He crossed himself for the first time in years. When you looked at all that goddamn fat, all the tired old wrinkles, you'd never know there was an altar boy in there, Frankie Bruno — a kid, a longshot artist. But if everything lined up just right tomorrow and Byron rose to the occasion, who's to say what could happen? Margolis — who was a showman, all right — might just see the light.

A forlorn hope, but hell, life's made up of fat chances. Bruno had gone from one wild hope to another, till finally he closed the book on such things. How he was pushing sixty and his wildest hope had walked right in out of nowhere. Here at last, his big shot — but deformed, afflicted, crazy as a loon. A certified weirdo. Wouldn't you know it!

Well, nothing would ever happen if Bruno didn't get the hell on over there. God knows, if he left the kid alone with those goons he could be comatose by morning. With a sigh, Bruno rolled out of bed, turned on some lights and started rooting around for something to put on.

At Buddy and Junior's, a dealer had arrived to do business. He was a muscular, long-haired biker with a heavily scarred face. Wearing a 'smile' T-shirt, he sat cross-legged on the floor across from Buddy and Junior. His briefcase was open, displaying rows of baggies full of pills and capsules. On the floor beside him was a loaded revolver.

'Okay, brothers,' he rapped smoothly, 'the Elvis Presley drug shelf — we got biphetamine, dex, quaalude, placidyl — got a good price on Mexican amphetamine today, very commercial.'

'Nope,' said Buddy.

'Okay, movin' right along —'

The front door opened and Bruno entered. The dealer reached quickly for his pistol.

'It's okay, man,' Buddy said. 'Just old Uncle Frank.'

The dealer relaxed and went back to business.

'Well, let's see . . . got some real nice turquoise, right off the reservation —'

'Nope.'

Junior intercepted Bruno and the two of them went through the kitchen and out the back door.

'A little acid today?'

Buddy broke into a giggle. 'Get serious, man. Do we look like hippies or what?'

In the garage it was dark except for the giant TV screen. Byron was slumped in a chair, watching an Elvis concert tape without sound. Beside him was a half-gone quart of beer. He couldn't stop trembling. Junior handed him two capsules.

'Easy on the booze with these.'

Byron swilled them down with the rest of the beer. Bruno watched with a worried look.

'He shouldn't have no more to drink,' Junior whispered to Bruno with a confidential nod and returned to the house.

'Frank, what's wrong?' Byron slurred. 'It doesn't let up. It's just like before — I can't stand up without getting dizzy. What's wrong with me?'

'Ah, you're okay,' Bruno rasped, trying to strike a hearty tone.

'I'm shakin' — I can't stop shakin' . . .'

Byron gazed at Elvis for a long time without blinking. Then his voice was very low and clear.

'Frank, I'm not gonna lose this thing, am I?'

'How can you lose?' Bruno was reaching for things to say. 'You got the fans, you've had the promotion, the word-of-mouth. How the hell are you gonna lose?'

But Byron was following his own train of thought.

'See now . . . I can't go back. It'd kill me to go back. Y'understand Frank? The past doesn't exist anymore, there's nothing to go back to. There's no Byron Bluford anywhere. I've gotta go forward, I've gotta go take my place. *Nothin'* can go wrong with this thing, y'understand?'

'Sure . . . sure.'

Byron gazed back at him like a hawk.

'No you don't', he muttered, turning away. 'You say you do, but you don't. She's the only one that understands me, goddamn it! She's my bottom line. Why the hell can't anybody else realise what I'm goin' through?'

He took a deep breath and extended his hand, watching carefully. The drugs were coming on. The hand was steady.

'Hey, there you go!' Bruno encouraged.

But Byron's attention had shifted back to Elvis, hooked by a series of sweeping gestures. Byron shook his head in grim determination.

'Look at him — look at those moves.'

He narrowed his eyes and turned back to Bruno with an eerie grin.

'You know what, Frank? If he wasn't dead . . . I'd have to kill him.'

Bruno's strategy was to talk him into going back to the penthouse, where Wendy could put him to bed. His big mistake was to leave the damn fool unattended while he went inside to call the girl — who didn't answer anyway. No sooner had he hung up the phone than he heard Byron fire up the limo outside — then he knew he had lost him. Bruno scrambled out just in time to see the goddamn black boat disappearing down the street.

'Damn!' He stomped the ground and shook both fists. 'Damn you, you fuckin' maniac!'

Byron came to a screeching halt in the parking lot of a luxury apartment complex. He slid out of the limo and took a few seconds to steady himself in the moonlight. Then he clomped up the outer stairs and pounded loudly on one of the apartment doors. After a long moment, the door opened.

'Elvis?' said Byron.

The Elvis Woman smiled and drew him into the apartment. She had thrown a flimsy bathrobe around her, but let it fall open as she led Byron to a plush easy chair and sat him down. She stared down at him for a moment, then swung one leg across him and leaned close, straddling him, teasing him with her breasts. Byron shook his head. 'Gimme Elvis, baby.'

He sprawled back, rigid with energy, as she unseated herself and continued on into the bedroom. A moment later she returned, hair slicked back, in a white satin-and-rhinestone jumpsuit.

Byron beckoned her over roughly. She knelt beside him and unbuttoned his shirt, letting her lips and tongue play down his chest, down to his stomach. Then she unzipped him and worked her way down, all wetness and hunger. Byron's eyes closed and his face became a mask of domination. He grasped her head and held it in place.

'Stay there, Elvis,' he muttered. It was half speech, half grunt. 'Right there, baby.'

Next morning, Byron pulled up to the Paradise garage and left the limo with the parking valet. He had slept a few hours. He felt good. Almost fresh. He had just enough time to pull things together before he was due over at the Roman Garden. He glanced at his watch as he sailed through the lobby — 7 A.M. Not bad. This was the day for it.

Upstairs he threw open the penthouse door and stopped short, jolted by what he saw: Wendy was fully dressed, standing there with her guitar and a couple of suitcases, staring back at him with her mouth trembling. At her side, just about to carry the bags down, was Eddie the bartender. Caught. They watched Byron without moving a muscle, waiting to see what he was going to do.

'Get outa here, man,' Byron growled. Eddie looked at Wendy and raised an eyebrow.

'Go ahead,' she told him. 'Wait for me downstairs.'

Eddie watched Byron warily for a moment, then set his

jaw and walked out.

Byron and Wendy eyed each other like two statues.

'Where the hell are you going?' said Byron finally.

'Austin.'

'With Babycakes there?'

'He's just gonna drive me —'

'Just a little drive to Texas, huh?'

Wendy's eyes flared. 'Don't kid yourself, man. Nobody's stealing me from you. I'm leaving. *Me, myself*. *I'm* doing this.'

Byron fixed her with an uncomprehending gaze. His head wagged slightly from side to side.

Wendy's voice softened. 'I've got to do something for myself Byron.'

'Today?' said Byron in a dazed mumble. 'You picked *today?*'

Wendy's face filled with guilt. 'Ah, Byron, what difference does it make what day? What do you need me for? I mean, who did you fuck last night. She'll be here for you. It all hurts too much. It's all for you. I'm worn out by your life. I've got my own. My feelings just aren't real anymore . . .

'You don't just stop loving somebody —' Byron recited like a kindergarten teacher.

Wendy laughed bitterly. 'What do you know about that? You love me like you love booze or food or drugs — just something you need to keep you going.'

So far, neither of them had moved. Now Byron took a step toward her.

'Stay where you are, Byron —'

'Unpack those damn bags.'

'No!' She picked them up and started around him toward the door. Eddie was right. She had to go *today*.

He stepped in front of her.

'C'mon, Byron,' she said, after a deep breath. 'I don't want to prolong this. My mind's made up.'

'Just unpack, will you? Jesus, I can't handle this, you're twistin' my head —'

'I'm not twisting anything. Your head's already so twisted you don't see what you've done to me. You don't even know me, Byron. As far as you're concerned, I don't really exist, I'm just *around*. Well, that's over,' she pushed against him. 'Now get out of the way.'

'C'mon, be realistic.'

She looked into his face and laughed. He pulled her to him and force-kissed her. She yielded stiffly, but held on to the bags. It was a cold, silent clinch. She turned her head away.

'You're telling *me* to be realistic?'

'Don't leave me mama,' Byron almost whispered.

'I'm not your mama, you're not my baby —'

Now he roared: 'Take a fuckin' walk, then! What do you think'll happen when you get to Austin? You think the whole town's gonna turn out to kiss your pretty ass? What do you think'll happen to you with your little second-rate ballads, singin' em through your nose like a coyote?'

Wendy's eyes seemed to freeze over. She spat words like poison darts.

'Don't ever say second-rate to me, man. Not you, with your two-bit rip-off of a dead man.'

Byron slapped her with everything he had. She staggered back stunned.

'Oh shit —' she gasped.

She put her hand to her mouth and drew it back, dotted with blood. Byron gawked at her, horrified. Suddenly he sunk to his knees, gripping Wendy's legs in a convulsive embrace.

'Jesus, honey,' he moaned, 'I didn't mean it.'

She broke into quiet sobs that shook her whole body.

'Forgive me, forgive me, forgive me,' Byron chanted.

Wendy stopped sobbing finally and was quiet. The silence held — she had no idea how long.

'It's not easy being Elvis, you know,' Byron began.

She shook her head. She didn't want to hear this.

'There's no way to rest, you never go far enough. Nobody could ever understand this trip, not unless they were close

178

to somebody that was on it.' His voice dropped. 'You're the closest I've got . . . you've seen me working at it. It's like havin' a heart transplant. The parts of me that weren't Elvis had to go . . . so they wouldn't reject the heart, you know . . .'

Wendy held on to consciousness with the desperation of a nightmare dreamer. Dimly she knew that she was young, she could survive this. That whatever mistake she might have made, she could turn it around, make this instant in her life the first moment of a new power. Even though he had the physical strength to crush her, she could walk right over him now. She could grind him into dust.

She pushed past Byron and out the door.

In the street below, Eddie was waiting with his car. He smiled when Wendy emerged, bags in hand. High above them, Byron was looking down from the penthouse terrace. They could hear him bellowing hoarsely above the breeze.

'It's just about to pay off, you damn fool! What the hell did you come here for? You're runnin' out on the whole goddamn dream!'

Wendy paused, halfway into the car, and looked up at him. For a moment she hesitated — he looked so small up there, there was such a helpless ring to his voice. She shook her head sharply to clear it of all thoughts. Then she got into the car and slammed the door. She looked at Eddie. She knew he saw the sadness in her face. She smiled.

'Let's go to Austin,' she whispered.

From the terrace, Byron watched the car speed off. A spasm of pain went through his head. 'You damn little fool . . .' he mumbled, leaning heavily against the railing.

After a moment, he pulled himself together and stood straight. His face hardened. He turned and walked back inside.

In the mirror above the bureau, he greeted his image with a determined stare. He breathed in and out several times. He held his hand motionless in front of him. It was steady. He cut the air with it several times, karate-style. Finally his lips curled into the sneer and Elvis was there. Whatever had happened today, whatever would happen later, there was no probem. *History doesn't make mistakes*, Byron thought, as he grinned at the mirror image with a glow of confidence.

Elvis was there.

Barnum and Bailey

The Battle of the Elvises began officially with a catered brunch for the impersonators, served in the Elvis Presley Museum. There was a buffet breakfast at one end of the main gallery. At the other, an open bar was doing brisk business.

Outside the museum, ragged bunches of fans held up signs for their favourites: 'ALL THE WAY ELMO!' 'TCB MIGHTY EL-MARVEL!' Some of the fan clubs had chartered buses others came in caravans of station wagons. Byron's 'home-town' following dwarfed the others — a full force cross-section of Las Vegas Americana. Retired heartlanders, rowdy oil-drillers, working girls, school teachers, casino workers, housewives from the residential areas of town, roughnecks and hang-out artists from Lords 'n' Ladies — a motley army of souls for Byron.

Later on, the award presentation would be videotaped inside, so TV technicians in headsets were setting up cameras, taking readings, hanging lights, and laying cable between the displays. The Elvis impersonators, fifteen or twenty of them, mingled with their managers and flunkies, chatting in small groups. It was a room full of Elvises — all dressed in their own elaborate versions of the jumpsuit, the hair, and in most cases, the wraparound shades.

The chat was mostly shop-talk.

A pretty Elvis with barely visible scars showed his half-smile to a stocky older Elvis and a short, wispy Elvis.

'I couldn't curl the lip before surgery. Now —' He demonstrated, a perfect Elvis sneer.

'Well,' said the other Elvis, 'my theory is you don't need plastic surgery if you know how to do your hair.'

'What do you use?' asked the short Elvis.

'Miss Clairol.'

A fast-talking Elvis was showing a scarf to a black Elvis. 'I got a wholesale place in Philly where I get 'em by the case.' he said, spreading out the scarf and dangling it in the air. 'Six cents a scarf — you can't beat that!'

'Shee-it!' said the black Elvis. 'Gimme the address, man!'

Over by the scrambled eggs and Nova Scotia salmon, Jerry Margolis was making introductions among several pot-bellied old men in cowboy hats.

'Colonel Hickman, Colonel Gonzales, Colonel Schrader — this if Colonel Pendergrass . . .'

The Colonels chomped their cigars and shook hands.

At the other end of the room, the hard-drinking Elvises were throwing down a few stiff ones to get the day going. A slim, well-built Elvis tugged at the carefully arranged coif of a hairy Elvis.

'Wig?' howled the hairy Elvis. 'This ain't no wig. Go on, give it a real pull!'

Down the bar a woozy groupie, spilling through the cracks of her blouse, fawned hungrily on a youthful Elvis.

'You ever shoot out a TV?' she whined.

The youthful Elvis shook his head wistfully.

'I'd like to sometime,' he mused. 'Just to see what it feels like.'

'You can shoot mine out any old time,' she offered, moving a little closer.

In front of the hotel, like a giant black silverfish, the Byronmobile shot across the expansive approach and pulled to a swerving halt at the front entrance, nearly sidesweeping the parking valet. Buddy and Junior, in their pin-striped suits and gangster hats, stepped out quickly and threw open the rear door. Byron emerged regally into the desert sun, eyes hidden behind his darkest shades. He wore the American Eagle Special by Estelle, Tailor of the Stars, its long satin cape dangling from the high, gold-encrusted collar. The .22 Savage, in its holster, was belted around the waist.

The little phalanx of three marched unsmiling through the patio and pool area, between the squirting fountain statuary of the Roman atrium, past the outdoor tennis courts, and around to the entrance of the Elvis Presley Museum. Holding formation, they strode through the lobby and into the brunch, drawing pop-eyed stares from the other Elvises. Byron picked a place well apart from the turkeys and stood there, arms folded, splendid and aloof.

One of Elvis's own jumpsuits, a priceless, jewel-studded, gold-lame-and-brocade wonder, was displayed under special lighting on a headless mannequin. The winner would take it home. Jerry Margolis called all Elvises to the display for a group photograph. Twenty Elvises with twenty-one sided grins clustered around the single headless Elvis.

'Okay, boys — smile!' Margolis shouted as each Elvis struck his own version of the King's definitive pose.

Byron put some distance between himself and the others and chose a smouldering frown instead of a grin.

Margolis was ready for a final word before moving to the hotel's main showroom for the competition. Beside him was the TV director, a thin, snippy fellow in his late thirties. Off to one side, looking supremely uninvolved with the whole thing, were Ed Gallagher and another middle-aged executive who yawned and checked his watch.

'I wanna introduce you to our judges,' said Margolis, extending one arm toward them in classic master-of-ceremonies style. 'Ed Gallagher and Marty Pressman of the Roman Garden Hotel chain. It's a great honour to have these two men participate. Give 'em a hand.'

The Elvises applauded politely.

'As for you guys — I wish each one of you could tour with the Fan Fair. I wish each one of you could win this incredible jumpsuit from the King's own wardrobe. You're all winners in my book, so go to it! Let's have a terrific show!'

Cheers and applause from the Elvises.

'Now —' Margolis put a hand on the director's shoulder. 'Rod here has a few changes to announce, so I'm turning it over to him. Rod?'

The director stepped forward, strictly business, peering at his clipboard.

'I just want to remind you: When the winner is announced in the showroom, all five finalists, all five, will immediately return here to the Museum for the presentation of the suit, interviews, et cetera, et cetera. Do not foget — or I'll step on your blue suede shoes.'

Groans from the Elvises.

'Okay,' he continued, suppressing a grin, 'here is the revised order, so listen carefully.' He read from the clipboard. 'First — Ken Matsuda's Elvis-Magic. Second — The Jonny Lipsky Elvis show. Third — Vester Oakly and This-Was-Elvis. Fourth — Jet Presley and the Elvis Soul Review. Fifth — Big Elmo and El-O-Rama.'

Byron sneaked a few glances around. He couldn't believe these louts. Elmo caught his eye and nodded cordially. More a smirk than a nod. *Howdy, asshole*. Byron looked away. A wave of angry hot sparks seemed to blow through his head. He was among the apes!

But it had to be part of the process, this humiliation, this suffering. Otherwise it would be too easy. Elvis had suffered every step of the way. How could Byron escape it? There were so many easier ways it might have been done. Frank was in contact with Colonel Parker — they could have brought the Colonel right to the Paradise. They could've had a press conference right here in Vegas. No need for this damned turkey trot. By now he could've been in Hollywood. He could've held on to his girl.

A nagging vision of Wendy flared up like a stove fire. It kept coming and coming, piercing him like an icepick, burning, stabbing at him. Suddenly he almost came unstrung at the knees — but that would be too much, to weaken and fall. Was the Beast on the way? Keep cool, keep clear, keep sighting the distance ahead. This was part of the test — to suffer, to lose your woman — to hold the future in your hands as they were chopping at your legs. Keep moving. Keep dancing. Keep all pain and sorrow off to the side of the mind. Don't sicken with the end in sight!

There had been nights at the Paradise when he felt a presence enter the room, and he knew (although he had never mentioned it, not to Frank, not to anybody) that Colonel Parker was there. Secretly. Disguised. No one could know; that would blow the whole drama. But of *course* he would be dropping in, of course! How could he not inspect the future! The Battle of the Elvises was a circus, but the Colonel was a circus man. He was doing things according to Barnum and Bailey. He could've stepped in and altered the natural course of things, but this was a circus man's way of introducing a new Elvis to the world, pretested. Parker knew his stuff, he was a pro. Maybe he figured a clean public runoff was the way to prove to the fans, once nad for all, there was only one Elvis — and that was Byron. But to let such a pack of dreary hound dogs be involved, to let 'em bring down the tone of the process, to insult Elvis this way — what a goddamn shame!

Byron shook his head to clear it. He realised he had to elevate the occasion with his own presence. He closed his eyes and tried to open a blank hole in his imagination, then fill it with moving images of Elvis. Wendy was gone — like a rat, she thought the ship was going down. But that's where she'd really been a fool. This ship was afloat! Leave it alone, now . . . let it be. *TCB*.

He felt ready. He was going to hold together for this. This was history. He was a force that couldn't be stopped. He had no fear. He was on target. All the way to the Colonel! That's what Frank had said. There was a hole in history and Byron would fill that hole. So now it was just a matter of events taking care of themselves, just like Frank had said. There was no way to stop him, no way . . .

The Roman Garden had furnished a line of powder-blue Cadillacs to chauffeur the impersonators around the corner to the hotel's main entrance — a distance of no more than a hundred yards.

Byron refused his and sent Junior for the Byron mobile.

The blue Caddies swept into the porte cochere, one by one, disgorging their Elvises and Colonels. A mobile TV crew, featuring a blazered interviewer who traded chitchat with each Elvis, covered the arrival.

Suddenly Byron's limo roared up from the wrong side and forced its way into the porte cochere, abruptly halting the line of blue Caddies.

Byron cackled gleefully as he watched the Caddies reverse and back up, bucking and jerking.

'Look at 'em, Frank!' he laughed. 'Asshole . . .'

Bruno, who wasn't looking good at all, screwed the cap back on a half-drunk bottle of Canadian Club and stowed it in his pocket. Byron stepped out into the glare of the TV lights and waved his fingers at the cheering crowd. He swept grandly forward, past the interviewer and into the hotel.

The Roman Garden Showroom was an elegant, multi-tiered luxury palace. It was packed with fans, most of them Byron's, but the front tables were a sea of white-suited Elvises and their managers, sweating, clowning nervously, naïvely anticipating each others' performances. TV cameras, boom mikes, floor managers, stage managers, and other technicians made it clear that above all else, this event was a TV taping.

At Byron's table, Bruno looked a little vague, as if he didn't know where he was. Byron peered closer at the old man. He looked like death had put a hand on his shoulder.

'You okay, Frank?'

'Yeah,' said Bruno weakly, 'I'm fine.'

Byron extended his own hand and stared at it. Steady as a rock.

'Lookit that!' he said, triumphantly. 'Granite . . .'

The stage was rimmed with a framework of flashing lights which spelled out: BATTLE OF THE ELVISES! Underneath it was a revolving set from which a circular runway sloped down to the playing area.

The emcee, a Wolfman Jack impersonator who called himself 'Wolfman Bob', stood off to one side, chatting with Jerry Margolis, as technicians scurried all over the stage making last-minute adjustments to the set.

In a glassed-in control booth at the rear of the house, the director and some engineers sat in front of a bank of monitor screens, waiting to cue the show into action.

'Stand by!' the director snapped, and began his countdown.

Lights dimmed and the stage was plunged into semi-darkness. A kettledrum rolled expectantly as the *2001* theme began, slow and majestic, building slowly toward its climax.

'Ladies and gentlemen,' growled Wolfman Bob into his mike. 'The Margolis Entertainment Network and the Roman Garden Hotel are proud to present . . . from Tokoyo, Japan . . . Ken Matsuda and Elvis-Magic!'

The set revolved, revealing the Japanese Elvis, his name flashing behind him in neon, and his band, already into a hard driving 'See See Rider.' Matsuda leaped off the moving set and bounded forward, singing phonetically and displaying perfectly timed versions of the classic Elvis movements.

The other Elvises watched with open-mouthed fascination, but Byron had seen enough of Matsuda in thirty seconds. He tilted his head back at a condescending angle and let his eyes play over the crowd of other Elvises. He watched them nodding, gaggling, mugging — a rhinestone-infested array of retards, lips going up at the drop of a hat. His own lip curled into a grin as it did whenever he took a good look at the poor saps.

The show flowed on, a river of Elvises. There was something wrong with every one of them. Jonny Lipsky, the fast-talking Elvis, had trouble staying on key and couldn't keep up with his band. A rotten performance. Jet Presley and the Elvis Soul Review looked like more James Brown then Elvis, and the band did Motown kicks. All wrong.

When his turn approached, Elmo rose to leave his table and go backstage. Margolis came trotting like a dog to meet him halfway and walk him over to the stage door. As Byron watched Elmo's back moving and bobbing along he had to suppress a supreme urge to draw his revolver and start blasting. Inside his head he saw Elmo exploding, just like a TV set.

He chewed his thumb uneasily throughout Little Dynamite, the World's Smallest Elvis — a squab-sized turkey. He hardly saw the little runt, knowing Elmo was next. A tiny muscle in his right eye started to twitch . . .

Then it was Elmo's turn. Byron stiffened and sat taller. What was it about the intro —? The Wolfman seemed to be putting a little something extra into it. Byron looked sharply at Bruno, then back at the stage.

'. . . a big, big welcome for . . . The Crown Prince of Rock 'n' Roll — Big Elmo and El-O-Rama!'

And the revolving stage offered up Elmo and his band.

Immediately Byron relaxed. From the first step Elmo took, Byron knew he was a loser. He didn't have it, not quite — and with doing Elvis, missing by an inch was missing by a mile. Either Elvis was there or he wasn't. And there was no Elvis in what this lunkhead was doing — stepping through his choreography like he was in a three-legged race, making the gestures, but empty, like a robot. And singing not from the gut, but from the top of his throat.

A couple of times Byron almost laughed out loud. He craned around and traded grins with Buddy and Junior, who were holding their noses and thumbing Elmo down. Byron leaned back in his chair, one foot propped against the table, his lip curled into a grin of contempt, as Elmo laboured through his set, steady, uninspired, plodding.

Now the path was clear. There was a red carpet rolled right up to Colonel Parker's front doorstep. Any fear that Elmo might get in the way was gone. There couldn't be a mistake like that now — Elmo was too ordinary. He looked a little like Elvis, but as for *being* Elvis, you might as well put Frank Bruno up there. No judge in his right mind would pick any of these turkeys to represent Elvis throughout the world. It was a clear field, all the way. No more interference, no more bullshit. No more wind-up Elvises. Byron was on the final stretch of his journey. He dominated them all.

'Ladies and Gentlemen — let's have a king-size welcome for . . . King Byron, the Emperor of All Elvis Illusionists!' The neon sign flashed: KING BYRON! The set revolved. Byron's band was throbbing with energy. The audience swung into view, whistling and cheering — Byron's crowd. The white suits sparkled out front like a field of daisies. And lights, everywhere lights! Byron, cocky now and bristling with excitement, bounded off the revolving platform, down the ramp to the edge of the stage, into the blinding light.

His presence was a complete contrast to Elmo and he knew it. For a moment he stood in sheer premature triumph, letting the royal presence emanate. Give 'em a picture they won't forget, he was thinking, don't rush it — give 'em a chance.

Suddenly he whirled and jabbed a finger at the Eternal Flames. He leaped in place and slung his mike through the air by its cord. Now he was all raw danger, mugging it up with kicks, pouts, macho stridings, commanding the stage, pulling off moves that had the people bursting into cheers like a hockey crowd. Even the other Elvises were grinning and whooping it up — all except for one old stone face. Elmo knew when he was being whipped. Byron grinned at him a couple of times just in case the point needed any going over.

Byron was lightning. Byron was a young stag, bounding and snorting. Byron was the boss, the enforcer, the humper, the mad leaper, the lover — everything he wanted to be, making new pictures every second, unpredictable but perfect Elvis, the husky baritone, the bumblebee tenor. The full range. The total experience. And he had the crowd —

jumping up and down, milling toward the stage, knocking into the TV people. King Byron was their Elvis.

Winding out with the showstopper, 'American Trilogy,' Byron was working the melodrama for all it was worth. As he swung into part three, 'The Battle Hymn of the Republic,' he pulled out the last stop. Sweat poured off him, soaking the jumpsuit. His face was rippling with strain. The fatigue of the last twelve hours was breaking through. He was hoarse, and for the first time, unsteady. But it only added to the intensity of the final moments. A storm of applause overwhelmed the last notes of the trilogy and Byron simply stood, exhausted, glowing, splendid in his cape, in the still centre of an emotional hurricane. Buddy dabbed at his eyes. Everyone was standing. Buddy and Junior jumped up and down hugging each other. It was all over.

There was an air of anticlimax about the announcement of the finalists. Who cared, anyway — Byron was the clear winner. Where was the suspense? All the same, they tried to whip it up, with drum rolls and fanfares and all the Elvises arrayed out front, supposedly on the edge of their seats with expectation. In a phony state of nervousness, Wolfman Bob made a big show out of receiving the envelope from the judges.

'All right — whew! And here it is . . .' He tore it open and glanced at the contents. 'This is a close one. We've got five finalists. I'm just gonna read the list —' He pointed at the house band. 'Boys, lay down some suspense.'

A kettledrum roll set the mood.

'Here we go! Ken Matsuda — Elvis-Magic . . . Vester Oakly — This-Was-Elvis . . . Little Dynamite, the World's Smallest Elvis . . . Big Elmo and El-O-Rama . . . and last but not least, King Byron, Emperor of All Elvis Illusionists!'

Each finalist leaped up with excitement as his name was called — except for Byron, who rose with dignity and ambled slowly to the stage.

The finalists waited while Wolfman Bob clowned around.

'And folks — we've got a winner!' he said finally, waving another slip of paper. His voice boomed: 'We've got a winner of the Battle fo the Elvises and that winner is . . .'

He stretched the pause for effect.

'. . . Big Elmo, the former Crown Prince, and now the New King of Rock 'n' Roll!'

A shock wave of nausea ripped through Byron. He watched in a state of blank disbelief as Elmo stepped forward and joined Wolfman Bob, raising both hands in a victory salute. Out front there was polite applause for Elmo, but the crowd was clearly perplexed. A handful of die-hards shouted from their seats, 'Byron! Byron!'

In the control booth, the director motioned quickly to his sound engineers.

'Sweeten it!'

The engineer reached for a knob on the control board. Out front, a blast of recorded applause flooded the room, drowning out the chants.

Bruno slumped into his seat, covering his eyes hopelessly with one hand.

Byron's face was a mask of silent rage — a volcano before the eruption. His eyes bulged as he watched Elmo savouring his triumph, waving, mugging with Wolfman Bob, grinning like a fool. His head snapped around trying to trace the source of the bogus applause.

Then, the show was suddenly over. The TV lights dimmed. The director's voice boomed over the talkback from the control booth.

'Finalists to the Museum. C'mon, c'mon. Let's go!'

They were being herded away, and Byron, struggling not to puke, was simply putting one foot in front of the other.

In the wings a fire exit opened into the bowels of the hotel, leading to the rear of the Elvis Museum. Margolis and a security guard stood by the door, hustling the finalists through. Byron was the last in line. He stopped and thrust his face close to Margolis's. Margolis looked back, hard-eyed.

'You took this away from me,' said Byron, trembling.

'You stole this from me —'

'Bullshit! C'mon, keep moving.'

Buddy and Junior reached the door, breathless, just as it was closing.

'Sorry boys,' said the security guard, stepping in front of them, 'performers only.'

Junior was about to shove the dumb shit aside, but Buddy held him back.

'Wait, man, wait,' he said. 'Let's see what's gonna happen . . .'

The fire corridor was a bare cinder block tunnel, fluorescent-bright, used only by hotel personnnel. After the limitless expanse of the showroom, it was stark and claustrophobic. The smallest sounds resounded off the walls — muffled whispers, clattering footsteps, the snuffling and heavy breathing of the finalists. Byron could even hear the sweat steaming off their bodies. His face was now chalk-white and he was having trouble finding air to breathe. Noises echoed through his head like bells. He couldn't take his eyes off Elmo, relaxed and casual, congratulated in hushed whispers by the others. 'Way to go, Elmo . . . gotta hand it to ya, man, great show . . .'

Somebody had farted. The stench, the glitter of the rhinestones and spangles, the sweat, the noise, made him sicker as the damn fool jumpsuits blurred together into a tangled mess. He was sweating cold mist now. Losing it. Struggling for breath. Fighting to keep his head straight. He felt the .22 Savage bouncing against his hip. With a premonition of what he was about to do, he felt himself reaching for the gun as if it were an animal that had to be set free. He drew.

Then, revolver in hand, he was shoving Elvises aside right and left as he scrambled toward Elmo. Reaching him, he locked him around the neck with one arm and held the pistol to his head with the other.

'What the hell —?' sputtered Margolis.

'Don't make me do it! Don't make me do it!' Byron shouted. His voice reverberated wildly through the corridor.

Now, his eyes were blazing with energy and purpose. *He* was the animal, ready to spring and strike at the slightest provocation. Sensing the immediate danger, everyone froze.

'Stay where you are,' Byron snapped at Margolis. Then, to the others: 'Down the hall and into the Museum. Go!'

Byron chased them along the corridor as Margolis watched helplessly.

'I'll burn your ass for this, you sonofabitch!' he shouted.

'You robbed me, man!' Byron's voice rang. 'You took what's mine. If anybody burns, it's gonna be you!'

They stared at each other up and down the long stretch of bare corridor. Margolis's voice took on an edge of panic.

'Okay, what do you want? What do you want me to do?'

Byron punched each word: 'Give me what's mine!'

So far, Margolis had reacted from pure shock. Now he hardened into a ball of defiance. His hands curled into fists which he waved in the air.

'Fuck you!' he bawled. *'Fuck you —!'*

Byron blinked. He was hardly even aware of Margolis. A little speck of nothing. A fat insect, squeaking and waving at the wrong end of a telescope. Margolis didn't matter anymore. Byron erased him. He turned his attention to the knot of Elvises waiting by the fire door to the Museum.

'Open it,' he said to Ken Matsuda, the closest. Matsuda looked painfully around the group.

'He don't speak no English,' said Vester Oakly.

'Well, *you* open it, then!' roared Byron.

Vester pulled on the door. It opened.

Inside, someone said, 'Okay, here come the finalists. Stand by.'

With Elmo still in a hammerlock, Byron motioned to the others.

'Get in there. Move!'

At the other end of the corridor, Margolis looked on, shaking with impotent rage.

'Byron, goddamn you!' he shouted.

Vester, Matsuda, and Little Dynamite crowded through the door. Then, still pointing the revolver at Elmo's head,

Byron raised a boot to his ass and shoved.

With one silent glance back at Margolis, Byron stepped into the Museum and slammed the door behind him.

Uncle

Inside the control booth, the director sensed trouble.

'Something's wrong,' he snapped, scanning the monitors.

On the museum floor, the crew was ready for the Elvises — mikes placed, cameras aimed, images flowing back to the control booth. The interviewer, in blazer and headset was poised for post-game interviews and the presentation of the priceless jumpsuit. Byron cleared him out with a quick shove that sent the bozo reeling toward the cameras. Then he jumped up on the presentation stage and wagged his gun at the crew.

'Everybody out! Go on — move your asses!'

There was a moment of stunned silence as the technicians exchanged glances. Nobody moved.

Byron levelled the pistol directly at one of the cameramen and cocked the hammer.

'*Do as he says!*' came the director's voice, shrieking over the talk-back monitor. 'Get out of there — now!'

Byron watched the TV people bolt for the door, leaving their cameras and mikes on, silent witnesses to the turn of events. As soon as they were gone, he swung back to face his four hostages. For the first time, there was a shade of confusion in his eyes.

'Well,' Elmo said, sensing Byron's hesitation. 'You got us, all right. What you gonna do with us?'

Byron heard the soft note of challenge. Instantly his confusion was gone. He grinned broadly.

'Gonna present you with your award, boy!'

He strode toward Elmo, the pistol pointed toward his

mouth, watching the coolness drain from his face.

'Open wide.'

Ghastly pale, Elmo allowed his jaw to drop. Byron brought the barrel to within an inch of his lips.

'Say uncle,' he whispered.

'Uncle . . .'

Byron whooped with pleasure and leaped into the air like a wild buck.

Jerry Margolis hustled down the aisle of the showroom, barking instructions to his flunky, an eager young PR guy in a three-piece suit, and his 'attorney', a dead-faced bodyguard.

'No cops, you understand? Put a lid on it — I don't want a scandal. And for God's sake, keep the press away. We're gonna handle this thing in private.'

Margolis was so intent on finding Frank Bruno he failed to notice the crowd, still grumbling over the verdict, had not made a move to clear the house. Trouble was simmering throughout the showroom.

Down front, where Bruno was slumped in his seat, the losing Elvises lingered, talking quietly with their managers. Bruno was nursing a new half-pint of CC. His eyes flashed darkly when Margolis found him.

'Sober up. That maniac of yours just pulled his pop gun and he's holding my finalists hostage!'

Bruno blinked and sat up. 'Jesus . . .' he whispered.

When he and Margolis entered the control booth, everyone was staring at the monitors.

'Well, what's it gonna be?' the director was yammering. 'Ritual mutilation? Cut their balls off — what?'

Margolis went directly to the control board and punched the talk-back switch.

'Byron —?' he said grimly.

On the monitor screen, Byron's head jerked around, looking for the source of the booming voice.

'Byron, listen to me. I'm giving you one chance to let those guys go. Then I'm gonna call the cops. It's kidnapping, Byron. You'll do a lot of time. Think about that.' He paused to let it sink in. 'Let 'em go.'

After a moment, Byron's voice came back:

'I want what's mine.'

Margolis was struggling to keep his composure.

'You're even dumber that I thought, Byron. You still don't understand. I represent *merchandisers*, you sucker. I need a singing public relations man. I've got no use for a fuckin' schizoid maniac.'

On the monitor, Byron's eyes seemed to disappear into pools of dark anger.

'If you don't want me,' he said tonelessly, 'you don't want Elvis.'

Margolis was losing it.

'You got it, asshole. I don't want you and I don't want Elvis. I want Elmo! He's dependable. I can trust him. This is business! I wouldn't touch you now with a fifty-foot pole — I don't care how many bush-hogs think you're Jesus Christ!'

The director tugged at him urgently. Margolis restrained himself.

'Okay, I'm giving you exactly five minutes to let those boys go, then I'm calling the cops.'

In answer, Byron suddenly aimed and fired his pistol at each TV camera. One by one, the control booth monitors went dead. In the appalling silence, Margolis stared at the darkened screens. A moment later, the audio signal was gone. Now there was no contact with the Museum.

'Oh shit . . . oh God,' wailed the director. 'Did he actually *do* that? I don't believe it — he did.'

At that moment, Margolis's flunky entered the booth. Through the open door spilled an alarming sound — the crowd, chanting: 'By-*ron*! By-*ron*! Byron!' A glass hit the stage with a crash and tinkle.

Margolis raised his eyebrows inquiringly.

'They won't leave,' shrugged the flunky.

'What else could go wrong?' sighed Margolis, dumping himself in the nearest chair. He grabbed his wrist. 'Jesus, my pulse . . .'

Frank Bruno had been silent till now. A sodden glaze had settled over his face and he seemed useless, numbed with guilt and confusion and the immense amount of booze that was sloshing around his mind. But suddenly, like a clearing sky, he stood up, focused, keen-eyed. Now he knew what he had to do. A slow, murky decision process had come to its conclusion. Now the bell rang — he was mobilised for action.

'Okay, enough's enough,' he growled.

Everyone in the booth turned to him, surprised by the steely toughness in the voice.

'Just gimme some time,' he said, hitching up his belt. He walked out without a glance at anyone.

'Who the hell was that?' said the director.

Margolis sighed hopelessly. 'Colonel Bruno of course — don't you know anything?'

Buddy and Junior were outside the booth, waiting anxiously for news.

'What the hell's goin' on?' demanded Buddy, grabbing a piece of Bruno's jacket with one hand. Bruno brushed him off with a stiff swipe.

'Get the limo. You're gonna drive me around to the Museum. I'll take care of the rest.' His tone was absolute, commanding.

Buddy and Junior hesitated.

'Go!' shouted Bruno. Grinning with confusion, they hurried off. Bruno made his way through the hotel lobby, wadding relentlessly toward his showdown with Byron.

Byron paced the museum like a cat, eyes darting back and forth between front door, fire door, anything that moved. His spine rippled with awareness and his ears seemed to have amplifiers attached to them. He had arranged the turkeys back-to-back in the Elvis Portrait Grotto; they'd be out of the way there, but he could keep an eye on them. Four jumpsuits full of Jell-O instant pudding. Not a peep out of them. They had just zipped right up. As he paced, a weird sensation made him seem to grow a foot or two taller. Time. What time was it? He had lost his reckoning of day and night, hours and minutes. But it didn't matter. All he had to do was wait.

Things were quiet now, but Byron knew it was just a matter of time till the scene would heat up. Margolis was most likely on the phone right now, explaining his ass off to Colonel Parker. Byron grinned, wishing he could tap in on that one. Well, the asshole got into this jam by himself. Let him sleaze himself out of it if he could.

He wasn't confused now. He had caught up with his action. He was clear as ice. This was how you corrected a mistake so huge it could mess up history and leave it bent in the wrong direction. You took a desperate action. Jerry Margolis thought he was clever enough to warp destiny, but Byron had simply jumped right over his fat ass in one bold leap, all the way to Colonel Parker.

Now there could be no mistake — the Colonel would have to step in to clear things up. Once he did, just like Frank had always said, there would be no contest. Only a simple recognition of who was Elvis and who was not.

'Hey, Byron.' It was Elmo. There were tiny lines of beaded sweat across his upper lip. He was scared. 'Better think about letting us go, man. The cops'll be here any minute. All hell's gonna break loose. We could get hurt bad.'

Byron just chuckled. How could you have a serious conversation with a chickenshit turkey like that?

'Listen, maniac —' Elmo blurted, trembling openly now, 'don't you know what happens when they send the cops in — everybody gets it!'

'Blood, huh?' Byron laughed.

'Yeah, goddman it — your blood, too!'

Now the laughter came in gulps and Byron was shaking with it, almost out of control. *Watch it, now. Cool down.* He choked it off and took a deep breath. He spat on the floor and cast a heavy look at Elmo. Then he whispered his contempt.

'You simple fool. You've got no notion, do you — like about how men like Colonel Parker pull strings from the shadows?'

Elmo stared at him in blank confusion. 'Colonel Parker?'

'All of you listen to this: Sometime soon a guy in a three-piece suit's gonna show up at the door. He's gonna be real polite. He'll say something like: "Hello, Byron. We've been reconsidering the situation —" and so on and so forth. Colonel Parker will be right outside waiting. There'll be a meeting, on my terms. Colonel Parker'll —'

'Byron!'

There was a banging on the front door.

'Open up!'

It was Bruno. Byron motioned to the Elvises to stay put and made his way to the front, protecting himself from view. He opened the door and Bruno pushed through.

'Well?' said Byron, shining with anticipation.

'Well what?'

'What's the situation?'

'There ain't no situation. You're fucked. Margolis won't give an inch.'

Byron waved the pistol impatiently.

'Aw, the hell with Margolis. That's just what he says. Everybody out there knows he ripped me off. The whole world saw it. Now I've got him by the balls — so don't tell me he ain't about to give me nothin'. I wanna know what's happening out there.'

'You just blew it, that's all!' Bruno's eyes were suddenly wide as plates. 'If you think you've got any career, any future left after this —'

'Don't worry about my future, man. You just put Margolis on the horn to Colonel Parker and get this thing straightened out, that's all.' Byron was waving the revolver around and showing the whites of his eyes. 'There's a lot more at stake here than my career — there's the Colonel's — there's Elvis's! Margolis is trying to put something over on the whole world with this Elmo asshole here —' He pointed the gun at Elmo. 'Well, the world ain't gonna bend over for that, and neither's Colonel Parker!'

Bruno drew back, unable to believe how far the fantasy had gone. He felt suddenly old again. He sighed heavily and his glance fell to the floor. Byron continued his declaration.

'I'm not budgin' with these jokers, Frank. Not till somebody gets him.'

Bruno's face twisted into a mad, exasperated grin.

'Well, then shoot 'em!' he concluded.

'Huh?' Byron looked back at him through a cloud of perplexity.

Bruno's voice rose sharply to the level of a shout. 'Yeah, shoot 'em. Shoot the clowns. Shoot 'em all — shoot me, too. Let's have a bloodbath. Let's get on the cover of *Time*. Go on, shoot!'

'Now, hold it, man —' said Little Dynamite shakily. Bruno ignored him and moved a step closer to Byron, jabbing a finger toward his face.

'Because I'll tell you one thing — it ain't gonna make any damn difference. Colonel Parker could care less if *any* of us lives or dies, including you. I really hate to tell you this, but he ain't watchin', he ain't interested — *he doesn't give a shit!*'

Byron gaped at him in dumb astonishment. Bruno anticipated his thoughts.

'Yeah, I lied!' His eyebrows flew up and he nodded wildly. 'I lied about it all because I'm such an old fool I even believed my own lies and it seems like they aren't even lies anymore. But I'll tell you the truth now: We're scavengers. We're livin' offa Elvis's crumbs and there ain't anything more to it than that!'

Byron blinked. He tossed his head in an attempt at bravado.

'Let's see what Colonel Parker says,' he mumbled.

But Bruno was merciless. He seemed to swell and grow unforgivingly, right in front of Byron's eyes.

'Get it through your head, boy. We'll never get so much as a whiff of Colonel Parkeer's ass. He don't *need* us. He's got Elvis! Elvis is alive. Elvis still makes money every day — he made more money today than you'll ever make in your life! Parker's got the boy — even if the boy don't breathe anymore!'

Byron just looked at him. He was staggering mentally now, groping at the frayed edges of a dream. Bruno was relentless.

'Waste 'em! Go ahead. Holding on ain't gonna get you a damn thing! Blow their fuckin' brains out!'

Byron laughed once, a loud guffaw. Then he went blank. He pawed at his eyes with his free hand and let the gun dangle from the other. An anxious pall spread over his face. He seemed to be waking up, disoriented, from a deep, ugly sleep. He turned and squinted at the Elvises, as if he saw them now for the first time and wondered what the hell they were doing there. He shook his head from side to side, covering his eyes with his hand.

'Let 'em go,' said Bruno gently.

'Holy shit . . .' Byron whispered.

'Let 'em go,' Bruno repeated. 'We gotta get you out of here. This was a bad move. If the cops get in on it, you'll be bustin' rocks in a federal pen.'

Byron was struggling to think. Bruno's words had imploded deep in his mind, burning away the whole machinery that had pumped and revolved and thrust him ceaselessly on to this moment. Now the force of the imposition was written across his face, and the meaning of it, slowly forming . . .

Colonel Parker didn't need him, didn't need a new Elvis. There would be no heir to the King, no such thing, none of them would take his place, nobody. The whole long trip, from all the way back in Portland, all meant nothing. The sure knowledge, the secret that *Elvis was there*, ready to flower again, the power that came with it, the power of the Elvis inside, it was all a hallucination. A lie. Bruno's lie. Byron's lie.

Turkeys among turkeys. Kneel down and eat your fantasy, boy! And who the hell were we even talking about now? Byron. Byron. Byron. Who the hell was that now?

He wandered through the silent Museum, stopping in front of the plastic statue of Elvis. He stared into its plastic eyes. He pushed the button in its base. The plastic Elvis sang to him:

'You ain't nuthin' but a hound dog . . .'

Byron swung back toward the portrait grotto, his eyes wide open now. The hostages flinched as he raised the pistol toward them.

'Go on!' he said, pointing it toward the door. 'Get outa here.'

They started immediately for the front.

'Just a minute!' Byron shouted. They froze in their tracks. 'You — Elmo.'

Elmo turned weakly. Byron gestured toward Elvis's jumpsuit.

'Take your prize, boy,' he drawled ironically.

Elmo returned for the suit, gathered it up, and followed the others out into the sweltering desert afternoon.

In front of the Museum, the beginnings of a crowd had formed. Fans who hadn't had seats for the show stood around with innocent tourists and curiosity seekers. Barry Hartz and a TV news crew from Channel 5 had arrived. Some print reporters had shown up and were working the crowd with their minicassette recorders: 'What's going on? It is true somebody's got hostages in there?'

Private security guards had just formed a ring around the entrance when the doors flew open and the Elvises emerged, breaking into a run. The crowd rippled into cheers and the reporters were on them like leeches, only to be hustled aside by the security guards. More guards herded the Elvises into a waiting hotel van, which sped off toward a rear entrance to the showroom.

Buddy and Junior watched it all from the limo.

'What now?' said Junior.

'Just wait.' Buddy searched the front door area with nervous eyes. 'Get ready to drive like a sonofabitch. We'll have to get him away from here.'

Back in the Museum, Byron had collapsed into blankness.

The life had drained out of his face and left it rubbery and grey. He looked weak, robbed of his spirit, without hope of renewal. With the revolver on the floor beside him, he sat by the plastic Elvis, staring ahead into empty space.

'Byron?' Bruno prodded. When there was no response he went over and shook him by the shoulders. 'C'mon, Byron. This is it. Let's get outa here.'

Inside the showroom, the confusion had escalated from mildly threatening to dangerous. The pro-Byron mob had gone out of control, milling around, refusing to disperse, tossing bottles and glasses, chanting, 'By-*ron!* By-*ron!* By-*ron!*'

'Ladies and gentlemen,' thundered an announcer's voice, 'Byron has left the building!' It was useless.

Margolis and his bodyguard were backstage, peering out at the commotion, when the director rushed up, in a state of hysteria.

'How the hell am I supposed to wrap this thing up?' he shouted in a piercing falsetto. 'You're the goddamn producer — clear the house, call the police, do something!'

Margolis raised both hands firmly.

'No cops,' he insisted. 'I don't want busted heads. There's gonna be no fuckin' scandal, y'understand? He's turned 'em loose. They're on their way. We'll do the presentation here. I refuse to turn this event into a national laughingstock!'

'It's already a laughingstock, you idiot!' yelled the director. 'Do you want a riot on your hands?'

A door flew open and the four ex-hostages crowded in, still shaken and dazed. Margolis looked around and spotted Elmo, clutching the prize jumpsuit.

'Elmo!' he shouted desperately. 'Gimme that suit and get out there! Let's do the presentation and get the damn thing over with.'

Elmo stared back as if cornered by a madman. He shook his head firmly.

'No way, Mr Margolis. I ain't goin' out there in front of that mob. They want Byron. Give 'em Byron.'

Margolis sputtered angrily, rubbing his bald head with both hands. His flunky slinked in and drew him aside.

'You've got to get this crowd under control,' he whispered urgently. 'Front office is very, very pissed. Mr Gallagher says to do something quick or else —'

'Or else what?' Margolis appealed to heaven.

'I don't know — boiling oil? How do I know?'

Margolis grabbed his pulse.

'Oh, my God, I'm dying,' he muttered. Then his voice rose to a shout. 'All right, damn it — get Byron! Do anything you have to — drug him, tie him up — but get his ass over here. *Now!*'

A Thousand Million Pieces

'Whaaa-hoo!'

Junior steered the ungainly black monster with his fingertips, skidding deftly around a blind corner, recovering in a storm of dust and smoking rubber, and firing off down the alley, pushing fifty. It took only the simplest road stunts to shake Barry Hartz and the TV truck: two neat 180-degree spins and there wasn't a trace left of Channel 5.

'Lost 'em.'

'They'll just show up at the Paradise,' Buddy grumbled.

'We'll just whip their goddamn asses, too!'

In the rear, Byron sat, unfocused, shattered. His eyes flicked back and forth. All at once he straightened up and his voice seemed to come from far away, but loud and distinct.

'I am a lunatic. You all know that.'

Buddy and Junior kept their mouths shut and looked straight ahead.

At the Paradise, they marched quickly through the lobby toward the elevators, gathering looks from the gawkers as usual. Except that now, instead of sweeping proudly by, Byron ambled, shoulders bent.

Upstairs, Buddy unlocked the penthouse door.

'Stay out here,' Byron said as he entered. 'Nobody gets in. Not Frank Bruno, not anybody.'

'Boss,' Buddy stammered. 'Let Junior come in with you — in case you need something —'

Stay out here! Byron roared, his voice breaking. With a fierce wounded look, he turned and slammed the door

206

behind him.

Was it night inside? His eyes adjusted and then he could see his way, at least in the spaces between the heart throbs that drowned his vision every few seconds. Thank God it was cool. He wanted to lie down. He wanted to sleep, sleep it off. Turn it all into dreams. He had no body anyway, it seemed. He was in one room, then another, without any sensation of how he got there. Couldn't seem to hang onto himself. He floated like a ghost. Now he was in the bathroom. On the toilet top was a snapshot of Wendy. A blast of memory shrivelled him, and he gasped for breath as the full force of what she had done rolled over him. For a clear moment he remembered the whole godawful thing. One clear moment of the purest pain, a buried wound, yawning open in the middle of the newer ones. Pain upon pain upon pain.

He stared at the face in the medicine chest mirror. There was numb confusion in the eyes — who was it? Who was this sweating, staring, dumb-struck fool?

The heart attack came while he was taking a long, nervous piss. It began as a hot grabbing in the centre of his chest, so sudden that it made him spray the bathroom floor. Then the Beast struck. Byron backed into the wall. He ripped at the invisible death-clamp on his throat. He struggled out of the bathroom, reeling, fighting the Beast for breath.

Was he dying now? He toppled helplessly on his back, in the deep meadow of the bedroom rug and stared at the twinkling stars of Paradise in the ceiling. Heaven. Well, let it happen. No better time than right now. Let his heart burst. He grabbed at his chest and felt it palpitating. Let 'em find him with his flab stiffened up, with his face purple and blue, just like they found Elvis. Let the lights go out — he was ready. He was ready to die.

But his mind kept chattering, like a machine that doesn't know the plug has been pulled. Is this the way you go out? Yacking and yammering idiotic, non-stop mental speed-raps? What happens inside your chest? The heart goes off like a car bomb. It rips and tears and gushes. It blows you to smithereens. But this pain, this pain —

A new thought broke through — the suit! Of course! The goddamn jumpsuit!

He grasped it suddenly at the chest, clawing it, tearing it away from his shoulders till he lay panting on the rug with the shreds of it beside him, a flayed mess of old skin with raw flesh underneath. He knew exactly what he was doing, like an animal that chews off its foot to escape a trap.

Out in the foyer, Buddy and Junior stood guard silently, unaware of the Boss's struggle. Once or twice Junior snuffled and reached under his shades to swipe at his eyes. Buddy kept his gaze on the elevator floor indicator. It took ten or fifteen minutes for the first invasion to arrive.

'Get ready,' said Buddy, watching the indicator climb toward *P*.

The elevator doors burst open and partially expelled Barry Hartz, with camera, mike, and a three-man crew, lights blaring. But before they could step fully out of the elevator, Buddy and Junior were shoving them back.

'Hold it now —' shouted Barry Hartz. 'Just a damn minute —'

The doors closed on them and the elevator started down. Buddy and Junior nodded to each other, mission accomplished.

Inside, Byron had drifted into calmness. He watched the clock inch forward. He was inching forward with it. The world was still there and the heart still beat in his chest. You either stopped dead or you just moved ahead with the world, second by month by year.

He rolled over on one elbow amd sighed heavily. His head hung from his neck, dripping sweat. Somehow he knew he wasn't going to die.

Then he was up, searching for those old rayon threads — the shiny purple slacks, the peach sports shirt with the turned-up collar — could it work? But he was too puffy. He couldn't fasten the pants now and the zipper snagged halfway up. His belly put a strain on the shirt buttons. He looked in the mirror again and saw a nobody, a paunchy aging scumbag.

Elvis was gone. The person Byron faced in the mirror was a stranger. His face showed the kind of strain that comes from pushing too hard on the edge of youth. The eyes were puffy and bloodshot and circled underneath with shades of fatigue. They stared back from the mirror with dull fascination. The face seemed to want to ask directions, plead for knowledge, be led to the end of a sorrowful journey. There was something pathetic in the way the strong, chiselled features added up to mush, fear, everything in a face that drives you away from the owner of that face, makes you steer clear of the desperate blankness that wants your soul because it has no soul of its own.

Byron was crying. Bending double with sobs. Mourning at last for Elvis. Crying for the dead boy that had flashed so bright, made such a strong run at being a man, and lost it. Manhood had risen up and smothered the King, like a snake from inside the guts, twisting his heart into silence, all the while whispering to him, a white, jewel-studded serpent of death, telling him he was still the world's boy. Byron and the face in the mirror wept like mourners and somewhere in it, Byron knew he was crying for his own craziness, his own waste of a life, the darkness that held his mind, the loss of his woman, the end of his youth, the crumbling of his dream. He was weeping for himself.

The phone rang. He let it. He was drifting in a vision of Maine, how the islands looked on a brightening summer day with the fog burning off, grey opening into green and deep blue. After a while he stuffed his legs into a pair of old jeans and jammed the BYRON softball cap on his head. The phone rang again, this time fifteen or twenty times. He let the ringing fill the empty space in his head. He sat in the dark, naked to the waist, waiting.

Then he heard talking outside. At first a commotion, a few shouts and some tussling around. The voices lowered and a few moments later Buddy and Junior threw the door open and came running in, all excited, followed by Margolis's flunky and the big goon he called his attorney.

'Bo"! You're the winner!' announced Buddy, beaming with the thrill of it.

'They want you!' Junior squawked like a fourteen year old.

Byron's right eye began to twitch uncontrollably. He stared hard at Margolis's men. The flunky stepped forward with a nervous attempt at a smile flashing across his face.

'There's been a new decision, Byron,' said the flunky. 'The people demand it and we're going with the people. The crowd over there is all yours, man and they're about to tear the place down. Let's go — we need you.'

Byron's eyes bored a hole in him.

'You tell Margolis to cram it up his ass. I ain't helpin' him out of no fuckin' jams.' He turned abruptly to Buddy and Junior. 'Clear 'em outa here.'

The flunky and the lawyer exchanged uneasy glances. Buddy and Junior looked from face to face, dumbfounded.

Then Buddy was seized by an inspiration.

'No, Boss, goddamn it! You're gonna get what's yours!'

Launching himself at Byron, he slammed him against the wall and pinned his arms behind him. The struggle lasted only a few seconds as the attorney produced a pair of handcuffs and clapped them on Byron's wrists.

'You goddamn traitor!' Byron screamed, wrestling them all the way out into the foyer.

'It's for your own good, Boss!' shouted Buddy. 'You've gotta show the world who's Elvis and who ain't!'

'The hell I do,' Byron gasped, struggling wildly as they forced him into the elevator and plunged downward toward the street. 'I don't have to show nobody nothing!'

Somewhere in the desert, Wendy and Eddie stopped at a 7-11 for a cold beer. They sat in the car and drank three apiece before their thirst was quenched. The sun was dropping and it would be cool before long. Eddie flicked the radio on and spun the dial till he got something — news. They weren't really listening. Wendy was just about to turn it off. Then —

'Finally in the news, Las Vegas: You thought you'd heard everything, right? But today, at an international Elvis Presley impersonators competition, one of the Elvises — a guy named King Byron — took four other Elvises hostage when he lost, and holed up in the Elvis Presley Museum. His demand? To see Colonel Parker, Elvis's legendary manager, in person. Well, King Byron's own manager, "Colonel" Frank Bruno of Las Vegas, talked him out of it and the hostages were released unharmed. Colonel Parker couldn't be reached for comment and Elvis, of course, is unavailable. That's news . . .'

'Jesus,' she whispered. 'Oh, Byron, Byron . . .'

Eddie lit a cigarette and blew a long stream of smoke out the car window, watching the hills turn red in the distance.

'Will they put him in jail?' she asked suddenly.

Eddie shrugged. 'Not for long. It'd make the Roman Garden look bad: they don't want that. They'll find some way to get the case thrown out. Everybody'll forget.' He looked at her. 'Anyway, he's crazy, isn't he? You don't put crazy people in jail.'

'Guess not,' she whispered. But her mind raced ahead of Eddie now. 'I knew this was going to happen —'

'No you didn't'

'I did. *I* must be crazy. It's just dawning on me what I've done.'

'No guilt trips. You got out.'

'That's right. I jerked the rug right out from under him and took off with it. I treated the situation like I could make it just disappear. He's a bastard, he's not perfect. But I don't care what he did — he's as much of my story as I am, his child is inside me, we're woven together. He's in trouble and I'm trying to get away with pretending he doesn't exist!'

'He's hopeless. Give it up.'

'He's not hopeless. He's alive. Life goes on. I tried to cut off part of my own body.'

'Damn it, what you cut off was a malignant wart —'

Something in his voice made Wendy want to punch him.

'You don't have any compassion, do you — you don't know what it is.'

'Why should I?' Eddie laughed sharply. 'That guy's an asshole. He's useless. Why in flaming hell should I get all upset if he destroys himself?'

Her face was suddenly seething with fury.

'Shut up and turn this damn car around.'

'Don't be stupid, Wendy.' Eddie's voice had gone hollow.

'I will be stupid. Turn this car around or I'm just gonna get out and walk it. You understand?'

She meant it. The lines in Eddie's face deepened, his cheeks seemed to sink. Austin, whatever it might have been with Wendy, was dying right in front of him.

'Come on, Eddie, stop saving me, man! I've got to go back. The story's just not over yet. There's more of it. More of Byron and Wendy, more of everything!'

Eddie saw the energy, the blind hope, the undeniable thrust of her dream resurging, regaining strength. It was a strength he didn't understand. He felt his own slipping away. With a shrug, he reached for the keys.

Byron had to be shoved through the backstage entrance and dragged to Margolis, kicking and struggling. Out front the crowd was still chanting? 'By-*ron!* By-*ron!* By-*ron!*' They banged the table with their glasses, rolled up their sleeves and shook their fists. With a mixture of a bar-room craziness and the stolid fervour of Americans bent on justice, they had held their places, refusing to be moved.

Margolis was cradling the prize Elvis jumpsuit. He held it out to Byron as if it were burning his fingers.

'It's all yours, okay?' he blurted. 'Now put it on and get out there!'

'No!'

'Listen to 'em!' Margolis pressed. 'They're your fans, goddamn it. Am I gonna have to move 'em outa here with a fire hose?'

Byron stopped struggling. For the first time he heard the

212

chants. 'By-*ron!* By-*ron!* By-*ron!*'

'You've won, all right? You can have the suit. You can have anything you want. Just get out there in front of the goddamn cameras and be *Elvis!*'

A slow, wary smile spread across Byron's face. He let the BYRON cap fall to the floor.

'That's it, that's it. Get him outa those cuffs!'

Yielding, almost serene, he let them help him into the jumpsuit. Someone was combing his hair and wiping his face. Then with a gentle push from the wings, he was out on the stage and the crowd was standing, the chants merging into a single roar. Every face was hot with anticipation. This had to be a moment nobody would ever forget!

Byron stood in front of the fans, magnificent in the glittering jumpsuit, his own face radiating emotional changes. He raised his arms to quiet the crowd. The roar continued, a surging waterfall of sound. He stepped to the mike. There was immediate silence as he bowed his head a moment, waiting for words.

'I want you to know — this is the highest moment of my life. I've got no further to go than right here'.

Thoughts were roaring through his head to fast they ran him down like trucks. He had exploded into a thousand million pieces, like seeds strewn through the universe. There was no Byron now, except in little pieces. If he could only tell them.

'We're all here because we love Elvis, right?'

The crowd broke into warm cheers. It was Elvis they wanted, whether or not they even knew it. They didn't want Byron. So let this piece of the King pass on from him to them — let it go. Let the fans have it. Byron unzipped the jumpsuit.

'Well, here he is. I'm wearing him. And it's itchin' me to death! So, hell . . . let's share him. Let's share Elvis!'

Then came the floating sensation. Like a hot air balloon pulling away from the earth, he felt himself rise off the floor. Slowly he stripped the jumpsuit and stepped out of it, naked and hairy and bare in front of the world. The fans went *oooh!* — a ripple of wonder. Things seemed to go into slow motion. Byron swung the suit in a circle around his head and let it spin through the air, unfurling, floating through the suspended moment, hanging high above the thousands of outstretched fingers.

In the wings, Margolis put his head in his hands and moaned like a stuck calf.

As the suit came down, tables pitched over, bottles and glasses shattered, bodies hurled through space to be where it had landed. Some fans got out of the way or were knocked aside. Men with bulging eyes and flailing arms fought their way into the crowd but were thrown aside and trampled by bunches of women propelling themselves blindly toward the suit.

Buddy and Junior went for it, springing from the wings and leaping off the edge of the stage. The Elvis Woman fought her way to ground-zero, ripping madly at the prize, her own jumpsuit half torn away, her breasts dangling openly as she held her ground.

Security guards rushed in, then shrank back, unwilling to wade into the centre of the riot.

Fists bounced off flesh and bones. Flecks of blood flew through the air as punches connected. And the rippling and flaying of the suit went on. Fragments sailed high, flipping and turning in the air, like pieces of a freshly killed sacrificial beast.

At last the metro police were there, entering at the rear of the showroom, surrounding the stage. Individual fans were running from the disarray, clutching what little bit of Elvis they had been able to rip free.

Byron saw the riot unfold out of the corner of his eye. It didn't concern him now. His role was played out. He floated above it, over it, free of it. He felt light and perfect, naked like a baby with no name, no past. He was brand new.

He saw Margolis jumping around as if someone had touched a cattle prod to his butt. He saw Frank Bruno standing in the wings like an old sack of potatoes. He saw

214

the metro police coming for him — friendly-looking guys, with grins on their faces, holding out hands to him. It didn't matter. He felt lighter already. He felt the flab falling away from him. There were no horrors now.

'C'mon Elvis, let's get you some pants on,' said one of the cops.

He faced them and raised both fists high in the air. He had no identity. His mind was blasted clean. For a moment, he had no idea who he was — *but he was free.*

He lowered his arms and met the cops like old buddies, letting them surround him, lead him off stage, help him into his jeans, move him toward the stage door. He didn't really notice when the new handcuffs went on, the ones with chains. He didn't care. Everything went by in a smear except for one clear moment, at the door, when Frank Bruno pushed through, grasped him with his fat arms, and planted the BYRON cap firmly on his head. The old guy looked beat and bloodshot, like he had just heard he was going to die.

'We made a good try, kid,' he said. 'We ran just as hard as we could, just got chewed up is all. God be with ya —'

Byron couldn't grasp what he was talking about. Chewed up? The rims of Bruno's eyes were wet. What the hell was wrong?

Then they were hustling Byron out of the door, straight into the desert sunset, in front of a crowd of fans, TV crews, photographers. Flash units were popping, reporters were shoving mikes in front of his face: 'Byron, why'd you do it? Byron, what happened in there?'

'Hey, Elvis!' a photographer shouted, trying to make him turn, sly fucking dog. But he walked straight ahead, toward the flashing blue cop cruiser, grinning full into the sunset, letting the chains dangle like snakes from his wrist.

Big goddamn fuss, for sure. Blink, flash — they fired like gunfighters trying to make him dance. But he was cool. There was no desperation, no sense of need, the bad news was over like yesterday, the gun-waving desperado had slipped into darkness forever. No depression. No show of horrors, no raging Beast. He was clear, like spring water, like window glass.

Beyond the chains, through the TV lights, he even thought he saw his girl, or a vision of her, squeezing desperately forward, clawing her way through to touch him.

'Wendy? Hey, baby —'

Before the cops could grab her she had broken through and smacked up against him with her whole body, like a soft little tailback.

'Listen to me,' she whispered just before they pulled her away, 'I'm going to be around, y'understand?'

Then she was gone, but it was enough. He was ready now, for whatever happened. He was clambering out of the blackness of a cavern, blinking into the sun. Elvis was gone now, ripped to pieces, given up, given away. But somewhere up ahead, with a touch of luck, the Byron of the future might be waiting in the mystery of history for his own dog-eared self to catch up at long long last.

'Any place special, Elvis?' said the cop behind the wheel.

Byron grinned at him through the chickenwire.

'Home, James.'